TI

JAMES SKIPP BORL
admitted as a solicit.
marrying in 1863 and moving with his new wife to Australia in 1864. He
spent five years there and also qualified as a solicitor and practiced law,
among other pursuits; however, his main lifelong interest seems to have
been writing. Over the course of a career spanning fifty years he penned
as many as a hundred serialized novels and an untold number of short
stories for newspapers and magazines in England and Australia, some of
which were also compiled and published in book form, such as *Stirring
Tales of Colonial Adventure* (1894). He died in Brighton in 1909.

CHRISTOPHER K. PHILIPPO has read, conservatively, over 1000 Christmas ghost stories and poems and takes especial pains to discover ones
not previously republished. In 2015 he uncovered the neglected grave
of Norman Tuttle (1787-1858), the original publisher of "A Visit from
St. Nicholas," and hopes to have Tuttle's family lot properly conserved.
His works in progress include a complete history of the cemeteries of
Lansingburgh and Troy, the complete works of H. C. Dodge, women
horror directors' movies, and the early film career of Alfred Hitchcock.
He has helped obtain historical markers for New York state suffragists
Caroline Gilkey Rogers (1837-1899) and Elisha Powell Hurlbut (1807-
1889), placed in 2017 and 2022 respectively, but has not obtained any for
Christmas ghost story authors . . . yet.

Portrait of James Skipp Borlase from the *Denbigh, Ruthin and Vale of Clwyd Free Press*, Dec. 24, 1887, 8. Facsimile signature from a letter from James Skipp Borlase to Mrs. Turner, Feb. 21, 1905, in the collection of the editor.

THE
SHRIEKING SKULL

and other

VICTORIAN CHRISTMAS GHOST STORIES

James Skipp Borlase

Edited by
CHRISTOPHER PHILIPPO

VALANCOURT BOOKS
Richmond, Virginia
2022

The Shrieking Skull and other Victorian Christmas Ghost Stories
First published November 2022

Introduction © 2022 by Christopher Philippo
This compilation copyright © 2022 by Valancourt Books, LLC

All rights reserved. In accordance with the U.S. Copyright Act of 1976, the copying, scanning, uploading, and/or electronic sharing of any part of this book without the permission of the publisher constitutes unlawful piracy and theft of the author's intellectual property. If you would like to use material from the book (other than for review purposes), prior written permission must be obtained by contacting the publisher.

Published by Valancourt Books, Richmond, Virginia
http://www.valancourtbooks.com

ISBN 978-1-954321-85-4 (hardcover)
ISBN 978-1-954321-86-1 (paperback)
Also available as an electronic book.

Set in Dante MT

Contents

LAW!   LAW!!   LAW!!!

DOCTOR BORLASE,

Attorney, Solicitor, and Proctor of the Supreme Court of the Colony of Victoria; Attorney of the Courts of Queen's Bench, Common Pleas, and Exchequer, Solicitor of Her Majesty's High Court of Chancery; and Doctor learned in the Law of the University of Frankfort on Maine,

May be consulted by letter, or personally at his office,

142 SMITH STREET, COLLINGWOOD,

Between 10 a.m. and 7 p.m.

—

DOCTOR BORLASE, in addition to his English Experience, has, for the past three years, given great attention to the intricacies of Colonial Law. He was formerly a pupil of the celebrated J. J. S. Wharton, M.A., and Barrister-at-Law, and still later has read with Halliday and Smith.

Doctor Borlase's great object in thus becoming an advertising Attorney, is to place a legal remedy within the grasp of the poor. Our Law has a noble maxim, *i.e.,* "There is never a wrong without a remedy." Hitherto that remedy has only been attainable through the medium of a long purse.

Doctor Borlase wishes to be the

"POOR MAN'S LAWYER,"

and the poorer classes shall have the benefit of his services at

ONE-HALF THE USUAL CHARGES.

He will give them

ADVICE GRATIS

between 10 and 11 a.m.

For the benefit of persons residing at a distance, Doctor Borlase may be consulted by letter, on enclosing a Post Office Order for 5s., payable to James Skipp Borlase, Solicitor, Melbourne.

—

N.B.—If you desire to provide for your family by making your Will or Insuring your life; if you wish to Sell or Purchase a House or Land; if you want to give a Bill of Sale over your Stock or Furniture; if you are driven to make a Composition with your Creditors, or go through the Insolvent Court; if you want your Debts Collected without heavy law costs; if you want to Prosecute or Defend an Action, first consult Doctor Borlase.

Divorce cases attended to.

—

The County, Warden's and Police Courts Attended.

—

Note the Address—142 SMITH STREET, Collingwood.

INTRODUCTION

The Christmas season is the most often selected for relating by
the fireside stories of ghosts and extraordinary adventures. If
they have a local association, so much the greater is the interest evinced in them.

Shepton Mallet Journal [South-West England], Dec. 23, 1887, 3.

A country parson "dealing out strange accounts of the popular superstitions and legends of the surrounding country, with which he had become acquainted in the course of his
antiquarian researches" acquaints the protagonist (and reading
audience) of Washington Irving's *The Sketch Book of Geoffrey
Crayon, Gent.* (1819) with the ghost-telling tradition of an old English Christmas. In "The Christmas Dinner" section of that work,
the parson's host likewise is "a great reader of old legends and
romances," and the women in attendance maintain oral tradi-
tions of "all kinds of ghosts, goblins, and fairies."

James Skipp Borlase (1839-1909), born in Truro, in southwest
England, would be similarly attracted in the early years of his
writing career to the surrounding country and legends for his
subject matter. Early pieces included the poem "My Native Bay,"
virtually a list of Cornish locations, and "Flora de Melville; or,
The May Queen: A Legend of Goodrich Castle," a serial appear-
ing in part in the Christmas Number of *Counsell's Miscellany*.[1]
Besides the general historical inclinations of Victorian times,
notable antiquarians in the family, including ancestor Dr. William
Borlase (1696-1772) and distant cousin William Copeland Borlase
(1848-1899), may have amplified Borlase's own historical interests.

Borlase was admitted as a solicitor in February 1862, but stead-
ily continued writing poems, stories, and serials. At the same

[1] *Royal Cornwall Gazette, Falmouth Packet, and General Advertiser* [Truro], Feb. 7, 1862,
4; "My Native Bay," *Cornish Telegraph, Mining, Agricultural, and Commercial Gazettte*
[Penzance], June 16, 1858, 4; "A Christmas Number," *Man of Ross and General Advertiser
for the Counties of Hereford, Gloucester, and Monmouth*, Dec. 9, 1858, 1.

time, he was an agent for a life insurance company and also lent money at interest. On September 1, 1863 he was married, and by October he had retired from law in Plymouth, the announcement coming so abruptly that his clients had to be left letters regarding their cases—not even posted but simply left at the former office.[2]

The couple departed for Australia in March 1864.[3] Borlase was admitted as a lawyer there in November, but by January 1865 he was arrested in Tasmania and brought back to Melbourne for deserting his wife. Reconciliation avoided a trial, though the marriage still didn't last. The scandal could have been a career-destroyer, but ultimately it was just a small news item that didn't make the front page. He grandiosely advertised his legal services in 1866-68, represented at least one insolvent debtor, and obtained admission in other Australian states.[4]

A couple of the stories in the present volume didn't have a Christmas association on their original publication but had Christmas elements added later, apparently to help ensure their republication. Retooling his own work was common throughout Borlase's career. The aforementioned "My Native Bay" would have its Cornish locations swapped out for Tasmanian ones a decade later, for example: any real native feeling giving way to ensure the poem's continued viability for print.[5] In looking for venues for his work, he was also adept at self-syndication or working with early networks in Australia and Great Britain.[6]

Borlase's Christmas ghost stories vary as to setting (Great Britain, continental Europe, Australia); the presence, allegation, or absence of the supernatural; suspense or comedy; happy end-

[2] "Wellington Life Assurance Society," *Western Daily Mercury*, July 25, 1863, 7; "To Lend, £9000," *Cornish Telegraph, Mining, Agricultural, and Commercial Gazette* [Penzance], Sept. 9, 1863, 1; "Public Notice," *Western Daily Mercury*, Oct. 31, 1863, 1.

[3] Lucy Sussex, " 'Bobbing around': James Skipp Borlase, Adam Lindsay Gordon, and Surviving in the Literary Market of Australia, 1860s," *Victorian Periodicals Review* 37, no. 4 (2004): 101.

[4] *The Age* [Melbourne], Dec. 2, 1864, 1; "Law!" *Telegraph, St. Kilda, Prahan, and South Yarra Guardian*, Dec. 8, 1866, 3; "Wife Desertion," *Argus* [Melbourne], Jan. 25, 1865, 3; "Wodonga," *Albury Banner*, Feb. 22, 1868, 3; "In the Supreme Court," *Sydney Morning Herald*, Sept. 21, 1868, 1; "Last Day of Third Term," *Sydney Morning Herald*, Sept. 28, 1868, 2.

[5] *Tasmanian Times* [Hobart Town], May 30, 1867, 3; *Albury Banner*, March 28, 1868, 4.

[6] Graham Law, *Serializing Fiction in the Victorian Press* (Palgrave, 2000), *passim*; Sussex (2004), *passim*.

ings or tragic. For this volume, some attempt has been made to mix them up from their chronological order for more variation. The Victorian reader might have read only two Borlase stories in a single Christmas season and fewer than ten Christmas ghost stories by any author. Relatively few years produced anthologies of them; rather they were scattered across multiple publications. Even the most patient and persistent habitué of newsstands and libraries might have found it challenging to find as many as twelve new ones in a single December. The modern reader might take a cue from that and consider spacing them out over the days of the Advent calendar and Christmastide, ideally letting each one linger individually awhile, hauntingly.

Melodrama, Gothics, Sensation Novels, and City Mysteries

The first example of Borlase entering the Christmas ghost story market was in 1867 for the *Albury Banner and Wodonga Express* of New South Wales, Australia. In this instance, he repurposed a story of his own from *The Odd-Fellows' Magazine,* the "Quarterly Magazine of the Independent Order of Odd-Fellows, Manchester Unity Friendly Society." Several of his works were published by the IOOF, and it stands to reason he would have been a member. Rituals involved skeletons as memento mori and ceremonial admonitions; somewhat notoriously, former IOOF lodges have required investigations when remains are found in them.[7]

The protagonist of Borlase's earliest Christmas ghost story was a law student, and given that Borlase himself studied law it is tempting to view some of the elements as semi-autobiographical. The unnamed character professes his admiration for "all the glorious romances of Scott and Bulwer." Walter Scott's "The Tapestried Chamber" (1829), reprinted in *The Valancourt Book of Victorian Christmas Ghost Stories, Volume One*, is an early example of a printed Christmas ghost story and features what would become a trope common to many such stories, that of a traveler being given a room of last resort in an old castle, a strange echo

---

[7] Cara Giaimo, "Stumbling on Skeletons in Old Odd Fellows Lodges," *Atlas Obscura,* Oct. 30, 2017, http://www.atlasobscura.com/articles/odd-fellows-found-skeletons.

of Luke 2:7's story of there being no room at the inn and having to resort to a manger, curiously (and gothically) depicted in some crèches as set in a stone ruin. Edward Bulwer-Lytton's occult romance *Zanoni* (1842) mentions a variation on the holiday tradition, comparing tricks of alchemists and necromancers to how "the showman enchants some trembling children on a Christmas Eve with his lantern and phantasmagoria."

Victorian readers' concept of "ghost stories" generally and "Christmas ghost stories" in particular was broader than the conception of some readers today. Mary Shelley, in her introduction to the 1831 edition of *Frankenstein,* released for the Christmas market, noted the novel's origin in a writing challenge following a reading of *Fantasmagoriana, ou Recueil d'histoires d'apparitions de spectres* at Lake Geneva in Switzerland. "'We will each write a ghost story,' said Lord Byron; and his proposition was acceded to." She went on to refer to her work as a "ghost story," and that description was widely reprinted in British newspapers at the time, perhaps one influence among many on Victorian readers' broad concept of "ghost stories" generally if not also "Christmas ghost stories" specifically. (A number of stage adaptations of the novel over the years were "conceived of as Christmas entertainment."[8]) The alchemical studies of Hermes Trismegistus and the admonition to the student in "The Fiery Skull" recall Victor Frankenstein and the warning about concentrating on Albertus Magnus and Paracelsus as he had done, suggesting a familiarity with the work.

Aside from Scott, Borlase had an admiration for Edgar Allan Poe—a number of whose works were first published in the annual *The Gift: A Christmas and New Year's Present*[9]—that he enthusiastically shared by doing multiple public readings of the author's work in both England and Australia.[10] Borlase also admired Mary Elizabeth Braddon,[11] a prolific writer and editor of ghost stories,

[8] Steven Earl Forry, *Hideous Progenies: Dramatizations of Frankenstein from Mary Shelley to the Present* (Philadelphia: University of Pennsylvania Press, 1990), 55.

[9] The Edgar Allan Poe Society of Baltimore, "Poe's Writings in *The Gift,*" March 31, 2012, https://www.eapoe.org/works/editions/agftoo1c.htm.

[10] "Mitcheldean," *Gloucestershire Chronicle,* Oct. 4, 1862, 5; "Mechanic's Institute," *Tasmanian Times* [Hobart Town], June 29, 1867, 2.

[11] *Hamilton Advertiser* [Scotland], June 27, 1891, 2.

something for which she was occasionally criticized:

> [W]hy fill Christmas books with ghost stories, and devil-hunts, and all that is superstitious, and silly, and absolutely bad? Will Miss Braddon or her publishers answer this?[12]

Borlase was also known to have a considerable familiarity with the "city mysteries" genre, having reportedly written a *Mysteries of Melbourne* and attempted to syndicate a *Mysteries of Sydney* by Adam Lindsay Gordon while in Australia.[13] In later years the *New York Mercury* would advertise across the United States that "a new and original series of THE MYSTERIES OF PARIS, covering the time of the second empire and the commune and revealing as with a master hand the follies of fair Paris, will be contributed by JAMES S. BORLASE."[14] The original *Mysteries of Paris* had a passage involving the truth of what happened to a well-dressed traveler who had stopped at a house on Christmas Eve for supper and a bed.[15] It seems as though it may have inspired Erckmann-Chatrian's *Le Juif polonais* (*The Polish Jew*) and one of the stories in the present volume, as well as having generally encouraged events of Christmas horror in other city mysteries, for example:

> "On Christmas Eve, at the hour of sunset—" shrieked the Astrologer, his features convulsed with anger, and his voice wild and piercing in its tones—"One of you will die by the other's hand! The winding sheet is woven, and the coffin made—you are rushing madly on your doom!"
>
> George Lippard, *Dora Livingstone, the Adulteress: or, The Quaker City* (London: G. Purkiss, 1848), 12.[16]

During this early period, Borlase also began making periodic

---

[12] "The Magazines," *Buchan Observer and East Aberdeenshire Advertiser,* Dec. 11, 1868, 4.

[13] Sussex (2004), 105.

[14] "The New York Sunday Mercury," *Tarborough Southerner* [N.C.], March 1, 1888, 1.

[15] Eugène Sue, *The Mysteries of Paris. Vol. 2* (London: Chapman and Hall, 1845), 338-340.

[16] Despite the challenge of adapting a sprawling text, the British theatrical adaptation of Lippard's novel made use of the Christmas prophecy as well. See Jamie Bridges, "Mysteries of an American City: The Monk's Hall Manuscript," *Victorians Institute Journal Annex,* http://www.nines.org/exhibits/Mysteries_of_an_American_City_.

use of the pseudonym J. J. G. Bradley, his father's real first initials, the surname just invention. "The Steel-Bound Valise" appeared under that name, while for all the others included here Borlase used his own upon initial publication (or republication if originally anonymous.)

Christmas Supplements and an Australian Gothic Interlude

In an anonymous story later republished in a revised form,[17] Borlase commented on the Australian's relation to British Christmas ghosts:

> when December comes, which is our midsummer, and blazing hot, I can tell you, we look out for "Peter Parley's Annual," and, dear me, how strange some of the stories do seem, and the pictures as well, to lads who have never seen ice or snow, and so can only guess what fun sliding, and skating, and snowballing must be. And then as to the ghost stories in some of the Christmas Supplements. Why, though our country is as big as the whole of Europe, and dotted all over with towns and cities, we haven't got a haunted house in one of them, that I ever heard tell of. Now that is an odd thing, isn't it?[18]

Aside from international periodical distribution, Australian papers occasionally reprinted British stories, or Australian authors chose to set Christmas ghost stories in the old home country. Nonetheless, others found ways to make Australia's characteristics work. "[R]ural isolation [...] nature itself, harsh and unforgiving [...] there's an *unheimlich* quality to this country's wilderness, which makes it clear that most characters—human or otherwise—are unwelcome. *Leave*, they seem to say. *You don't*

---

[17] Skipp Borlase, "Saved by Shadows: Adventures of a Man, a Boy, and an Ass with a Traveling Show in New South Wales and Queensland," *South Wales Echo*, Jan. 12, 1893, 4; Jan. 16, 1893, 4; Jan. 17, 1893, 4; Skipp Borlase, "Saved by Shadows," in *Stirring Tales of Colonial Adventure* (London: C. Arthur Pearson, 1894).

[18] Anonymous, "Through Many Perils; or, Adventures with a Magic Lantern," *Peter Parley's Christmas Annual* (1885): 109-156.

belong here."[19] Whether Borlase conceived it that way or not, it fits the bill—and tips the billycock hat to German tradition as well.

Christmas supplements and characteristically Australian ghost stories for them were uncommon during 1864-1869 when he lived there, however. For the most part he mined that part of his life for adventure and crime stories to be published in other seasons, and his efforts in actively marketing his speaking and writing there helped prepare for the more competitive market back in England. The only specifically Christmas writing he did while in Australia was a sunny, religious poem.

Folk Horror Made to Order

Borlase's earliest Christmas ghost stories, all written in the first person, suggested the influences of his reading and the publication market. However, in a self-publicity piece (written in third person), he remarked that starting in 1880 "he attempted a new style of writing, and with such signal success that he has worked the same profitable mine ever since."[20] Post-1880, his procedure seems to have primarily involved identifying short passages regarding ghosts, witches, deals with the devil, and so on from works of local history and folklore, then writing a longer story of his own from that germ of an idea and resetting the events around Christmas. In some ways this practice is similar to the story of Christmas itself: the actual Biblical story of Christmas is quite brief; much of the story as we know it today is the result of Christians' choice to expand on it in art and apocrypha, some of the latter coincidentally translated by the scholar (and Christmas ghost story teller) M.R. James.[21]

Potential sources for the title story of this collection are many;[22] the shrieking skull is a British tradition and also found

[19] Lisa L. Hannett, "Wide Open Fear: Australian Horror and Gothic Fiction," www.thisishorror.co.uk/columns/southern-dark/wide-open-fear-australian-horror-and-gothic-fiction.

[20] "Some Interesting Notes about Mr. James Skipp Borlase," *Beverley Echo* [Yorkshire, England], April 3, 1888, 2.

[21] Montague Rhodes James, *The Apocryphal New Testament; Being the Apocryphal Gospels, Acts, Epistles, and Apocalypses* (Oxford: Clarendon Press, 1924), 74-75, 172.

[22] *E.g.*, Henry Taylor, *Old Halls of Lancashire and Cheshire* (Manchester: J.E. Cornish, 1884), 69.

its way into F. Marion Crawford's 1908 "The Screaming Skull."
Another Borlase tale drawn from historical sources, "The Black
Cat," quotes details related to a 1661 witch trial that had been
infrequently reprinted and thus could only have been found in a
limited number of places:

> It was also decreed that "persones jmprisoned for witchcraft
> shall have no watch with them jn ther prisones, nor fyre nor
> candle, but that sex men nightly and dayly attend and watch
> them jn the vper tolbooth, and that the quarter-master shall
> order the watchmen to visit them at every three houres end
> night and day." James Cargill Guthrie, *The Vale of Strathmore:
> Its Scenes and Legends* (Edinburgh: William Paterson, 1875), 495.

Newspapers appear to have liked the idea of local stories; Borlase's (and other writers') would often be teased to readers prior
to publication. Some papers repeatedly returned to him year
after year for more. Additionally, a number of the stories would
have details and even their titles altered if it helped sales in other
markets. "The Witch Branks" could be of Loughborough, or
Forfar, or Stoke-Upon-Trent, or whatever was needed.

Borlase's Skeleton in the Closet: Victorian Re-Origination

In 1843, Charles Dickens sued regarding what was felt to be a
particularly egregious violation of his copyright, a work actually
titled "A Christmas Ghost Story. Re-Originated from the Original
by Charles Dickens, Esq., and Analytically Condensed Expressly
for This Work." It was one of only several instances of copyright
violations occurring just within the subgenre.

Borlase, for his own part, was never sued regarding his writing. However, after he had returned from Australia to England
an anonymous writer in the *Australian Journal* accused "Mr.
Skiplace" of having "furnish[ed] certain literary contributions"
that "bore more than a mere 'family likeness' to 'Ivanhoe'" and to
have been "lactating freely at Sir Walter's dairy." If the complaint
referred to published works, it's clear Borlase owed inspiration to
Walter Scott, but not direct plagiarism.[23]

[23] "Our Whatnot," *Australian Journal*, Dec. 1870, 219. [Quoted in Sussex (2004), 111-112.]

Evidence of borrowings from elsewhere was published in the *Bulletin of the Bibliographical Society of Australia and New Zealand* in 1997, with some stories conclusively found to contain fragments from nonfiction, and with the analysis of an anonymously contributed story in the *Australian Journal* that was also later republished in revised form under Borlase's name. The analysis determined that the two versions contained writing characteristic of both James Skipp Borlase and Mary Fortune, with the greater share belonging to the latter.

> But why is it that Mary Fortune seems never to have offered any protest? It may be that, having seen her story in print and having (presumably) been paid for it, she never learned of its after-history. It may be that she came to know but could see no prospect of effective redress. Or it may even be that she regarded Borlase's use of one story as a fitting recompense for his editorial labours on her apprentice-work. […]
>
> Whatever his motive, his part in this anonymous story was to be his last publication in the *Australian Journal* and may be the last legitimate product of an unacknowledged but fruitful literary partnership with Mary Fortune.
>
> Lucy Sussex and John Burrows, "Whodunit?: Literary Forensics and the Crime Writing of James Skipp Borlase and Mary Fortune," *Bulletin* 21, 2 (1997): 73–106.[24]

The editor has found instances of Borlase republishing revised versions of stories that had originally specifically been credited to "Waif Wander" (Fortune). "Surly Dick's Big Nugget" had been twice acknowledged as a work by her, published anonymously, then republished as Borlase's. "Kirsty Oglevie" had been credited to Waif Wander, then republished as Borlase's.[25]

There are asterisks to a couple of the stories in this volume

[24] See also Lucy Sussex, "'Whodunit?' A Postscript," *Bulletin* 22, 2 (1998): 111-113.

[25] "Answers to Correspondents," *Australian Journal* 1, 14 (Dec. 2, 1865): 223; "Notice," *Australian Journal* 1, 18 (Dec. 30, 1865): 279; "Recollections of a Digger.—No. II: Surly Dick and His Nugget," *Australian Journal* 1, 19 (Jan. 6, 1866): 292-295; J. J. G. Bradley, "Dick's Big Nugget," *Sheffield Independent,* Christmas Supplement, Dec. 23, 1876, 3; Waif Wander, "Kirsty Oglevie," *Australian Journal* 1, 42 (June 16, 1866): 661-663; J. S. Borlase, "Stories of the Bush. No. V. 'Kirsty Oglevie,'" *Essex Halfpenny Newsman*, June 13, 1874, 3.

that had originally appeared anonymously. "The Fiery Skull" had originally appeared under the title "The Student's Tale." In title and style, it bears resemblance to Borlase's "Sketch from a Law-Student's Diary," but that first appearance had credited its authorship to "Muta." The name Muta was attached to other contributions both accepted and rejected by the journal.[26] Unless it had been an elaborate ruse by Borlase to make the publishers or readers think the journal had more authors than in actuality, perhaps he only had a hand in editing it, if that.

"Bored to Death," before being credited to Borlase in 1875 and having the mention of Boxing Night added, among other changes, had appeared in the *Australian Journal,* and even before that in the New York City periodical *Harper's New Monthly Magazine.* Its reference to "Chapter One Hundred and Twelve of the 'Hobgoblin Husband'" seems like self-satire, given Borlase's career-long association with serials. He did have a gift for humor, one review of readings he delivered at a Mechanic's Institute in Tasmania observing, "As to the comic afterpiece, in 'The adventures of Mr. Timothy Tiggs on Salt Pan Plains,' (an old poem we take it, localised for the occasion) Mr. Borlase kept his audience in a roar of laughter for a quarter of an hour."[27] Borlase would even become the editor of *Fun, or, The Tasmanian Charivari* for a time.[28] He was published in New York papers a number of times over the decades, but a foreign acceptance so early in his career does give one pause, especially with there being another instance of an anonymous, humorous, Harper's publication being anonymously republished in Australia, then being credited to Borlase's pseudonym in the following decade.[29] Further research and analysis is clearly required.

Still, Borlase clearly wrote much that was his own. He estimated that he had "produced more than a hundred 60,000 to

[26] "Answers to Correspondents." *Australian Journal* 1, 11 (Nov. 11, 1875), 175; Muta, "Power of Words," *Australian Journal* 2, 71 (Jan. 5, 1867), 302-303; Muta, "Nemesis: or, The Deserted Claim," *Australian Journal* 2, 73 (Jan. 19, 1867), 327-328.

[27] "Mechanic's Institute," *Tasmanian Times* [Hobart Town], June 29, 1867, 2.

[28] "Local News," *Tasmanian Times,* August 24, 1867, 4.

[29] "What Dick Blaize Found at Church," *Harper's Weekly,* Sept. 9, 1865, 566; "What Dick Blaize Found at the Church," *Australian Journal,* August 18, 1866, 807; J. J. G. Bradley, "What Dick Blaize Found at Church," *Merthyr Express* [Glamorgan, Wales], August 29, 1874, 3-4.

90,000 words serials, and short tales ad infinitum,"[30] and that rings true when searching databases of newspapers and journals. Moreover, the fact that he set so many of his ghost stories during the season, rather than merely having them published then, make him worth consideration. He recognized a market and regularly supplied it with work practically guaranteed publication, and was received well enough to keep being invited back to do more.

As some bibliographers have printed the wrong year for his death, it may be worth including a notice of his death in full:

AUTHOR DIES AT BRIGHTON.

—

Mr. James Skipp Borlase, who died suddenly on Monday at 141, Queen's Park-road, Brighton, was a voluminous writer of stories for serial publication. Perhaps one of his best-known works was "Stirring Tales of Colonial Adventure," but he was also the author of "Daring Deeds," "The Night Fossickers," and many other stories. He was the eldest son of the late Mr. J. J. G. Borlase, a solicitor, of Mitcheldean, and was 70 years of age.

Brighton Gazette [Sussex]. November 6, 1909: 1 col 5.

Whether Borlase deserves a lump of coal as a possible plagiarist of "The Fiery Skull" or "Bored to Death" remains to be seen. Certain of his works outside the Christmas ghost story genre decidedly make the naughty list. However, this author's past ubiquity at Christmas is unquestionable and this first collection of so many of his Christmas ghost stories should provide an informative and enjoyable window into the tastes of the Victorian era.

CHRISTOPHER PHILIPPO
October 2022

---

[30] "The Author a Penzance Man," *Cornish Telegraph, and Mining, Agricultural, and Commercial Gazette* [Penzance], Sept. 10, 1902, 1.

NOTE ON THE TEXTS

The texts contained in this volume are reprinted verbatim from the sources listed below, with the exception of a small number of obvious printer's errors, which have been silently corrected.

"A Weird Wooing; or, The Ghost-Guarded Treasure: A Tale of an Old-Time Christmas and New Year's Days." *Runcorn Examiner*, Dec. 23, 1898, 3.

"A Bride from the Dead: A Tale of a Dreadful Christmas Wedding on the Cumberland Fells." *Yorkshire Herald*, Dec. 23, 1899, 13.

"The Shrieking Skull; or, Haunted Wardley Hall: A Tale of Two Lancashire Christmas Eves." *Marylebone Mercury* [London], Dec. 21, 1901, 14.

"The Black Cat, or The Witch Branks of Loughborough. A Story of Two Leicestershire Christmas Eves." *Leicester Chronicle*, Dec. 19, 1885, 10.

"Two Ghostly Swordsmen; or The Duel on the Moor. A Christmas Story of Brandesburton." *Hull Times*, Jan. 28, 1905, 2.

"The Fiery Skull: A Tale of Magic and Spiritualism." *Sheffield Daily Telegraph*, Christmas Supplement, Dec. 24, 1875, 4.

"Twelve Miles Broad." *The Australian Journal*, Dec. 1885, 187-188.

"The Haunted Silk Mill, or, The Ghost-Guarded Treasure." *Derby and Chesterfield Reporter*, Dec. 22, 1905, 2.

"The Steel-Bound Valise; or The Murder at the Old Stone Cross." *Sheffield Daily Telegraph*, Dec. 24, 1875, 11.

"Bored to Death." *Penrith Observer*. Dec. 21, 1875, 7.

"The Spectre Horseman: or, Haunted Wye-Coller Hall. A Christmas Story." *Luton Reporter* [Bedfordshire], Our Christmas Budget Supplement, Dec. 18, 1903, 6-7.

"Our Fellow Lodger; or, The Adventures of a Christmas Eve." *Albury Banner and Wodonga Express* [NSW], Dec. 28, 1867, 2.

"A Tale of Two Christmases." *Walthamstow and Leyton Guardian*, Dec. 7, 1907, 2.

A WEIRD WOOING;

OR,

THE GHOST-GUARDED TREASURE.

A Tale of an Old-Time Christmas and New Year's Days.

CHAPTER I.

THE WEIRD WOOING AT ST. ANTHONY'S CHAPEL.

The Christmas Eve, which fell on the Fifth of January, 1748, was, even as far north as Edinburgh, as mild and sunny as many a May Day; yet that was not the reason why Ivor Oliphant had begged Muriel Drummond to meet him at St. Anthony's ruinous chapel (which still stands at the base of Arthur's Seat, looking across what is now the Queen's Park, towards the grim and yet stately old palace of Holyrood) but because her stern, mercenary father, Sir John Drummond, had forbidden him admission to his mansion in the Canongate, as being a pardoned "rebel," whose already deeply mortgaged estates had been confiscated in consequence of his having drawn his sword, *on the losing side,* during the Civil War of 1745 and 1746.

This the young gentleman had done not so much out of loyalty to the gallant, but ill-fated Chevalier, as in the hope that he would thereby win name and fame and wealth that, united, would make him more worthy of the hand of the beautiful girl whom he idolised rather than merely loved, and whose constancy he believed, at the time, no misfortune could shake.

Alas, he had had, of late, grave reasons for doubting her once as firmly believed-in fidelity, and he had sought, entreated, aye,

even prayed for the coming interview, in order to put it to a final
test.

And yet he looked as handsome, frank, and *debonaire* a young
fellow as ever won a woman's heart, and kept it through weal and
woe; for he was tall and stalwart, fair of complexion, and perfect
of feature, with laughing blue eyes, a pleasant smile, a soft voice;
and, best of all, a dauntless heart.

There was no smile upon his lips, or laughter in his eyes upon
the present occasion, however, for he had come to St. Anthony's
Chapel to know his fate—to learn from the girl whose love he still
felt sure he had once possessed, whether the rumour was true
or false that she had, at last, yielded to her father's commands,
and consented to marry old and ugly Sir Ralph Restalrigg, whose
enormous wealth was the only recommendation he possessed.

The lady was already late at the tryst. In the early days of their
mutual love she had never kept him waiting half as long as she
was doing on this, he began to believe, ill-starred occasion; so he
shook his head, (which was crowned by the well powdered tie
wig and triple cocked hat of the period), sadly and dejectedly, as
his moody gaze wandered over The Hunter's Bog, and St. Margaret's Loch in turn, and hummed in low tones:

> "Now Arthur's Seat shall be my bed,
> Saint Anton's Well my drink shall be,
> Since my true love's forsaken me."

as sad of heart the while as had been the jilted lover who composed the words and gave them their pathetic tune on that very
spot a hundred years and more ago.

Presently, however, the expression of his face entirely changed,
for two men, bearing a sedan chair, had suddenly turned the
shoulder of the hill from the direction of Dunrappie's Loch, and
come to a halt beside the clear, for ever up-bubbling waters of
Saint Anthony's well.

Ivor Oliphant at once darts back into the little chapel ruins,
for it strikes him that Muriel Drummond may not wish her chair-
bearers to know whom she has come hither to meet; and there
he plays nervously with the hilt of his sword until, a couple of
minutes later, there entered the chapel in turn a young lady of

some nineteen years of age, and so wondrous lovely that the man might well have been excused for the committal of any act of folly whilst under the influences of her charms.

She was as dark as her lover was fair, with great star-like eyes, that could be as soft as moonlight or as dazzling as the lightning's flash; her figure was perfectly and somewhat voluptuously proportioned, her skin wonderfully clear, her features most delicately chiselled, her lips ruby red, and her teeth of ivory whiteness; but there were times when, influenced by sudden and violent anger, the latter would bite the former till little beads of blood rose thereon; for, though so lovely to outward seeming, Muriel Drummond was haughty, self-willed, passionate, and, worse than all, intensely selfish.

Some of her female friends called her, amongst themselves, "*The Leopard*," and she certainly possessed the innate ferocity of that animal, as well as its outward beauty and grace of motion.

There was much of that grace about her now, as she advanced towards her lover with both hands outstretched, at the same time saying:

"Well, here I am, you see, though why you subjected me to the pain of again meeting you I cannot tell for the life of me. You know that I love you, Ivor; but with no chance of your ever being able to afford to marry me what is the use of our carrying on our pitiful little comedy any further?"

"If you *really* loved me, Muriel, you could not speak to me in such a tone and way."

"I do love you, though, and with one solitary exception, better, aye, much better than I do anyone else in the world."

"And the solitary exception is, I suppose, old Sir Ralph Restalrigg, with whose name all Edinburgh has lately taken to couple your own?" rejoined the young man, bitterly.

"No, Ivor, the exception is myself. I love myself better even than I do you, and so I have, at last, made up my mind to marry Sir Ralph Restalrigg, solely because he can bestow upon me all that my love of luxury and pleasure have taught me to regard as essentials to my happiness."

"Muriel, I have tried hard to win wealth for your sake."

"I know it; but then, you see, you have failed."

"You would once have gladly shared comparative poverty with me. Oh, why did I not then urge you to do so?"

"Because you thought more of my welfare than you did of your own happiness. Ah! I was worth winning in those days. A young girl of sixteen has, in general, very few faults; but God help such an one three years later, if she becomes motherless and possesses a father such as mine."

Here tears filled the lovely speaker's eyes, and full of pity, Ivor Oliphant would fain have folded her in his embrace and kissed her fondly, had she not eluded him.

"No, Ivor, no," she said, in sorrowful tones. "With all my faults I am still pure; so I will not allow even you to press lips that of right now belong to another. I have told you what I really am in order to show you how little you lose in losing me."

"By the light of heaven I have not lost you yet, nor do I intend to do so until I have made one more determined effort to win you. Alas, had poor Prince Charley but succeeded in recovering his father's throne I should, ere now, have been the owner of unmortgaged lands, and, most probably, of a title as well."

"I warned you, Ivor, when you joined the Prince's standard, that six feet by two of English or of Scottish soil was the sole amount of land that you would ever win in his service; a service you entered as Master of Oliphant, and quitted a penniless and proscribed adventurer. Thank heaven that you had not to pay the further penalty of losing your head upon Tower Hill."

"That matter is an old song now, Muriel, so I prithee to sing it no longer. There is, however, a path to wealth still lying open before me, and I mean to tread it this very night," responded our hero, determinedly.

"Not the road, Ivor! Oh, not the road!" exclaimed the fair girl, with a shudder, "for, though it is a gallant calling enough, and followed nowadays by many young men of good family; nor is there, that I can see, any lack of honour in pursuing such a career so long as blackmail is only levied upon whigs and such like, yet the highway so often leads to the gibbet, that——"

"I was not thinking of adopting the profession of a highwayman, fashionable though it has become," exclaimed Oliphant, laughingly interrupting her.

"No," he added, suddenly becoming grave again, "but there is an old building in Edinburgh which is supposed to be crammed with wealth, belonging now to no one, and yet which it would require a bold and even well-nigh desperate man to appropriate, for the house I speak of has been closed, barred, bolted, locked and sealed for more than a hundred years, and *the Plague lies buried therein.*"

"No, no, Ivor, it was not the Plague but Death himself who was buried a century ago in that old house in Beth's Wynd."

"Death *him*self? What on earth do you mean, Muriel? For whoever heard of Death being of the masculine gender?" exclaimed Oliphant.

"Listen and you shall hear, for my great aunt on the mother's side, Mistress Eldspeth Macfarlane, who died in her hundred and sixth year, when I was a little girl of nine, was herself a little girl at the period of great pestilence, and told my mother the tale of that old house in my presence, as I will now tell it to you, in order to deter you from the desperate enterprise which you seem to contemplate."

"Tell it me, then, though mayhap it will only strengthen my resolve," answered Oliphant, with a scornful laugh.

"Well, when the fell disease was at its height, and floated about in the air in the shape of little golden-hued serpents no thicker than hairs; when huge bonfires blazed in every street to combat the awful stench of human corruption, and wherever two thoroughfares met a gibbet was set up whereon to hang any and all persons who managed to escape out of a house the plague had entered, and each one of which was branded with a great red cross painted on its front door, Death, owing to his countless victories over life, won the power of incarnating himself, that is to say, of assuming a human form, a tall, gaunt, livid-faced man, wearing a broad-brimmed black hat slouched down over his forehead even to his eyes, which gleamed like live coals, and, draped in a long, loose horseman's cloak, reaching to his feet, he entered every house wherein the infected lay at their last gasp, in order to bear their souls away."

"Go on, Muriel," urged Oliphant, with a ghastly smile, as the girl at this juncture came to a panting pause, owing to being well-nigh overcome by the horrors she had conjured up.

"Of course," she continued, with an effort, "whenever Death entered no one ventured to oppose him and few were bold enough even to look at him; but the idea at last occurred to a few that he might be privily followed to some house or other, and secured therein, so that he could do no further harm, and, eventually, he was, one night, so followed, and, happily, imprisoned in that old mansion in Beth's Wynd, where, at the time, the only remaining doctor in Edinburgh whom the Plague had spared, lay in his last agony. Well, a guard was instantly set at the front and back doors, and within an hour those doors, and every window as well, were boarded over, and sods were even laid atop of all the chimneys. The next day the wood-work was well tarred over, as it has been twice a year ever since. The Plague suddenly ceased its ravages so soon as Death was thus made captive, but a dreadful curse will assuredly fall upon that individual who opens his prison and lets him forth, most probably to bring the awful pestilence amongst us once more. Oh, Ivor, for God's sake, be not thou that man!"

"Muriel, your story makes no mention of the treasure."

"That was so unimportant an item compared with the others that I did not introduce it into my narrative. You must know that Doctor Davie Duncan, whose soul Death was going for when he was trapped, and forever, it is to be hoped, made captive, was a man whom every one revered for his probity and honour, wherefore nearly all the plague-stricken whom he attended confided their gold, jewels and plate to his care, lest they should be stolen by the drivers of the corpse-carts, when they came into their houses for their bodies, to convey them, uncoffined, and merely wrapped in the blankets whereon they had died, to the plague pits, wherein hundreds were interred before the yawning gulphs were covered over— But what are you laughing at now, Ivor?"

"I was laughing, Muriel, at the credulity of mankind, and at that clever fellow who frightened people into the belief that he was death incarnated. Why, can't you perceive, as clearly as I do, that he must have been a common thief, who went into dying folk's houses, not for their souls, but for their gold and plate? Under that long, loose cloak of his he could carry away any amount of booty, and he knew well enough that his sombre get up, and his fictitious character, would frighten everyone from molesting him. Ah, he doubtless hoped to make a fine haul at Doctor Davie Duncan's. Of course, the fact of the plague subsiding so soon as he was effectually bottled up was a mere coincidence, for, in all probability, the pestilence had by then worn itself out. Well, the Doctor and Death, as you dub him, are still in possession, I reckon, though reduced to mere skeletons by this time, I should say. Happily the treasure must be there also, and that treasure shall become mine ere the rising sun ushers in another day."

"The treasure may be guarded and defended by the ghosts of the two dead men, Ivor!"

"Now, out upon your old world superstition, though even if it were so, a couple of live men, armed to the teeth, would better guard it against me than a dozen ghosts. Muriel, my own darling, I will win that treasure, and through the treasure your own most adorable self. What say you? Is it agreed?"

"If you are quite sure that the Powers of Darkness will not be mixed up in the matter, it is agreed, Ivor."

"The darkness of the night will be the only darkness to be dealt with, my own darling, and that will be friendly instead of adverse. Come, bear a stout heart, and also quickly get you gone, for I have much to see to ere night arrives. Old Sir Ralph Restalrigg may now go whistle for a wife, whilst I will win the fairest and bonniest in all Edinburgh. Kiss me, Muriel, for, as matters stand, you may do so with a clear conscience. Kiss me and then away. To-morrow I will call at your father's house in Canongate, and demand of him your hand in marriage, without the slightest fear of being again turned from his door."

Carried away by her lover's sanguine hopes, and her own real affection for him, the kiss was given, and then Muriel Drummond ran down the hillside, and re-entered her sedan chair, to be borne swiftly away.

The weird wooing was ended, but the most woful wedding ever chronicled was yet to come.

CHAPTER II.

THE GHOST-GUARDED TREASURE IN BETH'S WYND.

Let not the reader suppose that our gruesome Christmas story is far-fetched and improbable, for, on the contrary, it has the merit, if merit it is, of being as true as it is strange.

In proof of how long-lived and hard to kill superstition is, we may here add that when the old house in Beth's Wynd, which, in imagination, we are now about to enter, was pulled down in the year 1808, to permit of the Advocate's Library being erected on its site, it was still furnished exactly as when the Plague had visited it in 1645, and all Edinburgh was alarmed lest the pestilence should burst forth out of its long sealed-up tomb therein, and work as great havoc as it had done nearly two centuries previously; many people, indeed, left the city, and returned not thereto until time had dissipated their fears; but now to return to our tale.

We have described the day as being sunny and almost summery; but, as night drew on, the wind suddenly veered round from south to north, and in the month of January that implies a great deal in such a high latitude as Edinburgh.

Consequently, the heavens were clouded over, and thick flakes of snow had begun to fall, when, close upon midnight, Ivor Oliphant, wearing a long loose cloak, and carrying a bag, which held, for the present, nothing but a well-greased saw and a dark lantern, clambered over a low wall in the rear of the old house in Beth's Wynd, and came to a halt in front of a boarded-over window.

He had encountered very few people on the way, for Christmas Eve is not the period of rejoicing, and too frequently of drunkenness, that it is in England; whilst, once arrived at his destination, our hero had little fear of his labours being interrupted, knowing, as he did, that no one would approach that supposedly accursed old mansion after nightfall for any consideration whatever.

So he laid his bag down amongst the rank weeds and the dead nettles which entirely hid the pavement of the narrow, walled-in courtyard from view, and taking out his saw, set zealously to work upon the black, tarred boards which covered the window through which he had resolved to effect an entrance.

The labour was comparatively easy, so decayed and worm-eaten was the wood, and when the clock of St. Giles's Cathedral began to boom forth the midnight hour, he had made a square orifice amply large enough to admit of his clambering there-through.

Breaking a pane of glass in the window, he inserted his hand, forced back the catch, and then, though not without considerable difficulty, and the putting forth of all his strength, succeeded in raising the lower sash.

A minute later he stood within "Death's Prison," and as he alighted on the floor, so dense a cloud of dust arose therefrom, that it nearly choked him; whilst, at the same instant, a hundred fiery eyes gleamed upon him out of the darkness, and then vanished, as the rats, their owners, with shrill squeals of alarm, darted into their holes.

As quickly as possible Ivor now lighted the candle in his dark lantern, and by its aid looked about him.

The room he had entered was furnished, and on the table stood the remnants of the last meal that had ever been partaken of therein; but the plates, dishes and glasses, were covered with dust and the air was full of moths.

Believing that the goal of his labours lay further and higher, Ivor Oliphant opened a door and then ascended a staircase that was full of treacherous holes, but those the light of his lantern enabled him to safely avoid.

The room which he next entered, at the top thereof, proved to be *the* room, and even our hero's iron will was powerless to prevent him from rushing out of it far more quickly than he had gone in, for there, in a bed, whose counterpane had grown yellow from age, was a corpse; and stretched out on the floor yet another, the latter lying on its face with arms and legs stretched out in the shape of a St. Andrew's Cross, and each hand grasping a bag, whilst stirred by the draught that came up the staircase and through the open door from the broken window, the voluminous black cloak in which the body was draped, fluttered as though he that it covered was still embued with life.

The face of the corpse in the bed, with the parchment-hued, dust-covered, moth-perforated clothes tucked up under its chin, was that of a mere skeleton; but stray locks of grey hair, and a long grey beard still adhered to the bare bones.

The countenance of the other dead man could not be seen, because it was buried in the carpet.

It doubtless, however, pertained to the robber, who, a hundred and three years previously, had posed as Death rendered incarnate, and, thus insolently mocking the dread King of Terrors, had been struck down by him in the midst of his sins in this awful manner; for, all round him, as he lay there, crucified as it were, to the floor, was the metallic gleam of gold, and the yet brighter sparkle of gems and jewels.

As Ivor Oliphant entered the room a second time—for his panic was only of short duration—it struck him that the robber must have collected all the treasure together, which had been entrusted by his dying patients to Doctor Davie Duncan for safe keeping, before discovering that he had been followed to the house, and firmly secured therein.

Then most probably followed a lingering death from famine, unless, indeed, the Plague had seized upon and consigned him to a quicker, though more agonising doom.

In either case his lust of gold had apparently caused him, eventually, to return to that chamber, so awfully tenanted, and die wallowing in, and greedily clutching at the glittering bait which had lured him on and on, to his destruction, no matter what previous efforts he might have made to effect his escape.

This conviction caused Oliphant to reflect with a shudder:— what if *he* had been seen to enter the old house (for he was well aware that many windows commanded a view of its rear as well as of its front), and the terrified neighbours had hurriedly dressed, run out of their homes, and were now securing him therein, just as that other poor wretch had been secured, more than a century ago; why, then, in another hundred years (it might be less or it might be more), another searcher after the treasure might be tempted to break into the old house even as he had, and would find three dead bodies in that room instead of two.

In deadly fear that such an event might really be happening, he rushed forward, black bag in hand, to secure the tempting treasure.

He fastened his hold, first of all, upon one of the bags of gold which was grasped by a skeleton hand; but, as he did so, a shriek smote upon his ears, and he let it go again with a cry that was just as eerie and shrill.

"Could the treasure really 'be ghost-guarded,'" he shudderingly wondered; but at the same instant the shriek was repeated, and then he knew that it was but the wind blowing in at the open window downstairs; so he set to work with a bolder heart, cramming the gold enclosed in the linen bags, and the hundreds of loose gold pieces, as well as the jewellery which everywhere strewed the dusty, rat-gnawed, moth-perforated carpet, into his own stout leather bag; and, what was left over, into his every pocket.

Then, his task accomplished, he staggered out of the room; for by that time the close, mephitic air of the chamber of death had well-nigh overcome him, and, after almost reeling down the crazy and dilapidated staircase, gained the window by which he had entered the ancient house half-an-hour previously.

It did not take him long to clamber through it, and glad enough he was to breathe once more the pure, fresh, outdoor air.

But he did not beat an immediate retreat from the premises. No, he first of all replaced the square piece of boarding which he had so carefully sawn away, and then, drawing from a pocket a small gallipot, containing a black sticky substance, he rubbed it over the saw marks, so that no one but a very close observer would be able to discover that the wooden barricade had ever been tampered with.

Then he clambered over the court-yard wall again, finding it not so easy a feat this time, so heavily was he laden with spoil; and, a quarter of an hour later, he had gained his lodgings in Baxter's Close off the Lawnmarket, where he spent the remainder of the night in examining his questionably acquired riches, which ended in the discovery that he was wealthy beyond even his wildest hopes.

CHAPTER III.

Ivor Oliphant has become, by one bold coup, a rich man. The jewels of at least a score of once leading Edinburgh families, cut off, root and branch, by the Plague, a hundred and three years ago, are now his, and for days he is busy picking out the stones and melting down the gold settings.

One ring, however, composed of the most lustrous diamonds, he thinks will exactly suit the wedding finger of the lovely girl whom he knows he has securely won, and he keeps it to place over the plain gold hoop that will mark his right of possession over her on the performance of the nuptial ceremonies in the old Grey Friars' Church, on the morning of the 24th March; for, as he had gained his fortune on Christmas Day, he had resolved that he would win his wife on New Year's Day; and, that he should so win her, Muriel Drummond's mercenary father was now well content, for he looked not so much to the man as to the dowry which he would be able to settle upon his daughter, wherefore, so soon as our hero had been able to satisfy him that he was far richer than Sir Ralph Restalrigg, Sir John Drummond gave that ancient swain a summary dismissal, Muriel also breaking her once reluctantly given promise to marry him without so much as the faintest qualm of conscience.

So Ivor took and furnished a fine house in the, at that time, most fashionable part of Edinburgh, for his bride who was to be, and New Year's Day (which then fell upon the day before Lady Day), at last came round, and with it, at all events to the parties chiefly concerned, the fondly and longingly anticipated wedding.

As the bridal cortège entered the gloomy old churchyard on foot, from Candlemaker Row, by way of the steep flight of steps just to the right of the "Martyrs' Monument," bride and bridegroom walking arm in arm, with three fiddlers playing a merry tune immediately in front of them, and the rest of the wedding party following two and two behind, the lovely Muriel shuddered, and when her lover anxiously inquired the reason, she responded, with an evidently forced laugh: "Indeed I cannot tell. Perhaps because someone is walking over the spot where my grave will be," her answer being prompted by a superstition which is not yet entirely exploded, though the bitter March wind would have been a far more reasonable excuse.

A minute later, her wandering gaze happening to alight on a high, weed-grown mound that rose bordering the long, straight path which led up to the church porch, and which they were slowly traversing, she asked, in a low tone, "Is not that the spot where those who died of the Plague were buried?"

"One of the *many* spots, my darling; but let not you or I speak ill of the Plague, for has it not given us unto each other?" Ivor Oliphant whispered back; but started and shuddered, in turn, as the last word quitted his lips, for he could have sworn that he heard a hollow voice respond, apparently issuing from underneath the ground, "Mock not at the Plague, for it is about to rend you two apart for ever!"

And now the grey old church is entered, the minister is awaiting them, the service is quickly commenced, and carried on until it reaches the point where the bridegroom has to place the ring upon the bride's finger.

He does so, and then he slips over it the flashing diamond one which he has so fondly dedicated to be its guard and keeper.

Muriel gives a little gasp of pain as he does so, for something in the ring has pricked her. (It is the tiniest particle of human bone, on the inner side, that has become fixed in the setting, and which Oliphant, often as he had examined it, has never perceived). The next instant, however, the bride is lost in admiration of the beauty of the gems, and the momentary pain is entirely forgotten.

The service is soon over, and the wedding party adjourns to the vestry in order to sign the necessary books and registers. Smiling congratulations are passed around. The minister hands Muriel her marriage certificate and Ivor Oliphant gives her a kiss, murmuring the while, in a low tone "Mine, mine for ever."

Then he suddenly notices how deathly pale she is, and that some strange-looking black spots have appeared upon her face and hands.

He says nothing to alarm her, but begins to feel terribly though vaguely uneasy, and is thankful when they are outside the church and on their way home.

Alas! that home, the home which he has been at such joyful pains to prepare for his lovely bride, is destined never to be reached; for half-way down the long, straight, graveyard-path, Muriel's arm slides out of the embrace of his; and, 'ere he can save her, with a low, gasping moan, she reels and falls right across the rank, weed-grown mound which covers the long-ago buried of the Plague.

With a cry of consternation Ivor Oliphant springs forward to lift her up, but recoils, perfectly appalled by the sudden change in her appearance.

The black spots upon her face, which he had noticed in the vestry, have already doubled in size, and are bubbling, as it were, with corruption.

"Keep away from me, I am dying! Oh, I know that I am dying, and it is from the plague—the plague!" she feebly moans.

All fled at the dreadful words; of friends and relatives not one remained behind, save the heart-broken bridegroom and the distracted father.

Poor Muriel, her suffering, though agonising, was brief. She never spoke again, and in ten minutes all was over.

Then Sir John Drummond would fain have had the poor corpse carried to his house in the Canongate, but by that time the City authorities had appeared upon the scene, and for the safety of the general community sternly forbade such a measure, but insisted upon the body being interred there and then, and their harsh fiat was duly carried out.

So Muriel Drummond was wedded and buried in the same hour, nor were father or husband allowed so much as to touch her remains ere she was hidden from their view for ever.

They themselves were straightway removed to the Tolbooth, and kept close prisoners therein until it became absolutely certain that they had not contracted the fell disease.

When they were set at liberty, the first thing that Ivor Oliphant did was to give all his recently acquired wealth to public charities, after which he enlisted in a Highland regiment, just ordered on foreign service, and a year later, he fell, leading a forlorn hope, at the capture of Arcot.

A BRIDE FROM THE DEAD:

A TALE OF A DREADFUL CHRISTMAS WEDDING ON THE CUMBERLAND FELLS.

CHAPTER I.

TWO SWORN FRIENDS BOUND ON A DESPERATE ENTERPRISE.

On a Christmas Eve, about the middle of the reign of that valiant little monarch George II., the last English king who ever fought for his crown and country in the forefront of battle, a gallant, both handsome and young, mounted on a powerful-looking horse, which had evidently been ridden fast and far, trotted up the long and struggling single street of Keswick in Cumberland, and drew rein at the door of the ancient bow-windowed hostelry of the "Saracen's Head."

"Hope I see you sound in mind and limb, Captain Kirkland, and I bid you a hearty welcome back to your ain countree. We've all heard of your brave deeds in the Lowlands of Germany, and we are bound to think that you are Cumberland born and bred," exclaimed the burly landlord, as he bustled forth through a doorway that was none too wide for his easy passage to and fro, for mine host was a man of some thirty stone weight.

"Thanks, Glassonby, for so kindly a greeting, and we'll have a long chat together when I am not so pressed for time. Is Mr. Dacre here?"

"Aye, sir, and has been for the last hour and more. He's eagerly expecting you, I fancy, for he's been stamping up and down my brand new coffee-room carpet, in his muddy jack-boots, ever since he arrived, just as though he was treading on nothing better than a sanded floor."

"Has he already supped?"

"Neither meat nor drink has passed his lips, in this house at any rate, and by the look of his nag I should say that he hadn't once drawn rein throughout a thirty miles ride, your honour."

"Then give each of our horses a quart of old ale to wash down their oats and beans, for we shall probably have to betake ourselves to our saddles again within the passing hour. As for ourselves, send us in the best that your house affords, together with a bottle of old-crusted port."

"I hope for your own safety's sake, that neither of you young gentlemen will quit 'The Saracen's Head' before to-morrow, Captain Kirkland."

"Why, what on earth is there to be afraid of?"

"Half a dozen as thorough-paced scoundrels, unless their looks vastly belie them, as ever sat round my kitchen fire. They aver that they are riding on the king's service, to account, I suppose, for their being armed to the teeth, but unless I'm altogether out in my reckoning it's their own business which they are bound on, and that a very black business at its best. Their leader—or at all events, their apparent leader—is own brother to the bonnie young lady whom your honour's heart was once so firmly set on, and who, if common report is to be believed, is about to be forced into a marriage, much against her will, with old Sir Archibald Dutton of The Howk."

"It is to prevent that marriage from being consummated that I am here, Glassonby."

"And perhaps it is to prevent you from thrusting your finger into this pie of the devil's own baking that those cut-throats are now in my kitchen and their horses all ready saddled in my stables, for their leader ordered that only the bridles should be removed," growled the landlord.

But this concluding speech of his was unheard by the individual to whom it was addressed, who ere its close, had darted into the hostelry, eager to greet his waiting friend.

"Kirkland, welcome home again!"

"Dacre, a thousand thanks for keeping this rendezvous."

Such was the mutual greeting, accompanied by a hand-grip that was as hearty as it was sincere.

They were both of them handsome young fellows of about twenty-five years of age. Richly clad, too, were they in the picturesque costume of the period, when gold or silver-laced velvet coats, elaborately embroidered waistcoats, knee breeches, silk stockings, silver-buckled shoes, powdered tie-wigs, patches, lace, wrist ruffles, and swords in velvet scabbards, constituted the outward visible signs of all men of good birth.

In place of silk stockings and buckled shoes, however, these gallants, being travellers, wore huge jack-boots, formidably spurred; and whilst Captain Kirkland had not yet relieved himself of his long, loose horseman's cloak and triple cocked hat, on which he wore the black cockade of the reigning house of Hanover conspicuously displayed, those belonging to his old schoolfellow and friend, Dacre, were thrown carelessly across a chair.

"What the deuce prompted you to ask me to meet you here, at a village inn, instead of seeking me at my own house, under Grisdale pike, where you would have been so heartily welcomed?" asked Dacre.

"Because I stood in too immediate a need of your services, and my going to Grisdale Pike, instead of your coming here, would have meant the loss of half a dozen, in all probability, precious hours. Dacre, I want you to venture with me into what may prove to be a veritable hornet's nest; and if the snow, which has already commenced, should happen to be a heavy fall, we shall arrive at our journey's end none too soon, though we leave here in an hour's time, for our destination is Murgur Dale, and our route will lie between the Saddleback Mountain and the Souther Fell."

"And what may be the object to be gained by our traversing in such weather as the present as abominable and perilous a track of country as any in all Cumberland, or, for that matter, in all England?" asked Dacre.

"To stop as infamous a marriage as a scoundrel and a coward ever concocted between them."

"Who is the scoundrel, who is the coward, and, above all, who the fair damsel who is apparently to be sacrificed between them; for it is very evident to me that your interest is centred in the bride rather than the bridegroom?"

"Why, that old roué and reprobate, Sir Archibald Dutton, of The Howk, is about to force Sir Ralph Oughterby, of Caldbeck Hall, to give his only daughter, my own affianced bride, and the loveliest girl in all Cumberland, to wife, under the threat that in case of refusal he will denounce him to the Government as having been deeply involved, the year before last, in the cause of the young pretender; and, furthermore, that he will bring his two sons to the gallows at Carlisle for more than one act of robbery upon the King's highway, of all which crimes and misdemeanours he asserts that he holds the most damning proofs; wherefore he is the scoundrel and Oughterby the coward I take it."

"Well, many people in these parts are well aware that the two young Oughterbys have turned highwaymen, though no one has thought much the worse of them on that account, inasmuch as they have only robbed their political enemies. A highwayman's career is, in fact, a somewhat fashionable one at present, and it is said that even the Lord Bishop of Carlisle has more than once ridden forth at night in order to levy blackmail at the pistol's muzzle from some rich Papist or other to help on the repairs of the Cathedral."

"It is a hangable offence, no matter how fashionable it may be, and in order to shut old Sir Archibald's mouth, and make their interests his own, Marjorie Oughterby's father and brothers have determined to force her into his arms. She is to be taken by them to his grim old moated Grange in Murgur Dale, this very night. Alas, we shall be too late to prevent the consummation of that outrage, whilst early on Christmas Day, which is to-morrow, she is to be wedded to him by special licence there."

"No clergyman will tie such a knot, my dear fellow, that is to say, if a young, lovely, and evidently persecuted girl appeals to him with sufficient eloquence to spare her."

"Many clergymen would not, but some few would, and if I am right in my conjectures the bevy of scoundrels who are at present carousing below stairs, are about to set forth on such a parson hunt, and if they can't secure a clerical scamp who will do their dirty business for them without any scruple, they will kidnap an honest one, carry him to The Howk by brute force, and once there, compel him to go right through with the marriage ceremony with a pistol levelled at his head by way of argument that there will be no withstanding."

"And how are we two to stop such a marriage, in heaven's name, opposed as we shall doubtless be by a score or more."

"We may still be in time to assist Marjorie to escape from The Howk in some way or other, ere matters arrive at so dire a pass. If too late for that, I may be able to make her Sir Archibald Dutton's widow within the same hour that she becomes his wife. You know that I am a sure shot, in fact I never yet missed my man. His death will render every member of the Oughterby family as safe as they would be were they allied to him by marriage, so that by shooting him I shall scarcely incur their very deep ill-will."

"And what would save your own neck, let alone mine, from the hangman's noose?" asked Dacre.

"As for yourself, I will only ask you to oppose force with force, so that, should you chance to kill a man, he will fall in fair fight, whilst as far as I am personally concerned I have the king's authority and license to slay, in whatever way I choose, the first scoundrel who happens to deserve such a fate at my hands," answered Captain Kirkland.

" 'The king's license.' That sounds to me most strange."

"I had the good fortune to save his Majesty's life, at the imminent hazard of my own, during the battle of Dettingen. Asked by him what boon I would accept as my reward, I proffered the request I have just named, for I had a presentiment even then that the very thing would happen which is now on the point of happening, and knew that Sir Archibald Dutton would never consent to meet me like a man, sword's point to sword's point. Well, my petition was granted, and hardly had I arrived in England, on a six months' leave of absence, when I received a letter from my darling girl, telling me of the dire fate that was threatening her, a fate which I had keenly apprehended, and, indeed, almost foreseen. Within an hour of the reading of her letter I had started for the north, and here I am at Keswick, resolved to save her from a doom which to her would be worse than death, or else to perish in the attempt."

"And in the prosecution of such attempt I am with you, hand and glove," exclaimed Dacre, with fervour.

"Spoken as I felt sure that you would both speak and feel. Ah, here comes our supper. After we have done it justice we will set out on our journey."

"Those rascals have departed, bag and baggage, Captain Kirkland," remarked the landlord, as he placed a very appetising repast on the table, "and what is better still, they have ridden south instead of north. They looked somewhat suspiciously at your horses, but I don't think I gave them any opportunity of tampering with them."

CHAPTER II.

A WILD RIDE.—STOPPED BY SNOW.—A BRIDE IN BONDAGE.

When the two friends set forth from "The Saracen's Head" on the desperate, and what would have seemed to less daring natures well-nigh hopeless enterprise, the snow was falling thick and fast, and the wind, icy cold and from the north, was blowing in a way that threatened to pile it into deep drifts in many parts of their long and rugged journey.

"I'm by no means sure that the longest way round wouldn't, in our case, taking this snowstorm into consideration, prove to be the shortest, and it would most certainly be the safest," remarked Dacre, as he glanced somewhat anxiously at the leaden-hued sky. "Where a wheeled vehicle is able to go there wouldn't, in all probability, be anything that could stop us, even on such a night as this, but that mere bridle track between the Saddleback and Souther Fell, with mountain streams to be crossed in the darkness, streams that at this time of the year are speedily swollen into torrents, and tarns hundreds of feet in depth, right up to their precipitous margins, that we may inadvertently plunge into at any moment, should we but chance to get a few yards out of our proper path, which the snow will be sure to hide, affords such a variety and plenitude of perils that we can scarcely hope to escape them all."

"God will guard us, be sure of that, comrade, for we go to right a most greivous wrong; aye, He will protect and guide the chosen ministers of His vengeance, if we seem not to doubt His power by diverging from the shortest and most direct route," was Captain Kirkland's retort.

Dacre shrugged his shoulders, but made no other rejoinder, and for a little while the two young men rode on side by side in silence.

Presently the sound of the distant church bells, evidently ringing a joyous Christmas peal, was borne towards them from a distance, but seeming dull and muffled, so heavy was the atmosphere owing to the dense, low-scudding clouds, and the snow-laden air.

That was the last sound they were destined to hear for many hours, for they presently entered upon the dreary and utterly desolate region of moors and mountains, with no light to guide them along their obscure way save that of the tiny lanterns which dangled from each of their stirrup irons, according to the custom of the country and of the period; for so thickly fell the large, soft snowflakes around them by this time that the feeble rays of those lanterns scarcely penetrated more than a yard or so beyond their horses' heads.

Ere another half hour had elapsed it had become evident to them that they were off the bridle-track, for more than once the shivering of the ground under their horses' hoofs proved that they were on the margin of a morass which was probably capable of swallowing steeds and riders in the twinkling of an eye, did the former happen to flounder any deeper therein.

The instincts of the sagacious brutes, Cumberland born and reared, saved both themselves and their masters from so lugubrious a fate, however, and led them on to safe ground once more, at all events for the time being.

"Our shrouds will be white and pure enough should it come to the worst," Dacre observed at last in somewhat of a desponding tone.

"If we are destined to wear them, may kind heaven bestow upon Marjorie Oughterby just such another shroud on her way to The Howk, for Death, I know, would be to her a far more acceptable bridegroom than Sir Archibald Dutton. For all that I have little doubt but we shall pull safely through our present troubles, and also save her from her threatened fate," answered Captain Kirkland in tones of conviction.

"Is it your intention to proceed straight to The Howk?"

"No, to an inn called 'The Black Sluggard,' a short half-mile on this side of Dutton's old ramshackle mansion. It is a place of resort for drovers and pack-horse drivers, so that there we shall most probably be able to pick up some information that will be useful in helping us to decide upon what will be the best course for us to follow," answered Kirkland.

They had now reached a narrow defile, or pass, between two mountains, whose precipitous walls bulged outwards, and almost met overhead, but they had not penetrated it for any great distance when a vast mass of snow fell from the summit of one of them, piling itself to a height of at least a dozen feet, directly in their path, thus rendering their further progress impossible.

Captain Kirkland gave vent to an ejaculation of despair, and then exclaimed: "You were right, Dacre, for it would certainly have been far wiser to have taken the main road to Murgur Dale, indeed we shall have to retrace our way and follow that route after all."

He wheeled his tired horse sharply round as he spoke, but had scarcely done so when there descended another avalanche of snow from the mountain top, blocking up the narrow path in that direction also, so that it was now as impossible to retreat as it was to advance, for the horsemen were imprisoned between two snow barricades, each of which rose many feet higher than their heads.

"The power of the Devil has proved supreme, and that of God has gone to the wall," exclaimed Kirkland with an oath.

"Do not blaspheme," rejoined his friend, sternly. "You may rest assured that the Almighty will deliver Miss Oughterby from her persecutors in a much more effectual manner than our feeble hands or brains would have managed the business. Lose not your faith in God, no matter what else you may lose; for see how he has provided for our safety, and that of our good steeds as well, from what, but for His special mercy, might have proved a death-trap to the four of us, for we could not have passed the long night out in the open without being frozen to death before morning."

Dacre pointed, as he concluded, to a huge rift in the limestone rock close at hand, which was evidently the entrance to a cavern of some extent, and a minute later the horsemen had ridden into it, and discovered the cave to be dry and comparatively warm.

We will leave them there and forthwith shift the scene to the grim old moated mansion of The Howk, in whose oak-raftered, cobweb hung hall, which is warmed by a huge turf fire, two old men are conversing.

The tall, stalwart sexagenarian, with iron-grey hair, a military moustache and florid complexion, is Sir Ralph Oughterby, who has somewhat the aspect of a lion temporarily held in subjection by the whip and eye of its trainer, yet ready and eager to rend and tear that trainer should an advantageous opportunity for so doing only offer itself; whilst his companion, a huge, bloated, Caliban-looking individual of about the same age, with bleared, blood-shed eyes, a coarse, purple, pimpled face, thick sensual lips, and a ponderous body, smooth shaven, wearing a well curled Ramilies wig, and shabby, ill-fitting clothes that are thickly sprinkled with snuff, is Sir Archibald Dutton: "Simpering Dutton" as he has got to be nicknamed, because he is always smiling or chuckling at something or other, not, be it understood, owing to sheer good-nature, or a happy temperament, but from mere habit, as in the case of the "laughing" hyena.

He holds in his right hand—for he has just been perusing it for about the hundredth time—the special licence, under the hand and seal of His Grace the Archbishop of York, which authorises him to wed within the walls of his own house or elsewhere, "Mistress Marjorie Oughterby of Caldbeck, in the County of Cumberland," but folding it up with one of his usual chuckles, he observes to that young lady's father, "I will now go and visit the pretty wild bird that you have helped me to cage, Sir Ralph, and if possible woo her into a good humour for the ceremony of the morrow."

"For the sacrifice of the morrow, you mean," growled Sir Ralph, with an oath; and then he added in tones of suppressed fury: "I can't think why I have refrained from ridding myself of you by a sword or a pistol bullet, rather than give you my only daughter in marriage. I doubt, even had I paid some hireling to murder you, whether such a crime would have been so foul an one as that which I am on the point of committing."

"It would have been a more foolish one, though, for the evidence that would consign your neck to the block, and those of your two sons to the halter is safely deposited in the hands of a friend, sealed with my own seal, but to be opened and used in case I should die a violent death. So you see, I have provided against all possible treachery," and chuckling and grinning at his own sagacious forethought, Sir Archibald hobbled out of the hall on his gouty old feet, with as evil an expression in his protruding, gooseberry-hued eyes as ever distinguished those of a beast of prey.

Up the wide, black oak staircase he went, with ponderous tread, and a minute later he had thrust a rusty key into the lock of a door, turned it with a harsh scroop and entered a gloomy room, on the wide window seat of which sat a lovely young girl, gazing with tear-dimmed eyes, out through a thickly-leaded casement upon a range of rugged mountains, and a deep, leaden-hued tarn or small lake, which nearly filled the valley that lay between them.

Blue as a summer sky were those eyes and delicate as the wild rose bloom the cheeks which the tears trickled down; her cherry-hued lips were quivering with the agitation that caused her rounded, milk-white breasts to rise and fall as though she was breathless from hard running; whilst the heavy masses of her golden hair enveloped her slim, yet perfectly proportioned form like a veil, with its superfluous length trailing along the cushioned window seat.

"A merry Christmas, my sweetest, and I also wish you a happy New Year, as the mistress of my heart and home!" exclaimed Sir Archibald, with a low, albeit somewhat of a mocking bow.

"You might just as well wish me a happy new year in my grave, for such will this grim old place prove to be unless I can manage to escape from it," was the maiden's prompt answer.

"So every wild bird thinks when newly caged; but after it has been fed upon nice sweet sugar for a little while, it will sing as sweetly, and take matters as blithely as though it were still free of the wild woods, my pretty one. As for escape from this place you will find that a sheer impossibility."

"I am not quite friendless, even though my own father and brothers have turned against me, and I believe he who possesses my heart is on his way to succour me even now; yet more than on him do I trust to God to preserve me, if need be even by a special miracle, from the life of misery to which your treachery and infamy would fain consign me."

"The age of special miracles is for ever past. Neither God nor the Devil will be able to wrest you from my arms, Marjorie; whilst, as for your old lover, Captain Kirkland, to whom you evidently allude, unless he should approach The Howk with two score armed men at his heels, I flatter myself that we shall be able to keep him outside its walls, not only till after our marriage, which is to take place at nine o'clock to-morrow morning, but also until I have tamed my wild little hawk, and changed her into a perfect ring-dove. Goodbye, for the present, birdie, for you will be a far pleasanter companion after the parson has made us one flesh, because you will by then have realized the fact that what can't be cured must be endured," and with those words Sir Archibald left her.

CHAPTER III.

A WEIRD CHRISTMAS FEAST.—A BRIDE FROM THE DEAD.

Long and weary was the night spent by Captain Kirkland and his friend Dacre in the cavern, whose widely yawning mouth had invited them to escape therein a death from cold, or from another snow avalanche in the narrow defile.

Even there, every half-hour or so they had to leap to their feet and walk briskly up and down for a few minutes in order to maintain some degree of animal warmth, for there was nothing that they could make a fire with, and all this while their thoughts were as dark as the cave itself, when once the candles in their stirrup

lanterns had burnt themselves out, which they did not take long
to do.

Captain Kirkland was oppressed with the most poignant anxiety concerning Marjorie Oughterby, and Dacre was full of fears
that the snow would confine them as helpless captives within
their present shelter until they perished from hunger and cold
combined.

With the earliest grey of the dawn he rushed out of the cavern
to reconnoitre, and intense was his relief upon discovering not
only that the sky was clear and bright, but, better still, that the
two snow hills which had enclosed them in what had threatened
to be a veritable death trap, the night before, had been consider-
ably flattened down by the wind and furthermore frozen so hard
that it would be quite possible to clamber over either of them on
foot.

He rushed back with the good news to his companion, who at
once exclaimed, "Let us push on then, in heaven's name, for we
may still arrive in time to prevent the marriage. Our horses will
be snug enough here until we get a chance of sending for them or
of returning this way ourselves."

They started at once, bending their course north-easterly, with
the mountain peaks for their sole guides, for every trace of the
road was obliterated.

Soon they came to the Glendermacken river, fast locked up in
ice.

They crossed this without mishap, and at length Murgur Dale
lay stretched before them, and at its further end, a good league
away, they could clearly descry the grey walls of The Howk, with
the smoke ascending from its tall, quaintly twisted chimney stacks.

But now the upper surface of the snow began to melt under
the sun's rays, so that their onward progress became, perforce, as
slow as it was laborious.

The spirits of the two young men also grew as heavy as the
trackless waste they were traversing, for neither of them had yet
been able to think out a way of forcing an entrance into the grim
old mansion which they were approaching uninvited.

"We will succeed in planning a feasible scheme, no doubt, over
our breakfast at 'The Black Sluggard.' I am as hungry as the pro-

verbial hunter, and when my stomach's empty my brain is always in the same condition," exclaimed Dacre at length, assuming a tone of hopelessness he was very far from feeling.

But, to his extreme chagrin, his friend declared that no time must be lost in calling at 'The Black Sluggard,' and that he meant to push straight on for The Howk, carve a way in with his good sword if his entrance was opposed, and then shoot down its owner at the head of his own board, whether the marriage had been already consummated or no.

"By heaven, I believe that this trouble has turned his brain, but, be that the case or not, I can't desert an old schoolfellow and life-long friend, whatever pickle he may be leading me into," muttered Dacre to himself.

So they continued to stalk on in silence, until The Howk rose close before them, the mediæval drawbridge still spanning the moat of slimy, fœtid water, all the narrow, diamond-paned windows dim and dirty, a woe begone-looking mansion, having the appearance of being utterly deserted.

"What an uncanny looking place," exclaimed Dacre, with an involuntary shudder. "One could imagine it to be filled with the ghosts of the long-departed, rather than by a Christmas wedding party."

"Its weird appearance causes me a strange and unaccountable uneasiness," answered Captain Kirkland. "Come down into this little hollow, Dacre, whose depths none of the windows can possibly command, and there let us make our final plans."

"I prithee do not let us be long about them," remarked his friend, "for now that I look upon our goal I am most anxious to reach it. The fact is that I am ravenous with hunger, and, even if it be peopled only by ghosts, yet would I rather sit down to a good meal in company with the dead than remain in a state of semi-starvation any longer."

"A good meal awaits you, sir, and the dead are already seated at the board," exclaimed a low, sweet voice close at his elbow, and turning sharply round Dacre beheld a most lovely girl standing there, clad all in white, and with a face every whit as colourless; a strange smile dwelt upon her lips, and there was a wild light in her eyes which seemed to bespeak insanity.

At the same instant Captain Kirkland also became aware of her presence, and springing forward with a glad cry, and the single ejaculation "Marjorie!" he would have clasped her in his arms had not the young lady drawn herself proudly up and rejoined with cold hauteur:—

"I have not the honour of your acquaintance, sir, but if you also are hungry, you are welcome to accompany your friend. It is Christmas Day, you know, and Christmas is a season for showing hospitality. All the other guests are dead, but your companion has said that he does not mind that, and really they are much nicer dead than they were when alive, which was but half an hour or so ago."

"Mad! My poor, persecuted darling has been driven raving mad by their vile machinations," said Kirkland to Dacre, in an awesome whisper.

"All the more necessary that she should be humoured, so let us obey her in everything and contradict her in nothing," was his friend's equally low-toned reply.

"Yes, it struck me that you were a little mad, both of you," remarked the girl in white, who had caught a word or two of their discourse. "Not that it matters, in the least," she added heartily, "since you are both hungry and it happens to be Christmas Day, so now come along quickly, or the roast beef will be quite cold, I fear. Fancy hot joints and vegetables, with beer as well as wine, for a wedding breakfast at ten o'clock in the morning; but that's an old Cumberland fashion, and my husband was such a hog that I'm really thankful that he thought fit to gorge himself to death before we had been wedded for one whole hour."

Thus she rattled on, smiling and merry, until the grim old house was reached; which entering by the wide-open front door, Kirkland and Dacre found themselves all at once in a most dismal-looking hall, wherein at least a dozen individuals, all of the male sex, sat around a big table that was spread with bountiful but coarse fare, the great sirloin of beef, half demolished, but still faintly steaming, as were also some of the dishes of piled-up vegetables.

The hall was illuminated, for the most part, by a luridly-glowing turf fire, that was heaped up as high as a hay cock on the flat hearthstone, for the snow of the night before had so beaten against the windows, and then frozen hard against the glass, that they admitted scarce any light whatever.

Deep as was the prevailing gloom, however, it was nevertheless easy to perceive that every one of the dozen men who sat at the table was as dead as dead could be, even though most of them looked as though they were merely asleep.

"Sit down, gentlemen, for there is plenty of room," and their fair hostess placed chairs for them as she spoke. "The parson is unable to say grace because, as you can see for yourselves, he is just as dead as any of the others. But I suppose I should introduce you to them all," she rattled on. "This is my husband, and I thank heaven that he has made me his widow without any unnecessary loss of time. This is my father, this is my brother Ralph, and that one my brother Reginald, the others I don't know the names of, and even the parson is a perfect stranger to me. But why don't you commence your meal, for I thought that you were very hungry? I know I heard one of you say that he would rather breakfast with the dead than not breakfast at all."

At this juncture a chorus of voices suddenly arose from somewhere or other in the house; angry voices, astonished voices, wailing voices, shrieking voices, whilst one of them sounded shrill and clear above the others, exclaiming in tones of mingled fear and horror:—

"I did it, I tell you all. It was monkshood that I made the sauce with, instead of horseradish. I've warned the master again and again that he shouldn't have the poisonous stuff growing in the kitchen garden along with wholesome vegetables, but he was that fond of the dark blue flowers that he couldn't abide them being rooted up. God grant that he hasn't paid for the foolish whim with his precious life."

Then a door at the further end of the hall was suddenly thrown open, and half a dozen servants, both male and female, came pouring in pell mell, the red faced cook, looking far from sober, in front of the others, and no sooner did she catch sight of the strange positions and contracted faces of the erstwhile revellers, than she gasped out: "Just as I feared it would be," and fell with a heavy thud to the floor.

"Marjorie, have you taken any of the horseradish sauce?" asked Captain Kirkland, anxiously, as he turned towards the so speedily widowed bride.

"No, no, I don't think so, indeed I am sure not. I—I never could touch it. Oh, Giles, so it is you who have come to my help and I did not even know. The horrors of this morning must have turned my brain for awhile. My poor father, my poor brothers," and with a flood of tears Marjorie fainted in her lover's arms.

"That is well, Kirkland, but you must get her out of this charnel-house as quickly as possible. Hark to the distant merry peal of Christmas bells. You have won a bride from the dead, my friend, but death or lunatic asylum may claim her if the return of consciousness finds her still in this awesome hall and amidst its grim company. Take her home to Caldbeck. The old house-keeper there was her nurse in childhood, and she loves her almost as though she was her mother. I will remain here, for I have still my wits about me, and these poor servant folk seem to have alto-gether lost theirs," said Dacre.

Captain Kirkland perceived the sound sense that was con-tained in his friend's advice.

"A carriage and horses at once, with a sober driver. I will give ten guineas to whoever sees this lady and myself down in safety at Caldbeck Hall before mid-day," he called out, in that stern, clear voice, which had ever won such prompt obedience from the soldiers under his command.

Nor did its accustomed power fail him now, for some of the male servants flew to obey his behest, and within ten minutes an old yellow chariot stood all ready at the hall door.

Marjorie, still happily unconscious, was lifted into it by Kirk-land and Dacre, and a minute later the horses, whose shoes had fortunately been roughed on the preceding day, were whipped up into a trot, so that by the time the newly-made wife and widow opened her blue eyes and looked wonderingly around her, The Howk, with all its horrors, had been left far behind, and an hour later she was weeping for her father and her brothers in the arms of her dear old nurse, and safely sheltered in her childhood's home.

Poor Marjorie was ill for a long time, for the mental shock she had suffered from was a very severe one, but the tender care and devoted attention of her old servant and of her lover, who had taken up his quarters in the village inn close at hand, at last led to her complete recovery, and then, as may readily be imagined, this wife of a single hour did not remain a widow for very long.

She was, in fact, wedded to Captain Kirkland, in the six-century-old church of St. Kentigern, at Low Caldbeck, in whose graveyard her father and the two brothers lay buried, in the following May, and it is believed that, in the words wherewith old-fashioned romances were usually concluded, "they lived happily ever after."

Lest the reader may think that the poisoning of a number of people at a meal by partaking of a sauce made with monkshood (i.e., aconite) instead of horseradish is a far-fetched idea, we may state in conclusion, that such a tragedy has happened more than once, for the roots of the two plants are exactly alike, and in winter there is no foliage above ground to distinguish the one from the other.

An entire dinner-party at Bristol thus perished some forty-five or forty-six years ago, and when discovered, an hour later, still seated around the table, some leaning on their elbows thereon, and others reclining in their chairs, they merely looked as though they were asleep.

The only way of distinguishing the two roots, which are very similar even in taste, is that whereas aconite, when shred, will speedily assume a pinkish hue, horseradish will still retain its natural colour.

It is a most foolish and reprehensible thing to grow the plants together in the same ground.

THE SHRIEKING SKULL;

HAUNTED WARDLEY HALL.

A TALE OF TWO LANCASHIRE CHRISTMAS EVES.

─────

CHAPTER I.

A COURSE OF TRUE LOVE THAT RAN VERY FAR FROM SMOOTH.

What can tempt lovely, eighteen years old Ruth Brierley into the gloomy depths of a pine wood this sunny but bitterly cold Christmas Eve of the year 1650?

For the snow is frozen hard upon the ground, and icicles hang in millions from the branches of the trees.

She has stolen away from grim, grey Wardley Hall, with fear and trembling, lest her departure should be observed and her purpose suspected, and now, though she has left it a quarter of a mile in her rear, she often glances nervously round at its long lines of glittering windows and feels as though not one of the many hundreds of tall, straight, mast-like tree trunks that surround her on all sides is big enough to conceal her from inquisitive and hostile eyes.

For her stern, harsh, Puritan father, and the man whom that father has resolved that she shall marry, and who is at present an honoured guest at Wardley, have heard a rumour that her youthful lover, Sir Ralph Osbaldiston, is haunting the neighbourhood, and they have both come to the conclusion that he being a Cavalier who had fought at Worcester, and afterwards escaped to France in the company of his royal master, Charles Prince of

Wales, no temptation less powerful than that of love could have lured him back, no matter how apparently impenetrable his disguise, to a country where a prison, and perchance the gallows might await him, and above all, to a neighbourhood where he was so well known as that part of Lancashire.

For Wardley Hall was his ancestral home, until it and its broad estates had been confiscated by Cromwell, and bestowed on Colonel Brierley, as a reward for the latter's leal services to the Commonwealth, for he had proved himself a gallant soldier at Edgehill and at Marston Moor, and a capable leader at Naseby and at Dunbar, whilst to recompense a faithful and a valued follower with the lands and the riches of others is always a deal more pleasant than to do so at one's own expense.

When Ralph Osbaldiston was the youthful owner of Wardley, and Edward Brierley had but his military pay wherewith to maintain himself, the latter had warmly encouraged the former's love suit, but so soon as the battle of Worcester had been fought and lost, Osbaldiston outlawed, and his mansion and estate bestowed upon himself, Colonel Brierley began to look out for a more fitting husband for his motherless girl, and presently found a man after his own heart in Sir William Cunliffe, of Colne, a greybearded, morose, and extremely ill visaged Puritan, who had once been his comrade-in-arms, was reported to be extremely rich, and who, after having lost and buried two wives, fell in love, at the age of fifty-two, with Ruth Brierley, and immediately made up his mind to wed her whether she was willing or no.

It is, perhaps, needless to say that our pretty heroine was very far from willing to become the third wife of the already much married Baronet, and her father's frequent threats of solitary confinement, on a bread and water diet, and even of a sound horse-whipping, if she continued obdurate, had hitherto failed to make her obedient to his wishes, whilst now, in response to a note surreptitiously placed in her hands by her faithful maid, she had come to the lonely pine wood to accord her outlawed lover a clandestine meeting.

He did not keep her long waiting, for she had not reached the rendezvous five minutes ere the full thud of a horse's hoofs upon snow heralded the young cavalier's approach, and in half as many more he had flung himself from his saddle and clasped her in his arms.

"Ruth, dearest Ruth," exclaimed Sir Ralph, with passionate fervour, "this is a time for action rather than for words. Remain here, and, sooner or later you will be forced to wed that sour, hypocritical old beast Cunliffe, but, fly with me, and we will be married at Manchester before sundown, and, ere the week's end you shall shine as the brightest star at our good King's court of Saint Germain-en-Laye. I have arranged everything—license, parson, relays of horses all the way to Dover, and a fishing boat to bear us across the Narrow Seas from thence to Calais. Come, love, do as your dear mother would have had you do under the present cruel circumstances, were she still living, for we were betrothed with her full consent, and even with her warm approval. There is no time to be lost, for to me every moment is fraught with deadly peril. For the first couple of miles we must ride double, but at that distance away a second horse is waiting for you in charge of a trusty groom. We can talk as we jog along. You will come, won't you?"

"Aye, with right good will, and in perfect truth, to the world's end, if you wish it, dearest Ralph," was the prompt answer.

"Good girl! Brave girl! you shall never regret the confidence that you now place in me;" and, as he concluded, the young Royalist, whose hair was close cropped and who wore the severest Puritan garb by way of disguise, mounted his powerful horse once more, and then held forth his hand, and stretched out his stirruped foot by way of stepping stone on to his good steed's crupper.

But, ere Ruth Brierley could place her tiny foot on his, another hand seized her roughly by one of her soft round arms, and sent her reeling to the ground, whilst a gruff voice at the same time exclaimed:—

"Away, if you value your life, Osbaldiston. I don't want your blood, so set spur to steed before my sense of duty overpowers my inclination to spare you."

It was Colonel Brierley who spoke, whilst by his side stood Sir William Cunliffe, sneering of lip yet stern of eye, his right hand fingering the stock of a pistol which was thrust into his broad leather belt.

"Needs must, I suppose, when the devil drives," retorted the young cavalier with a bitter laugh, "for you two have not dared to face me unsupported. I can hear the tramp of at least a dozen armed men coming fast at your heels, wherefore discretion becomes the better part of valour. Hear me vow, however, before I go, Colonel Brierley, that the day on which you give your daughter in marriage to the grim wolf who stands beside you, he dies the death of a wolf, or else henceforth lives the life of a tortured fiend in hell, for we Osbaldistons have ever possessed the gift of second sight, as doubtless you have heard."

So saying Sir Ralph wheeled his horse sharply round, and galloped away, a bullet from grim old Cunliffe's pistol humming a good yard above his head the while.

"Confound you, Brierley, what made you knock up my arm and so spoil my aim? Had you not done so he would now be a dead man," growled that worthy, as he returned his still smoking weapon to his belt.

"I did it because I chance to be the possessor of the young fool's confiscated estates, and know very well that my tenants, who were once his, would, in some way or other, avenge his death upon myself, if once they got to know that I had had a hand in, or even winked at, his destruction. Tut, tut, man, there's no need for you to be scared by his words, for threatened men live the longest, 'tis said, and I vow that Ruth shall be yours ere the happily abolished Popish festival of Easter again comes round. Ah! the wench has thought fit to faint away I perceive. It is just as well that she did not see you fire that foolish shot. And now I prithee tell those fellows of mine who are hurrying up that their services are not needed, and, were I you, I would not call at Wardley Hall for a day or two, for it will take me all that time, I suspect, to break my daughter's stubborn will, and compel her to bow her head to the inevitable.

"But you surely believe that you *will* be able to do so?" said Cunliffe somewhat anxiously.

"Even the fiercest of wild beasts can be tamed and made obedient to their trainer's will, and I, who have commanded men, will not, you may depend upon it, be defied by a mere slip of a girl, who is, moreover, my own child," replied the ex-colonel of "Ironsides."

"I beseech you, nevertheless, to subject your daughter to no discipline that will mar her beauty."

"If the worst comes to the worst she shall receive no chastisement the marks of which will not be wholly obliterated in the course of a week or two; but spare the rod and spoil the child says wise King Solomon, and the precepts of the Bible are surely worthless if they be not followed," was Colonel Brierley's answer.

CHAPTER II.

WON BY MURDER. ENTER THE SHRIEKING SKULL.

In a rough and ready, yet, withal, in an effectual manner, Colonel Brierley got his daughter out of her swoon, and then took her home, where he sentenced her to solitary confinement in her own room, with a Bible for her only reading.

There she spent the whole of Christmas Day, or rather what should have been Christmas Day, for even to celebrate Christ's birth, or death, or resurrection, was regarded as a crime in the dark England of those days.

But though kept for some weeks a close prisoner, subject to constant lectures on the sin of disobedience, and to almost as frequent flagellations, according to the precepts of Solomon, administered by her father, Ruth Brierley would not give her consent to wed Sir William Cunliffe.

"My faith was pledged, with my dear dead mother's and your own full approval, to Sir Ralph Osbaldiston, and whilst he lives I will bestow my hand in marriage on none other," was her invariable answer; a most unfortunate one for all parties concerned, as after events proved.

For her decision was communicated, at last, to Sir William Cunliffe, who almost immediately thereafter quitted Lancashire for London, where he was well aware, from the reports of trusty spies, that his rival was in hiding, as well as what were his favourite haunts.

Did he repair thither in order to betray the young Cavalier to the authorities, so that axe or rope should remove him from his path, the reader may naturally wonder?

Not so, for Oliver Cromwell, the Great Protector, had, within the past few days, been stricken down by an illness which was like to prove mortal, and his son Richard, who would in such case succeed him, was known to be weak, irresolute, and remarkably tender-hearted, wherefore, so soon as he should stand in his father's shoes, the offices of both headsman and hangman were likely to become mere sinecures.

On these accounts a duel to the death, or else a cowardly assassination was far more likely to serve Sir William Cunliffe's turn.

At last he came home, looking grimmer and greyer than ever, and the next day visited Wardley Hall with the news that Sir Ralph Osbaldiston had been slain in a drunken brawl.

The intelligence had come to him through a relative, who was an alderman of the City, he declared, and he was even able to produce an account of the tragedy, as published in the *Flying Post,* the only newspaper which England at that time possessed.

How he had procured its insertion, and at what price, himself alone knew, but he professed a certain degree of regret at his rival's untimely fate, taking due care not to overact his part.

And now there was added to Ruth Brierley's sufferings an ever bruised heart as well as a frequently bruised body, and ere long, deep grief, as it often does, crushed her high spirits and her hitherto indomitable will, so that, ere Eastertide came round, owing to not caring a whit what now became of her, she, in order to escape the thong of her father's lustily applied whip, not so much on account of the pain that it inflicted as for the degradation it cast on her girlhood, consented to become the wife of Sir William Cunliffe, hoping that the misery of such a fate would soon kill her outright.

It was a sombre wedding, the face of the girl bride being as white as the dress she wore, and the solitary bridesmaid, a spinster sister of the grey and grizzled bridegroom, a Minerva-like looking woman of some fifty years, who, from the expression of her countenance might have been officiating as chief mourner at a funeral.

The ceremony over, much to the inward satisfaction of bridegroom and father, who had both entertained grave fears that their joint victim might have plucked up sufficient spirit to resist her weird destiny even at the last available moment, the bridal party returned to Wardley Hall to breakfast: a substantial meal devoid of all modern elegancies.

The bride, on reaching her for long miserable home, was trembling as well as pallid, for whilst traversing the park, with her hand within her old husband's arm, a face had suddenly appeared to her from behind a huge laurel bush which she had immediately recognised, or fancied that she recognised, as that of her dead lover, and she did not doubt but that it was his ghost which had come to mutely upbraid her for having, apparently, so soon forgotten him.

Notwithstanding the agonising distraction of her mind, however, no sooner had she entered the banquetting hall than she noticed a small, square, corded box, standing upon the well-spread table, which her father observing at the same moment, he exclaimed, with a laugh: "A wedding present, Ruth, arrived rather late 'tis true, yet doubtless still acceptable," and, as he spoke, he cut the cords, and then prized open the lid with the dagger which he always wore at his side.

Taking carefully out of the box a something hard and round, that was wrapped up in tissue paper, he cleared the latter away, and in the next instant gave vent to an oath, close followed by almost a scream, for he held in his hand a grinning skull, traversed by a deep cut, apparently inflicted by a sword blade.

At the sight, Sir William Cunliffe's usually mahogany-lined face turned as grey as lead; his eyes looked as though they were about to leap out of their sockets, and his burly form fairly shook.

"Pah, what a silly, unbecoming jest," exclaimed Miss Cordelia Cunliffe, who possessed the nerves of a rhinoceros; but, strange to say, the hour-old bride became, suddenly, the calmest of the party, as she stooped to pick up a sheet of paper, which, unobserved by all but her, had fluttered from the box to the floor upon the taking out of the skull.

On it she now read, in a cramped, stiff looking writing:—

"Keep me,
I guard thee,
Heartily, cheerily;
Discard me,
I warn thee
Of treachery, cruelty;
I come to my home
Never from it to part,
And that home shall be thine
With my brother's true heart,
Since buried is mine."

No sooner had she read the doggerel rhyme than, with flashing eyes and compressed lips, Ruth passed the paper on to her father, who having perused the lines in turn, uttered a harsh, but unnatural laugh, and then shouted out, "This is a snare of the devil! Avaunt Satan! I defy thee and all thy works!" and picking up the skull he hurled it out through the open window on to the lawn.

But, no sooner had he done so, than he felt a heavy buffet on his left ear, a fearful shriek rent the air, and the next instant the skull rested grinning on the mantel-piece.

Everyone present was now overcome with horror. Two or three servants who had entered the room in order to wait at table, rushed out of it again with cries of fear, and Miss Cordelia Cunliffe exclaimed in a wild wail:—

"The devil is assuredly amongst us."

"That he is, and there he stands, in the person of your brother," retorted Ruth, drawing herself up to her full height, and pointing an accusing finger at Sir William Cunliffe.

"Villain!" she continued, "your assassin stroke is still imprinted on the head of my betrothed. You have parted me from his body but from that which remains of him you shall never separate me, so help me God and his own unquiet spirit. He has come home, as he has written, and he evidently intends to stay, for even my father has been unable to evict him, and here he promises to guard and protect me so long as I make it my home also, as I intend to do."

"Your future home is my mansion at Colne, madam, and thither I intend to take you at once," growled Sir William.

"I warn thee, for thine own sake, not to do so," calmly replied the bride, "for I am no longer a timid girl, but a fierce and vengeful woman, and it would be certain death for thee to close thine eyes in sleep under the same roof which covered me, since most assuredly I would reward treachery with treachery, and stab thee to the heart at the first convenient opportunity. Take a tigress to thy bed, and thou wouldst find her a less perilous mate."

Scarcely had she uttered these stern, determined words, when another shriek pealed through the room, this time with a something exultant in the tone, and Sir William, clapping his hands over his ears to shut out the, to him, horrible sound, rushed, in abject terror, from the room.

A minute later he was joined by Colonel Brierley, who gasped out, "What does it all mean, and what is to be done?"

"It means witchcraft and sorcery of the blackest kind. Send at once for that godly and pious minister, the Reverend Zerubbabel Meekly, and have the foul fiend exorcised out of that accursed skull, after which it may be buried, and then will trouble us no more. I shall take my sister off home at once."

"And Ruth?"

"You may keep her yourself until she ceases to be dangerous. Break her spirit or break her bones, I care not at this moment which, but, by heaven, time shall make her mine, despite every fiend in hell."

"Cunliffe, did young Osbaldiston really perish by your hand?"

"Yes, thanks to your daughter's vow that she would never wed anyone else whilst he lived. His blood rests on her head rather than on mine. I followed him on to London Bridge at midnight, slew him in fair fight, and then lifted up his dead body and pitched it into the Thames. Do you doubt my word?"

"No, but you had better return to Colne as you propose," and Cunliffe did.

CHAPTER III.

THE SECOND CHRISTMAS EVE.—WIDOWED AND RE-WEDDED.

Although Sir William Cunliffe left Wardley Hall with his spinster sister, in his lumbering old family coach, full of craven fear, and very much after the manner of a whipped cur, he had not the slightest intention of abandoning his lovely girl bride for very long.

He trusted to wise King Solomon's counsel, carried out by the agency of her father's whip, to reduce Ruth to reason, and Colonel Brierley would, without doubt, have frequently had recourse to that old world recipe for the correction of rebellious children but for the skull, which, every time that he attempted to reduce precept to practice uttered such unearthly and blood-curdling shrieks that he invariably lost nerve and abandoned his cruel intentions in abject terror.

For the Reverend Zerubbabel Meekly had failed to exorcise from out that grim relict of mortality the evil spirit which was supposed to tenant it, and, consequently, no matter how often it was removed from the house, sometimes to be cast down a well, and sometimes to be buried deep underground, it never seemed to experience the slightest difficulty in re-entering Wardley Hall, no matter how securely its doors might be barred and its windows fastened.

At last Ruth had a little recess especially constructed for its reception, in the thickness of the wall half way up the broad, black oak staircase (*where it may be seen to the present day,* for even in this twentieth century it cannot, it is said, be got quit of; indeed a picture of skull and staircase appeared, no later than last year, in that popular weekly, *Tid Bits*), her father not daring to withhold his consent, for by that time he was fairly frightened of his most unwelcome guest, and would willingly have given half his fortune to have been able to get rid of it.

The great Lord Protector died, his very common-place son, Richard Cromwell, succeeded him, and plots became everywhere rife for the restoration of the King; yet these events, any one of which, had it happened a year ago, would have had as stirring an effect on the old Colonel of "Ironsides" as a trumpet blast has on a war horse, scarcely attracted his attention, for the Shrieking Skull, and the doggerel rhyme that had come with it engrossed all his thoughts, and seemed to be hurrying him fast towards his grave.

The last lines—

> "And that home shall be thine,
> With my brother's true heart,
> Since buried is mine,"

caused him to remember that Sir Ralph Osbaldiston possessed a twin brother, his junior by something less than an hour, who, because the Wardley Hall estates had been thought, by the parents, to be too small to bear dividing, had been educated in Catholic schools and universities in France and Belgium, with the ultimate intention of his becoming a priest.

Colonel Brierly recollected to have heard that the brothers resembled each other to a most remarkable degree, and now he could not help but perceive that the elder being dead, every reason for the younger one's entering the church was thereby extinguished, and he could even realise the strong probability, if Prince Charles Stuart became King of England, that he might be reinstated by the new monarch at Wardley Hall, and he himself be outlawed in turn.

Thus the rhyme which had accompanied the skull might, in addition, prove a prophecy, and his daughter become mistress of the old hall and its wide domains, by a marriage with her dead lover's brother, he (her father) being, the while, a homeless fugitive, with, possibly, a price set upon his head.

As he thought over the matter possibilities seemed to grow into probabilities, so that at length his feelings underwent a thorough change, and he began to wish Ruth a widow: not but what, in the fulness of time, she could be easily made one, for if the Royalists once got the upper hand he was well aware that Sir William Cunliffe had been guilty of many acts, during his term of power, which under the new regime, would render him amenable to either axe or rope, though the old Colonel never so much as guessed that a cold blooded murder was one of them.

However, his reflections made him kinder to his daughter, and less complacent towards her husband, conduct which so raised the latter's ire, who was as stubborn as a mule, and, so far as political events were concerned could never see beyond the bulbous end of his own rubicund nose, that when, at last, Colonel Brierley evidently grew reluctant to surrender up to him his daughter, he resolved, his terror of his wife being, by then, entirely dissipated, to carry her away from Wardley Hall by force.

It was on the second Christmas Eve of our story that he made the attempt, and it is only now left to us to chronicle how it failed.

Sir William rode over to Wardley Hall at the head of twenty stout retainers, and at the back of his saddle was strapped a pillion, seated in which he was resolved to bear his bonnie bride home to Colne.

He entered her father's house with a blustering swagger, and with many oaths made plain his intentions, declaring that if Ruth would not go with him willingly he would carry her off by force.

Thereupon the skull in the staircase niche instantly began to shriek, but Sir William had so thoroughly primed himself, on his way, with Dutch courage, from out a square bottle of Hollands which he carried at his saddle bow, that he feared neither skull nor devil, much less his "virago of a wife," as he hesitated not to call her, when, led into his presence by her father, she defied and threatened him, much as she had done upon their wedding day.

"I heed thee not. I refuse to obey thee. If the need occurs I doubt not but that even the dead will arise from a bloody grave in order to protect me," she at length exclaimed, in the accents of a woman suddenly inspired.

What made her utter such words? It is impossible to tell. She felt, herself, as though they had been forced from her, and, to her infinite surprise, no sooner were they spoken than the hurried tramp of many footsteps was audible without, the door of the banquetting hall was dashed violently open, and into the room rushed, sword in hand, a party of some two score cavaliers, headed by, as a single glance compelled her to believe, her dead lover.

Sir William Cunliffe was evidently under the same impression, for the mulberry hue of his great, fat face changed to a ghastly pallor, and it was with a trembling hand that he lugged his sword from its scabbard.

He had better, perhaps, have left it there, for the next instant Osbaldiston's blade crossed his own, and, no sooner had it done so, than, seized with a wild panic, Sir William Cunliffe relinquished his first half formed intention, and, with a sharp cry of despair, turned to escape by way of a wide open window immediately in his rear.

But the movement was fatal to him, for, with a quick bound forward, his antagonist's blade descended upon the back of his head, and cleft it open to his very brain.

"So perishes the cowardly assassin of my brother Ralph, stricken where he was stricken, though not by a stealthy and invisible foe," exclaimed Raymond Osbaldiston, as he wiped his good steel clean on the buff jerkin of the dead man and returned it to its sheath.

Then, looking round, he observed, first of all Ruth, stretched unconscious on the floor, and, secondly, her father, standing, stern and grim close by.

"Colonel Brierley," then said the young cavalier, doffing his plumed hat, "that you are a rebel I am well aware, but you are by no means the infernal scoundrel that that dead carrion once was. He foully assassinated my twin brother, less than a year ago, on London Bridge, and I have just avenged that brother in pursuance of a solemn vow to that effect. I have now to inform you that Prince Charles was yesterday proclaimed King of England, and that by his Letters Patent Wardley Hall again belongs to an Osbaldiston. For the sake of your daughter, once my dear brother's betrothed bride, I have secured you immunity for all treasonable acts which you may have committed in the past, and your old comrade, now General Monk, and standing high in the royal favour, sends you greeting by me, and on your taking the oath of allegiance will give you the command of a regiment."

Is there any need for us to make this story any longer, for cannot the reader guess how it ended just as clearly as we could tell it, to wit how Colonel Brierley turned his coat with as much facility as the celebrated Vicar of Bray was wont to turn his cassock, and how his lovely daughter, after a decent interval of time had elapsed, became the wife of Sir Raymond Osbaldiston, who was the exact counterpart in age, looks, and even disposition of her first ill-fated lover?

Of course, "they lived happily ever after," that goes without saying, for the prophecy which accompanied the skull had to be fulfilled in every particular, or, as a prophecy, it would have been more or less a failure. That—

> "I come to my home,
> Never from it to part,"

is proved by the fact that the Screaming Skull is in undisputed possession of Wardley Hall to this day, though now it never shrieks save when some dire fatality threatens its tenants.

THE BLACK CAT,

OR,

THE WITCH BRANKS OF LOUGHBOROUGH.

A STORY OF TWO LEICESTERSHIRE CHRISTMAS EVES.

At the merry Christmastide of 1634, the period when our story opens, Loughborough was, as now, the second largest town in Leicestershire, though it had scarcely yet recovered the effects of being nearly depopulated by the Sweating Sickness seventy-three years previously, and it had no railways, canals, coaches, nor even roads, or at all events what we should call roads, neither had it lamps, or pavements, or manufactures; but to make up for all these wants it had highwaymen and witches galore, with a gallows to hang the former on, and a stake to burn the latter at, and which was much more frequently in use than the gibbet, for did not the Bible declare "Thou shalt not suffer a witch to live," and had not Englishmen fought and suffered much for the liberty to read their Bibles and interpret them each man to his liking, which was, of course, in the most literal way possible.

Then, too, there was the scolding cart, the stocks, and the pillory, the first-named kept in the rear of the old market house, and the last two standing in front of it, and seldom tenantless, and last, but by no means least, there was the witch branks (which we shall presently describe) and the ducking stool, and a most rare and excellent invention was that latter, for what more effectual way could there be for curing shrewish wives than sousing them head over ears three times in the Soar, since in ninety-nine cases out of every hundred it made "the wife subject unto the husband," and left him the head of the house with a vengeance. We wonder how many henpecked husbands of this levelling age, when wives are more than ever disposed to wear the br....es, would vote for the restoration of the ducking stool, if they could only do it in secret—say by ballot?

However, we have naught to do with ducking stool, scolding cart, stocks, or pillory in our present story, though with the witch stake and the witch branks we unfortunately have, so now for a description of the latter.

It was then a hideous iron mask, with a spiked spur to enter in at the mouth and keep down the tongue, so that it might be able to utter no spell that would overcome the pain of the burning.

In the year 1624 Muriel Fenton and Madge Calvert were the rival belles of Loughborough.

Both were the daughters of independent men, and so set themselves down as belonging to the aristocracy of the dull old historic town, though they nor theirs mixed with the great county families resident at Prestwold Hall, Garendon Park, or Walten Court.

Still they enjoyed a pleasant little society of their own, and many well-to-do and gentlemanly young fellows were puzzled to tell which of the girls was the more attractive and winsome, the animated brunette Madge Calvert, with her large dark liquid eyes, ruby lips, rich warm complexion, sparkling white teeth, and lithe sylph-like form, or the more gentle and less self-asserting blonde Muriel Fenton, with her heavy masses of pale golden hair, her blue eyes as deep, calm, and unfathomable as the summer sea, her exquisite complexion (for the very flush on her cheeks suggested the idea of roses blushing through milk), her full voluptuous form, and her plump neck, arm, and shoulders, that were as white and as pure as cherry blossoms.

Sir Vivian Willoughby, who, although a Papist, was young, rich, and handsome, and considered a great catch by all the eligible maidens in North Leicestershire on those accounts, for the sole reason, perhaps, that men in general fall in love with their exact opposites, had, for a little while, shown a decided preference for Madge Calvert, but all at once he changed round and became the devoted admirer of Muriel Fenton.

Not because she had lain herself out in any way to tempt

him to change his allegiance, for she was not the girl to take any delight in cutting out or humbling another, but for the reason that he had either discovered in Madge something that he disliked or disapproved of, or that the attractions of the blonde were so overpowering and irresistible that, in his opinion at all events, they caused those of the brunette to pale and fade before them.

It was not long before Madge Calvert discovered that she was both forsaken and supplanted, and amongst so small a community she would have been dull of comprehension indeed had she not quickly discovered who was her favoured rival.

Madge Calvert hated Muriel Fenton from that hour.

Had she shown her hate she would have been a safer foe, but that was not part of Madge's nature.

Graceful as a cat in all her movements (for no one had ever beheld her even as a child in a clumsy pose or attitude), she possessed a cat's nature as well, for she could purr and kill at the same time.

So, the more she hated Muriel the more she fawned on her, and patted her, and called her "dear" and "darling," and wound herself into her confidence.

This last was no difficult thing to do, for Muriel being innately good herself, was slow to impute evil intentions to others; and besides, Madge Calvert was twenty-three, whilst she was only eighteen, so that Muriel placed the most implicit confidence in her friend, and would sometimes call her "little mother," and Madge pretended to love the name, though it caused her to wince every time that it was pronounced.

One day Madge called on Muriel, ostensibly to "keep her company and cheer her up," but in reality to discover by judicious pumping how the love suit was progressing.

She found her rival fondling a little black kitten.

"La, what have you there?" she exclaimed with a shudder. "Why, I declare, it's a black cat."

"Hardly a cat yet, though I think it will grow up to be a very fine one in time. Fancy, Madge, exactly as the church clock was striking twelve last night I heard a plaintive little miaw, and looking down out of my bedroom window into the yard I espied a little black spot upon the white snow. I saw it move, and knew then that it must be some poor tiny living thing that would die if left out in the bitter cold all night. So I went down and brought it indoors, and this is what it turned out to be. But the strangest thing of all, dear Madge, is how it could have got into our yard, for there are high walls all around it, you know. Clearly it must have fallen from the top of one of them."

"It's a pretty little creature, Muriel, and I should rear and keep it were I you," said Madge Calvert, feeling as she spoke so fierce and malignant a light coming into her eyes that she drooped her long ebon lashes to screen them. "Black cats are supposed to bring luck with them, you know," she continued, "and as this one came to you in so unaccountable a manner there must be something in it. Oh, I should most certainly keep it, and, in fact, I think you will be very foolish if you don't, for perhaps it may be a gift from your good fairy."

"You don't think that my having a black cat will make people take me for a witch, Madge, do you? But Molly Bagnall and Dorothy Whitmore, who were burnt to death last week for being witches, both had black cats, and the fact bore hard on them. Oh, dear, suppose this should be a kitten of one of those very cats?"

"I should have thought, dear Muriel, that you would have been above such foolish superstitions."

"And so I am; but what matters that if the rest of the world, our little world of Loughborough especially, are not? Everyone believes in witches now-a-days, even from the King and the Archbishop of Canterbury downwards. Aye, and so also does Sir Vivian Willoughby, notwithstanding all his book learning, and shrewd common sense. No, I don't think that I'll keep the kitten after all, Madge, for the fact is I'm afraid. And, besides that, I know that he would object to it, and as we are to be married so soon it is but right and proper that I should consult his wishes in the matter."

"To be married so soon, dear? This—this is the first time that I have heard of it," faltered Madge.

"Dear me, what have I said? I did not take you into my confidence before, Madge, because—because—well, in fact for the reason that I thought that you once cared for him, and therefore that the news might pain you."

"You thought that I once cared for Sir Vivian? Indeed, you were never more mistaken in all your life, dear little Muriel. I amused myself with him for a little while, that was all, and you know what a sad flirt I am. But I assure you that my heart has never been touched yet, so tell me all about it, dear."

"Well, then, we are to be married on New Year's Day, or in other words, to-morrow week, for this is Christmas Eve."

"I'm sure I wish you joy, my love. And so you already hold your future husband in so much awe that you dare not keep even a little kitten lest he should take you to task for it? If you would follow my advice, dear Muriel, you will show more independence of spirit, and just do as you like in the matter."

"No, I won't keep the kitten, indeed I won't. I tell you again that I'm afraid to do it, Madge."

"Why, Muriel, who would burn such a beautiful young girl as you for a witch? Well, you are a little coward, I must say. The mere idea of such a thing. It sounds so absurd that I really can't help laughing."

"Oh, Madge dear, I have more reason than you think for to be afraid. I—I feel that I must tell someone, or that my heart will break. I have no mother or sisters to confide in any more than you have, Madge, and you and I have been such friends from our very childhood that I could trust my very life in your hands."

"Why, of course you could; so out with it dear, and lift the weight from off your mind as quickly as you can."

"Then look at what has come to me within the last week, Madge. I never had spot or blemish of any kind about me before, and, oh! that one should at last appear in such a place as this;" and, unfastening the front of her dress with trembling fingers, Muriel Fenton lifted up one of the roundest and snowiest of bosoms and pointed with a finger of her disengaged hand to a little brown mole not much larger than a pin's head that was just underneath it.

"The witch mark!" exclaimed Madge Calvert, starting back aghast.

"Oh, don't call it so," cried Muriel, bursting into tears. "I so hoped that I might be mistaken about it."

"Would to heaven that you were, darling; but it is what is called a witch mark, and it is in the exact spot where they always come, so that if John Penkhul, the Leicester Pricker, were but to hear of it, 'twould not be long before he came over to Loughborough to plunge his cruel needle into it, and if it did not bleed, then you would be in danger of fire and faggot with a vengeance, for John Penkhul gets well paid for every witch he consigns to the burning. But don't shudder so, darling, for no one will suspect you of possessing such a thing, and I, your 'little mother,' will guard your secret as a sacred trust. I don't think, however, that I should keep the kitten under the circumstances were I you, so, as it is too pretty a little creature to destroy, you shall rear it for me, and as soon as ever it can lap I will take it from you and adopt it myself."

"Oh, thank you; that will be kind, and I agree with all my heart. But let us now change the subject for a more agreeable one. Sir Vivian is coming to take me for a skate upon the frozen lough to-night by moonlight, for, as you are doubtless aware, the waters cover the meadows like an inland sea, and are frozen hard as well. Indeed, it has never been frozen so hard since the Wars of the Roses, when one night two hundred Lancastrians, retreating from Leicester, towards Nottingham, got upon it unawares in a thick snowstorm, and imagining that they were still crossing fields, were suddenly engulphed and drowned.

"Then, if this time is like *that*, I shouldn't wonder if their ghosts were to appear upon the lough, Muriel."

"The possibility won't frighten *me* from going on it. Won't you stay to tea and accompany us, dear Madge?"

"No, but I may join you on the ice later on, for the lough is almost as near to our house as to yours, and I daresay many others will be going in the same direction. If I come I shall find you two out, never fear."

She took her leave, and she kept her promise. Most *fatally* kept it, as it turned out in the end.

She in fact went upon the frozen lough with her black, cruel heart bent on murder.

"I will lure him to his doom, and then I will bide my time and destroy *her*," was her double resolve.

Phrases such as these she had muttered to herself many a time during the evening, and she made but one mistake, a common enough one with her sex—she imparted her intentions to a confidante, her maid, Mary Boethen, whose loves and hates had always been identical with her own, and in whom she felt that she could implicitly rely.

The ice on the lough was that night in splendid condition.

The girls skimmed over it without an undulation or a sound, yet beneath the weight of Sir Vivian Willoughby, who was a herculean young fellow of six feet four in height, and broad and robust in proportion, it cracked somewhat ominously in certain places, proving that after all it was not so hard and thick as when it had opened to engulf the two hundred heavily armed Lancastrians; indeed the sinuous channel of the river through its midst was marked out as *dangerous*.

There were a great many skaters upon the ice, but the inundation was of so large an extent that they looked to be few, and Madge Calvert noted it all with keen though secret pleasure.

"Now who'll race me straight across to Cotes?" she presently cried out, indicating a half-submerged village on the opposite side of the Soar.

"The ice is too thin on the river. The current has as yet prevented it from forming thick enough to bear. Stay where you are safe," answered the young baronet, at whom the challenge had been more particularly aimed.

But Madge Calvert responded with a shrill and mocking laugh.

"Oh, you're afraid to follow me—you are afraid of the drowned Lancastrians' ghosts, but ice will bear up two that will break under two hundred, and the Meadow Reeves and the Bridge Masters are regular old women with their needless cautions, so follow me or be set down a coward," and she shot away with the speed of the wind itself.

"Save her, or she will perish," thereat exclaimed Muriel Fenton incautiously, and Sir Vivian, with the response of "The fool almost deserves it," was off in pursuit before his betrothed could find words wherewith to beseech him to be mindful of his own safety.

She herself was a wretched skater, and, unsupported, could hardly move a dozen yards over the ice without a fall, whilst to add to her present dilemma the full moon was suddenly obscured by a thick mist, which almost in a single minute shut the picturesque old town, with its high pitched roofs and pinnacled and embattled church tower, and whitewashed windmill, as well as the steep hill at its back, from her view, and left her far out on the gloomy lough, not knowing which way to turn, and in a state of mind bordering on distraction.

In vain she listened for the voices of her companions.

She could hear no sound of human life whatever.

Presently, indeed, she thought that she heard a crackling and bubbling noise at a distance, and then a sound as of mocking laughter.

But the conviction that the latter was unreal made her doubt also the reality of the former.

She again and again raised her voice to let her friends know whereabouts she was, but there was no response, and arriving at length at the conclusion that they would not be able to discover her in the still thickening gloom, she endeavoured to regain the shore and find her way home.

She had just got her skates off when the striking of the church clock providentially guided her in the right direction, and by the time she was off the ice she was also at the commencement of the narrow and dimly lighted streets, having gained which she ran all the way home, and straight into her little parlour, where the first object that she beheld was Madge Calvert calmly sitting in front of the fire.

"Oh, so here you are at last," said she. "But where is Sir Vivian? Hasn't he returned with you?"

"I haven't seen him. I expected to have found you two together, *if I found you at all,*" answered Muriel.

"Why, he was too great a coward to accept my challenge, or else you wouldn't let him. The ice on the river was all right, you see, or else I shouldn't be here," and Madge concluded with a disagreeable little laugh.

"It may not have been all right for him, though it was for you, for you are so lithe and light that almost anything would bear *you* up, whereas he—the fact is *you lured him to his death, woman, and you knew it.*"

"I am really much obliged to you for your most charitable opinion, Muriel Fenton," retorted Madge, rising to her feet. "I may have been giddy and thoughtless, but I've been nothing more or worse, and it's certainly not for *you* to call me a criminal—you, who live in such a fragile house of glass to throw stones at *me* is altogether too absurd and ridiculous."

And, putting on an air of offended dignity and conscious innocence, Madge Calvert pushed past Muriel Fenton, notwithstanding her supplications that she would forgive her hasty and unconsidered words and remain, and swept out of the room and house.

Hour after hour passed away, but Sir Vivian Willoughby came not.

'Ere morning dawned Muriel was in a burning fever, and raving in a wild delirium.

Therein she let out much that had happened, and it was these unconscious admissions of hers which led to a vigorous search being instituted for the missing baronet.

But, though the river was dragged, and divers ventured down through great holes cut for the purpose in the ice, not a trace of him was to be discovered, so that it was hard to say whether he had been drowned or no.

Anyhow, he had entirely disappeared from the town and neighbourhood.

Madge Calvert held firmly to her first statement, that the young baronet had not followed her across the ice towards the river, whilst Muriel Fenton just as positively averred that he had done so, and reiterated her conviction that he must have sunk through the thin ice, and been carried far down by the current 'ere he was drowned.

This, of course, after she had recovered from the terrible effects of the shock, and was once more in full possession of her reasoning faculties.

The estrangement between her and Madge Calvert had never been made up, and Muriel had no desire now that it should be, for, though she absolved Madge in her own mind from all criminal intention in the matter, she nevertheless could not forgive her for having been the direct cause of her lover's death, through her rash and presumptuous daring and almost wicked recklessness.

But was Madge Calvert going to be content with a *single victim?* No, far from it.

She now hated Muriel even for the privilege she possessed of donning mourning for her affianced lover, whilst *she* had no way of showing her own grief—a grief that she really felt—for she had loved the man whom she had deliberately lured to destruction—loved him with that fierce passion that would sooner destroy the adored object than see it possessed by another, and now she longed to consummate her vengeance on poor Muriel because she regarded her as the immediate cause of the wicked deed which she had herself committed.

Every time that she beheld in imagination the agonised and despairing face of Sir Vivian Willoughby as his hands grasped at the fragments of broken ice whilst he was sinking in the deep waters (though, truth to tell, she had never beheld the sight, for when she had heard the ice break in her rear she had not dared to look round), she hungered to see the lovely face of Muriel Fenton expressing equal or even greater anguish.

So that at last she took unto herself a fearful vow, that as he had gone out of the world by water, she should do so by fire; and that as he had perished on one Christmas Eve, so that she should perish on the next, *dying the death of a witch.*

"Hasn't she placed herself wholly in my power?" she asked herself, "by voluntarily showing me that accursed mark under her left breast?"

But Madge resolved that she would leave nothing to *chance.*

Muriel had kept the black kitten until it had grown a cat. Poor girl, she had nothing else left to love now, for her father was a stern, hard man, and had never exhibited the smallest particle of human tenderness in his nature.

Madge determined that *the black cat should seal her rival's doom.*

The second Christmas Eve had arrived when Madge said to two or three special friends and cronies, "I wonder what Muriel Fenton goes up to the churchyard every night to wander amongst the grave stones for?"

"Goodness me, and does she?" was the universal exclamation on hearing this.

"Aye, that she does, and all the time nursing that great black cat of hers. It seems to me a most un-Christian and witch-like thing to do. I'll warrant you that we should see her there to-night if we only had enough curiosity to go and look. Shall we?"

Of course one and all declared that they would only be too delighted to go.

All these were morning callers, so that there was plenty of time for preparation.

Hardly had her visitors gone when Madge Calvert said to her confidential servant:—

"Mary, you must manage to steal or lure away Miss Fenton's black cat during the afternoon or evening, keep it a close prisoner until nearly nine o'clock to-night, and then carry it in a bag to the church-yard, and place it amongst the tombstones. You will then call at Miss Fenton's, and ask her if she has lost her cat? She will of course say 'yes,' and you will make such answer as 'I thought 'twas yours that I saw over the church-yard wall as I came along. It seemed to be very bad, poor thing, but it wouldn't come to me, although I called it several times.' Do you understand?"

"Yes, Miss Madge, and what am I to do next?" asked Mary quietly.

"Why nothing at all except come straight home. If she asks you to go back to the churchyard with her to show her where-abouts you saw the cat, which by the bye you'd better fasten up somehow, so that it can't get away, say that your mistress requires you at home very particularly, and that you daren't delay. Here's a guinea for you, and many more may be earned by serving me well, added to which I intend to double your wages!"

Mary took the glittering coin, and performed her allotted task, alas, only too faithfully.

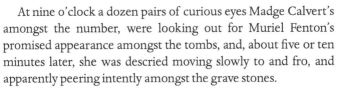

At nine o'clock a dozen pairs of curious eyes Madge Calvert's amongst the number, were looking out for Muriel Fenton's promised appearance amongst the tombs, and, about five or ten minutes later, she was descried moving slowly to and fro, and apparently peering intently amongst the grave stones.

Suddenly she was heard to utter a cry, and seen to stoop down, and when she had approached near unto the spot where the watchers were posted, behind a grim sepulchral monument, which is still standing, she was observed to be straining a black cat to her breast.

"She is a witch," whispered one.

"Yes, she *must* be a witch," assented another.

"The old churchyard has always been a noted place for witches," said a third.

"And black cats are their favourite familiars," remarked a fourth.

"Perhaps she has come to dig up an unbaptised child, as Marion Bond, Eldspeth Adams, and Bridget Dawson did, so that by eating some of it she may never be driven to confess her wickedness," suggested a fifth.

Then somebody said, "Isn't it our bounden duty to expose such wicked goings on?"

No one could exactly make out who spoke those words, but the next instant Madge Calvert's voice could be distinctly heard, exclaiming in accents hardly raised above a whisper:—

"Oh! don't call upon *me* to do so, for we were once such friends, and I still love her so dearly. I have known for years, though, that she possessed the witch mole under her left breast, but affection has chained my tongue, and it ever shall."

With these words Madge deserted her friends, and hurried away home alone.

Those who remained behind were not so particular, and as poor Muriel passed close by their place of concealment they called out after her,

"Witch! Witch! Witch!"

The lovely girl started as though a bullet had stricken her in the heart, but on looking round and perceiving nobody, she ran towards the churchyard gate with her recovered pet, and from thence through the streets all the way home, where she sank down in an easy chair in the little parlour, trembling in every limb.

"Oh, the horrors of last Christmas Eve, and the still greater horrors that menace this one," she moaned to herself. "Seen in the churchyard after dark, and with a black cat in my arms. Oh, it is enough to doom me to the stake."

This train of thought was at length interrupted by a loud and peremptory knocking at the street door.

She heard the servant open it, and then a rough voice exclaim, "Your mistress is in, and I must see her."

A minute later into the room where she was seated stalked a tall, stern, and terrible-looking man, carrying in one hand what resembled a huge iron head piece, or rather head-cage, with orifices for nose, eyes, and mouth, and with a spur receding inwards from the latter, the whole hideous contrivance being attached to a long and strong chain.

Poor Muriel had no need to be informed what this frightful thing was, or the name and office of him who bore it, for she knew that the one was the *Witch Branks,* which, when not in use, were in general kept in the belfry of the church tower (a tower which then possessed four pinnacles of great beauty, each bearing a gilded coronet atop of its weather vane), and he who carried it John Penkhul, the witch pricker, of Leicester, whom the neighbouring magistrates (her own father amongst the number) had invited to "take up his lodgment for a certaine time in those parts, in order to help discover and extirpate ye hellish crew of witches and wizards that so foully infested ye townes of Loughborough and Kegworth, and divers villages in their vicinities," in payment whereof he was to receive "one pound English for every proved witch, and an extra gratuity if he did ease and free the neighbourhood of ever so many."

"Mistress Muriel Fenton," said this fellow, with a whining and hypocritical drawl, "it is of the Lord's mercy that the honest gentleman, your father, is engaged on the town's business at Leicester, and that we will be able to get this black matter over before he returns. You will come with me before his worship the Headborough."

"What am I charged with, and who are my accusers?" asked poor Muriel, timidly and tearfully.

"Thou art charged first of all with bewitching to love thee, and then mysteriously spiriting away, so that he hath never since been heard of, one Sir Vivian Willoughby, of the Grange. Thou art also charged with possessing a wicked familiar spirit, having the outward form of a black cat, and of wandering with it in the churchyard amongst the graves of the dead, for some Satanic purpose at present unknown."

Muriel was about to make some kind of reply to these most foul accusations, when the witch pricker sprang upon her, dashed her back in her chair, and with cruel force drew the iron brank down over her head, pressed the big steel dart or spur into her mouth, and locked the machine at the back, so that for her to speak a word or even to make an articulate sound was quite impossible.

"*That* will prevent thee from muttering the *hocus pocus* which would change thee into a lion or a mouse, or summon thy broomstick steed, or thy cursed familiar to thy aid," said Penkhul. "And now," rattling the chain which was attached to the brank, and whose other end he had twisted around his right wrist, "I will take thee to the Court Leet Chamber over the shambles and prick thee in presence of the Constable and the Headborough, the Meadow Reeves, Street Masters, and Bridge Masters, and if thy witch mark gives no blood to the bodkin, we'll bring in Christmas with a good bonfire, my lass."

She was hooted, pelted, and spat upon as she was dragged through the streets in the direction of the old market house—she who had always delighted in the performance of kindly actions, and who all her life through had never committed a cruel one.

But what were *these* trials compared with that which was yet to come?

The Court Leet Chamber was soon crowded, and down on

the great table in the centre she was thrown and held by force, whilst the *Pricker*, with his huge coarse red hands tore her body raiment from off her, and bared her plump and milk-white bust to the waist, a minute later to point with malignant triumph at the little brown mole that was universally known, thanks mainly to King James's most learned and abstruse work on the subject, to be one of the most sure and certain of witch marks.

He now drew out of a case a long steel stiletto or sharp-pointed bodkin, and this he *seemed* to plunge thrice into Muriel's lovely body up to the very handle, just where the mole spot was situated.

Each time it came forth clean, bright, and untinged with blood, and each time, too, the poor palpitating victim (who had been previously blindfolded) showed no token, either by writhe or shudder, that the apparently deep and cruel stab had occasioned her the least pain.

Nor had it, for the witch bodkin was so made as to slip right up into its handle at the slightest pressure; so that, in fact, it never even punctured the skin of those whom it seemed to be plunged so deep into, whilst the absence of bleeding and the apparent insensibility to pain caused the beholders to feel that there could be no earthly possibility of the accursed one's innocence after so open and apparently so severe and crucial a test.

"She is indeed an accursed young witch," said the Head-borough, who had sat at her tea table scores of times—who, indeed, had dandled her on his knee as a child, and always professed the very warmest and almost paternal affection for her.

But his conduct was not to be wondered at, for in the times of which we are writing parents hounded their own children to an agonising death, and also children their parents, husbands their wives, and wives their husbands, if they but took it into their heads that they were witches or wizards, and consequently in close league with Satan.

Muriel Fenton, the witch test over, was allowed to re-don her torn raiment as best she could, whilst the witnesses against her were called up in turn to give their evidence on oath.

Madge Calvert seemed very reluctant to speak against her former friend, and yet she suffered her testimony to be drawn out of her in a way that told against Muriel far more terribly than if she had tendered it willingly; so that when she had done nobody present doubted but that it was Muriel who had tempted Sir Vivian Willoughby, and Madge Calvert also, to attempt to cross the frozen river on the preceding Christmas eve, and with the object of offering them both up as a sacrifice to her master the Devil.

The Soar, just opposite to Cotes, had borne a bad name ever since the two hundred unfortunate Lancastrians had been engulphed in its flood hundreds of years previously, for local superstition, ignoring the fact that the depth of the snow upon the ice had prevented them from knowing whether they were on water or on dry land, had laid the blame of the mishap upon a corpse candle, borne by a water kelpie or fiend, who had, of course, led them astray purposely.

The spirits of those drowned Lancastrians had, it was averred, often been seen hovering along the banks of the river just before the midnight hour.

So when Madge Calvert testified to the sudden mist and darkness that had obscured the moonlight directly after Muriel had encouraged Sir Vivian and herself to start off on their race across lough and river to the Cotes shore and back, when she swore moreover that as the ice broke up directly behind her she heard Muriel's clear ringing laugh, mingled with what she now believed to have been her lover's death-cry, and furthermore deposed to having seen shadows and ghostlike forms flitting along the river bank, and an old woman, mounted on a broomstick, flying over the tree tops in the direction of Mare Hill and Prestwold, as she turned on her skates and made her way back across the lough towards the town, at a right angle to her former course, there was not a single individual present but who believed every word she had uttered.

Then a travelling pedlar deposed that on the night in question, whilst approaching Loughborough from the direction of Hoton, he had seen the shadowy and indistinct forms of a number of armed men, doubtless the spirits of the drowned Lancastrians, dragging along a young man in their midst, who closely resembled the frequent descriptions that he had since heard given of Sir Vivian Willoughby.

Then came forward in turn those who had seen Muriel Fenton wandering amidst the tombs in the churchyard with the black cat in her arms, and when all the evidence had been heard the Court declared that a clearer case had never been laid before them, and Muriel Fenton was solemnly sentenced to suffer death on the morrow in the public Market-place—*death by fire and faggot*.

She was immediately thrust into the little dungeon or Black Hole, which was then situated at the upper end of the Market-place, and there she was kept all night according to the rules made and provided by the criminal law, that "persones imprisoned for witchcraft shall have no guard with them in their prisones, nor fyre, nor candle, but that sex watchmen nightly and daily attend and guard them without the place of their captivitie, and that yet other watchmen shall visit and look in upon them at every three hours end, both daie and nicht."

But even more than ordinary and usual precautions were taken in Muriel Fenton's case, for the window of her cell was boarded and nailed up, and even the key hole of the door plugged, so that no evil spirit should come to her aid; and the iron branks were kept on her head, with the cruel goad or spur pinning her tongue down in her mouth, so that she should be able to utter no fell spell, nor to curse them who had either witnessed against or sat in judgment upon her.

All night long in the centre of the Market-place, close to the pillory and the stocks, Muriel Fenton's funeral pyre, in the shape of bundles of well-tarred faggots, was being erected about and around the grim black post or stake, chained to which so many wretched creatures had already been roasted alive for the same imaginary sin.

And as the volunteer labourers sweated at their task, they laughed and joked, and looked forward to a glorious Christmas Day on the morrow, for there was nothing as praiseworthy and so amusing in those "good old times" as the burning of a witch.

Christmas Day dawns bright, frosty, and healthful, and, an hour from the rising of the sun, Loughborough Market-place presents the appearance of a sea of human heads.

Presently the doomed witch is brought out of the Black Hole, and preceded by the Pricker and the executioner, flanked by the

Meadow Reeves, the Street Masters, and the Bridge Masters, and followed by the Headborough and the Constable, all clad in their robes of office, she is guarded towards the place of doom.

Five minutes later she is being bound to the stake, already almost lifeless from terror, for what death can be so terrible as that by fire?

But notwithstanding all and everything, Muriel Fenton looks both interesting and lovely, for the branks have at length been taken from off her head, and the whole of her exquisite countenance is consequently exposed to view, a countenance now almost as white as her full round soft arms, that are bare to the very shoulders.

And now the red-rusty iron belt that is permanently attached to the stake is fastened around her slender waist, and another is locked around both the post and her fair white throat, so that she shall be held firm and immovable whilst she is being consumed; and whilst all this is being done, the town authorities take their places, and a pin might have been heard to fall as the crowd waited in rapt suspense for the igniting of the tarred faggots, that waist-high surrounded her, and the swift after rush of destroying flames.

It was at this most critical juncture that a female came tearing through the crowd like one demented and calling out at the top of her voice, "Make way! make way! I must and will out with it, for if I don't my soul will be more certain of burning in Hell's flames than that poor creature's body in earthly ones. Let me pass! Let me get to the authorities! Let me hold speech with the Headborough. I can and will clear her, for she's as innocent as a new-born babe of everything she's been accused of."

But whilst all this was happening, and apparently happening in vain, in one direction, a man on horseback was making his way towards the stake in a much more effectual manner from another, inasmuch as he little heeded how many people he knocked down and trampled under his powerful animal's hoofs in the passage.

When he had arrived so near to the place of execution in this most unceremonious manner that he thought his voice could be heard by them whom alone it was any use addressing, he shouted out:—

"Hold, on your lives, for here is Vivian Willoughby whom you have falsely accused that girl of making away with."

Sir Vivian Willoughby it was indeed, and as he spoke and took off his hat he was recognised by hundreds to whom his face and form were perfectly familiar.

A ringing cheer consequently rent the air.

Another minute and Sir Vivian was in excited and angry contention with the authorities.

"It can't be done, Sir Vivian. If she didn't bewitch thee, that's no evidence that the rest of the charges made against her are false. Wandering with a black cat in her arms all over the churchyard, and at night too; why, who but a cursed witch would do such a thing as that?" argued the Headborough.

"Oh, your worship, it was I who stole the cat and put it there; it was I who told her where to find it, and it was my mistress, Miss Madge Calvert, who made me do that and a score of things more in order to destroy poor Miss Muriel, who she has of late most bitterly hated. Her heart has been set on Miss Muriel's destruction this many and many a month. That I can swear to, and, what's more, I can prove it as well."

"And it was Madge Calvert, your mistress, who tried to destroy me on the night of my disappearance. It was she who tempted me to my too probable destruction, and all this misery and wickedness would not have happened had I not been pounced upon directly (after being first half drowned by the ice giving way) I gained the opposite side of the lough by a gang of rascals, who made me their prisoner in order to obtain the reward money paid by the Government for the arrest of every Catholic gentleman found more than five miles away from his settled residence. For this offence I have been kept in prison ever since, debarred from holding the slightest communication with a single relative or friend, and it seems that I have been at last set free only just in time to prevent a judicial *murder*."

And as he concluded the young baronet bent on the kneeling and repentant Mary Boothen a glance of mingled gratitude and disdain.

But *she* was nevertheless the most eloquent of the two in her impassioned pleadings for Muriel Fenton's freedom, since she felt that she had a great and a deep atonement to make for having taken part against her in the past.

Upon the united evidence of both, the Loughborough authorities *could not* but command their beautiful victim's immediate and unconditional release, their decision being welcomed and approved by the most tumultuous cheering on the part of the crowd.

Muriel Fenton had fainted dead away *before* the appearance of either Sir Vivian Willoughby or Mary Boothen upon the scene.

She was now released from her terrible position and carried home, where she was at last restored to consciousness by her lover, and, as soon as she could safely bear it, told of everything that had occurred to them both.

We have just space sufficient remaining to add that Muriel, 'ere the next Christmas Day came round, was Lady Willoughby; that Mary Boothen was her personal and favourite attendant; that Madge Calvert suffered a long and weary term of imprisonment for the joint crimes of perjury and criminal conspiracy, and that she died of a generally shattered constitution the very day that her sentence expired; and lastly, that John Penkhul, the Witch Pricker of Leicester, had, at length, the secret of his infernal stiletto, or "witch test," discovered, and as a reward for having sent some scores of miserable wretches to the stake in order to obtain their "head money," suffered himself on the gallows, though why the milder doom was meted out to so vile and diabolically cruel a wretch history telleth not.

The *Black Cat,* it is to be presumed, died a natural death, and as to the old *Witch Branks of Loughborough,* we believe that a future Headborough called Stacey had them cast into the river as a disgrace to the town, but there is an almost exactly similar one preserved at Leicester to this day.

TWO GHOSTLY SWORDSMEN;

OR,

THE DUEL ON THE MOOR:

A CHRISTMAS TALE OF BRANDESBURTON.

CHAPTER I.

A BEAUTIFUL FIEND AND A DIABOLICAL PLOT.

That part of East Yorkshire known as Holderness is more prolific in weird and ghostly legends than any other portion of
England even twelve times its extent.

Yet a native of Holderness was once asked if he had ever seen
a ghost, and his reply was: "Ah've nivvor seed ought wuss than
mysen, but," sinking his voice to a hoarse whisper, "ah believe ah
yance seed the divvil!"

Unfortunately, further particulars are not recorded, so we are
left somewhat in the dark as to the countryman's experience.

About fifteen miles from Hull, between Driffield and Hornsea, lies the village of Brandesburton, outside of which spreads a
wild stretch of barren land called the Moor.

Near the centre of this moor is a hollowed-out sandy amphitheatre, almost surrounded by a curiously-shaped mound, which
has a most weird history attached to it.

For it is said to have been the scene of a duel, or affair of
honour, between two gaily-dressed cavaliers, in the reign of King
James the First.

They fought with rapiers, a combat to the death, each falling at the same moment, thrust through the heart and throat respectively, and all on account of a lady fair who was unworthy of either.

The blood which drenched the ground from their mortal wounds can, it is said, to this day be plainly seen owing to the earth being there of a far darker shade; and on the anniversary of the event, which occurred on the Christmas night of the year 1604, all who are born at the witching hour of midnight, and at that same hour have sufficient courage to visit the eerie and unhallowed spot, will be spectators of a spectral encounter, fearfully realistic in every detail.

They will see the dire tragedy which was acted there, now three hundred years ago, re-enacted by two ghostly swordsmen, the clash of steel and the hoarse shouts of the combatants being clearly audible, the spectral vision only vanishing as each sword is finally plunged into either duellist's panting body.

But the real facts of the matter do not entirely agree with the above legendary account, and those fresh facts, which have but lately come to the author's knowledge, he will now endeavour to weave into a Christmas story of the East Riding of Yorkshire, than which a more thrilling and terrible one has assuredly never yet been either penned or told.

A young gentleman who is poor has but little chance of winning for his bride a young lady of good birth and family, who happens to be also poor, yet has an overwhelming affection for a multiplicity of pretty frocks, glittering jewels, and luxuries and pleasures such as only wealth can supply her with.

Thus Sir Haigh Rowley of Southcoats, aged twenty-five, though as brave as the immortal Roland, as handsome as Adonis, and owning a "handle to his name," of which some fair ones would have thought much since it is far more satisfactory to be called "My Lady" than plain "Mistress" or "Dame," felt an uneasiness which rapidly grew into alarm when Maggie Mortimer, of Routh, who, a year previously, at the wishing well of Meux, had plighted him her troth over a crooked pin and a broken six-pence, of which latter each of them had ever since worn a half, suddenly turned upon him a cold shoulder and began to show much more favour to a certain Mr. Cornelius Crooks, of Brandes Burton, who, though fat of body, forty in years, and fiery both as regarded hair and temper, was by far the richest man in East Yorkshire.

Sir Hugh felt sure that so uncouth a Caliban would never suc-ceed in winning the lovely Maggie's heart. No, that would ever be his own, the poor fellow tried to comfort himself by believing. Yet he could not help coming to the conclusion that a heart with-out its pertaining body would be but a shadowy possession at the best, wherefore his conviction, flattering though it was, gave him very little solid comfort.

Mr. Cornelius Crooks had won his great wealth as one of the old merchant adventurers of Hull during the long and glorious reign of Queen Elizabeth, or, at least, so he represented matters; but there were those who averred that for some years he had commanded a scout ship, in person, and when legitimate trade was slack, had not scrupled to indulge in a little piracy upon Spanish gold-laden galleons on their homeward voyage from the New World. Be that as it may, at the period of our story, he owned many thousands of acres of land to seaward of Hornsea, Bariston, and even Bridlington, and within that spacious domain had erected one of those fine Tudor mansions, than which no ordinary human habitations are more picturesque or beautiful.

But though the lovely Maggie Mortimer had secured so stout a string for her bow, both in a literal and a metaphorical sense, she, like many other ladies, by no means objected to having two strings thereto, and though decidedly "on with the new love," she still postponed being "off with the old one," for the latter she really loved, whilst for the former she did not care a rap, that is to say apart from his possessions, for which reason it was that one lovely summer's evening she met Sir Hugh Rowley in the little wood hard by Routh, which had for long been their favourite trysting place, and that in as loving a manner as though no more advantageous suitor had ever come between them.

She looked inexpressibly beautiful in all the glory of her nineteen years, her golden tresses streaming to the breeze, and her eyes as blue as the very forget-me-nots which she trod underfoot, but so lightly that they rose again as soon as the momentary pressure was withdrawn.

"Maggie," exclaimed Sir Hugh, advancing to meet her with extended arms, which presently clasped her exquisite form in a warm embrace, "Maggie, I was half afraid that, after all, you would not keep the tryst. Your parents, I know it well, are urging you to cast me aside, and to accept in my stead Cornelius Crooks, for a lover in the present and a husband in the near future. Yet am I loth to believe that you could ever bring yourself to love such an ogre as he is."

"Hugh, all my life through I shall love no one but you," retorted the fair girl with a sigh; "yet," she added, hesitatingly, "for all that I am going to marry Mr. Cornelius Crooks, and, in addition, almost immediately."

Sir Hugh Rowley looked for a moment as though he was stunned with a heavy blow; then recovering himself by a strong effort he remarked, with a miserable attempt at sarcastic mirth:

"Some poet declares that 'tis better to have loved and lost, than never to have loved at all. I shall not apply the lines to myself, however, but to my at present apparently more fortunate rival, for he shall lose you and his own life into the bargain, ere the time comes for him to lead you to the altar."

"No, Hugh," responded Maggie Mortimer, whose musical voice suddenly became harsh and strident, whilst her face, hitherto angelic of expression, in an instant resembled that of some beautiful fiend. "Take his life after he has led me from the altar, and then you may wed, instead of a pauper, than which you are little better yourself, the richest woman in Yorkshire. Aye, perhaps the wealthiest in all England, for Mr. Crooks has already made his will, which is to be signed immediately after the marriage is consummated, and therein he leaves me, his wife, everything of which he dies possessed, and I can assure you that the eyes of even a princess would glitter with greed at the thought of inheriting such unbounded wealth. Why, he owns all Holderness from Hornsea to the sea. The towns of Redmare, Tharlethorp, Frismarch, and Potterfleet, are all his very own, and—and those glorious possessions will be ours if you will make me first of all his widow and then your wife."

Sir Hugh Rowley shivered as he listened to this mercenary yet, for all that, impassioned speech.

"Maggie," he fairly gasped, "I never would have believed that you could have either thought or spoken as you have just done. By heaven, I would far rather wed you now, poor as you are, than I would as the wealthy widow of Cornelius Crooks."

"But I will not be poor when I have so good a chance of being rich. I have had more than enough of what is called genteel poverty, which I regard as poverty of the very worst kind, throughout the whole of my nineteen years of life. Hugh, you will have to win me as a wealthy widow or to lose me altogether," and the expression of Maggie Mortimer's face convinced her lover that she was in deadly earnest.

"And how would you have me carry the matter through?" he therefore asked; for, rather than fail to secure so beauteous a bride he felt himself capable of committing even a crime.

"Oh," laughed Miss Mortimer, almost hysterically, "the programme would be a simple one enough, and I have even thought it all out. At the first convenient opportunity you must insult Cornelius Crooks in such a way that he shall challenge you to fight him. Then tell him that you accept his challenge, but that as the challenged party you have a right to choose your own time and place for the duello, and to that he must perforce agree. Then leave the neighbourhood for a while, whereupon he will esteem you a coward, and think that you have run away in order to shirk the encounter."

"Confound it all, Maggie, he'll have good reason for deeming me a coward, whilst as for myself I cannot so much as guess what you are driving at."

"You will see everything very clearly if you will but hear me out. He and I are to be married in All Saints' Church at Routh, the wedding breakfast will be, of course, at my father's, ere which the will that I have spoken of will be signed. An hour later my husband and I are to set forth to pass the first month of our married life (and I prithee, Hugh, let it be only hours) at his house at Brandes Burton, called The Hollies, for the magnificent place which he has built a league on the sea side of Hornsea will not be ready until then to receive us. Well, directly darkness has set in, on the day on which we reach The Hollies, call there, demand a private interview with my husband, and thereat inform him that, as the challenged party, you have chosen your time for the duel between him and you as then, and for the place of meeting the hollow, sandy, mount-surrounded amphitheatre a quarter of a mile away on the moor. As the husband of so beautiful a bride," added Maggie, sarcastically, "he may plead for twenty-four hours delay, but having both right and inclination on your side, of course you will not listen to such a proposal. Take him straight away to the place I have mentioned, and there kill him, for in heart I hate and loathe Crooks every whit as much as I love you. The deed accomplished, you may claim me for your own true wife as soon as you see fit, and we will be rich and happy ever after."

"But if, on the other hand, he should kill me?" queried Sir Hugh, with a somewhat uneasy sounding laugh.

"He must not kill you," retorted Maggie, with flashing eyes and an impatient stamp of a tiny foot. "You are no unskilled hand with the rapier even now, but between the period of his challenge and the actual duel you must take lessons from the most renowned swordsman you can discover, even should you have to travel to London to find him. If I did not firmly believe that, after due preparation and constant practice, you could kill Crooks in a fair fight, without receiving more than maybe a mere scratch or two yourself, I would bribe two or three professional cutthroats to rid me of him in a less honourable fashion; yet I naturally shrink from so base an action as that, if by any possibility it can be avoided."

"I should think you did, indeed," exclaimed Sir Hugh Rowley vehemently; immediately adding, "Even my love for you, Maggie, though God wot 'tis as deep as the ocean, and as strong as its storm-lashed caves, would melt like a fog does before the sun's heat did I learn that you could even countenance so foul a crime as murder. But, my darling, since you will have it so, your husband of an hour shall die like a gentleman at point of sword, and in exactly the way you have indicated."

There is no need that we should follow the words or actions of these strangely assorted lovers any further; indeed, in the course of a very few minutes more they quitted the wood together; whereupon Sir Hugh Rowley mounted his horse and rode thoughtfully home to his house at Southcoats.

CHAPTER II.

"I WILL KILL YOU AT THE CLOSE OF THE HAPPIEST DAY OF YOUR LIFE."

Sir Hugh Rowley already knew Mr. Cornelius Crooks's favourite haunt in Hull, or rather, as it was then called, Kingstown-upon-Hull.

One of these was a hostelrie named the Green Griffon, standing close to the Guild House of the Holy Trinity, of which he was a high official.

Here, one afternoon, Sir Hugh found his intended victim drinking with half-a-dozen other kindred spirits.

The bluff sea dogs seemed to resent the intrusion of a mere landsman, and still more his joining in their conversation, as Sir Hugh presently did.

Upon one of the oldest presently introducing the subject of the Spanish Armada, Sir Hugh observed it was little wonder that the King of Spain despatched such an expedition after a lot of rascally English pirates had made a constant practice of attacking and plundering Spanish ships whilst the two countries were at peace, and when the crimes of such sea robbers were known all Europe over to have been openly winked at by the English Government. Indeed, instead of being hanged, as he richly deserved, he continued, "I am much mistaken if one of those blood and gold lustful pirates is not at this moment in this very room."

As Sir Hugh concluded he darted a contemptuous glance full upon Mr. Cornelius Crooks.

That worthy at once sprang to his feet with a mighty oath, and his fiery-hued hair and beard bristling with rage.

"Do you mean me?" he roared in a voice of thunder.

"Oh, as for that, if the cap fits your head you are at perfect liberty to wear it," retorted Sir Hugh coolly.

"The cap fit my head? No, sir, it does not fit it," came the furious retort. "But, by the devil's horns, aye, and by his tail as well, I will see how the edge of a cutlass blade fits into your throat, you jackanapes in velvet ribbons and point lace."

"Am I to accept your words as a challenge to mortal combat?" asked Sir Hugh Rowley disdainfully.

"Yes, and as your sentence of execution in addition," was the reply.

The party addressed rose from his chair at those words, and doffed his plumed cap to the whole of the assembled company in the most gracious manner, after which he delivered himself as follows:—

"Mr. Crooks, I accept your challenge with the most infinite pleasure; but, as the party challenged, I have the right to select time, place, and weapons. As for place, that I will decide upon in due course, the weapons will be rapiers, and as regards the time, I propose doing you the great honour and affording myself the intense satisfaction of killing you at the close of the happiest day of your life."

So saying, Sir Hugh treated his auditors to another polite bow, and then gracefully made his exit from the room, everyone therein being too astonished to hinder him.

CHAPTER III.

THERE, WITH A HAND PLAYING WITH HIS RAPIER HILT, STOOD
SIR HUGH ROWLEY.

When Mr. Cornelius Crooks got the better of his rage, which wasn't for some hours, he was sorely puzzled to decide if the young cavalier who had so direly insulted him was mad, or whether he had been in earnest in provoking the quarrel, and then had lost courage to the extent of shirking its otherwise inevitable consequences; for the worthy ex-merchant adventurer and ex-pirate felt certain that he could have killed him as easily as he could have crushed an empty egg-shell.

He knew perfectly well who the young man was, and also all about his past relations with the lady whom he intended to make his own wife; on which account he was willing to allow, in his cooler moments, that Sir Hugh had had some reason for trying to pick a quarrel with him.

"Only," went on his reflections, "the whipper-snapper hadn't sufficient pluck to carry his anger beyond words. As for the youngster's boast what he would do in the future, that was a mere idle threat, uttered in order to enable him to retire with a show of swagger, and—well, there was an end of him."

This comfortable conclusion was confirmed when, a couple of days later, Crooks learnt that Sir Hugh had suddenly left his old mansion house at Southcoats, attended by his single man-servant, bound for London, with sufficient baggage, borne on an accompanying pack-horse, to indicate that his absence from home would be a long one.

"A sensible fellow to avoid further quarrel with one who has killed more men in desperate fight than he numbers years. And, I am really obliged to him for going, since the fair Maggie would love me none the better, I opine, for my cutting a former lover's throat, especially that of so handsome a one. By the devil's hoofs, had he been but half as rich as I am, I might have whistled her to heel in vain, I reckon," mused the ex-pirate, with a chuckle.

So, easy in his mind about things in general, Mr. Crooks procured Maggie Mortimer's consent to wed him without, as he put it, "any ridiculous fuss or loss of time," and the event was finally fixed to come off on Christmas day, which, at that period, was considered to be the luckiest day in all the year for the celebration of so important a ceremony.

Needless to say, Miss Mortimer took a very different view of the luck of the matter from what Crooks did, since she hoped to be made a wealthy girl-widow on her very wedding eve, whilst he expected to be the proud and happy possessor of the loveliest wife in all East Yorkshire for many a year to come.

Well, the all-important day arrived at last, and in the profusely holly and ivy-decked little church of All Saints', at Routh, Cornelius Crooks and Margaret Mortimer were made "one flesh," as the marriage service coarsely dubs it. One flesh, indeed, when his was as red and coarse as a brick and hers as soft, white, and sweet as a lily! Why, the utterance inside a church of such an impossible lie almost amounted to a sacrilege.

Anyway, the ill-assorted couple were fast bound in the bonds of wedlock, and that without much fuss or bother, for Mr. Crooks had no desire to invite invidious comments about "May and December," and Maggie's parents, though they counted themselves a good old country family, were too poor to make an undue display on the occasion without suffering for it afterwards.

But, far more to the point than the smiles of gaily-arrayed bridesmaids and the popping of champagne corks, the all-important will was signed and witnessed, and then entrusted to the safe custody of the bride's father, and, a little later, husband and wife set forth, mounted on a sturdy cob, Maggie being seated on a pillion behind her lord, for the latter's neat little house at six-miles-distant Brandesburton, where they were to reside until his grand new mansion rising a league to the seaward of Hornsea, and called Santissima Trinidad, after a gold laden Spanish galleon which he had once attacked and captured, was ready for their joint reception.

At "The Hollies" the bride was received by two grim-looking middle-aged female servants, and a decrepit gardener, but a cheerful fire burned brightly in the oak-wainscotted dining-room, and the table was ready spread for dinner.

When the meal was served it looked a tempting one enough, but the bride had but a poor appetite, which was little to be wondered at considering what she confidently expected to close follow the repast, for it was already half-past four o'clock, so that darkness had closed in, and in an hour or two at most she fully believed that the husband who now sat facing her in the soft mellow light of four great wax candles, would lie a bloody corpse 'neath the yet milder radiance of a newly-risen full moon, for by frequent letters she had kept Sir Hugh Rowley well informed in London of all that was happening, and about to happen.

The cloth had been removed, and decanters of wine, with glass dishes containing fruit and nuts, stood reflected in the glittering mahogany of the carved table, whilst her ugly, beetroot complexed owner had drawn up his chair close beside his lovely bride's, intent upon indulging in "soft dalliance" with the captive of his bow and spear, or, to be more exact, the prey of his lengthy purse, when a tremendous knocking came to the outer door, causing Maggie's cheeks to pale and Mr. Crooks's face to turn an even deeper red than it had been before.

Then the front door was heard to open, spurred feet to tramp along an outer passage, and enter a neighbouring room; whilst a minute later a servant appeared with the statement that a gentleman had called who insisted on seeing the master of the house, and would take no denial.

"What name did the fellow give?" asked Crooks angrily.

"He would give no name, sir. He said there was no need to do so, because he had an appointment with you to-night, and you would, therefore, be expecting him," was the reply.

"By the devil's horns he lied, and I will send him out of my house a deal more hurriedly and unpleasantly than he entered it," growled the ex-pirate, and whipping up a candlestick from off the table he set forth to discover who his pertinacious caller might chance to be.

"Ah, Mr. Crooks, I presume that the close of the happiest day of your life has at last arrived, and, according to promise, I have come to kill you," was the cheery greeting with which he was received when he had entered the adjoining room, and shut the door behind him with a slam, by way of convenient vent to his rage; and there, bowing and smiling before him, one hand holding his plumed hat, and the other playing with his rapier hilt, stood Sir Hugh Rowley.

CHAPTER IV.

THE DUEL TO THE DEATH.—OVERWHELMED BY THE SEA.— CONCLUSION.

"The devil take you," roared Crooks, turning somewhat pale.

"No, no, my dear Sir, it will be a case of the devil take you, on account of the number of poor Spaniards you killed during your piratical career of, I am informed, many years."

"You have resolved to fight me then on a false issue, and pretend that a lost love has nothing to do with the matter?" growled Cornelius with a sneer.

"Mr. Crooks, a love once given to me could never be transferred to such a man as you," rejoined Sir Hugh, laughingly, "and you must be a fool if you deem such a thing to be possible, even though you are dressed for the nonce as a cavalier of good birth, and wear at your side, which, under the circumstances, is fortunate, a rapier in lieu of a cutlass."

"I not only wear a rapier, but, since I saw you last, I have made myself skilled in its handling."

"Then we shall have all the better sport, for during the past three months I have taken daily lessons in the use of the weapon from the most eminent swords-man in London."

"In that case had we not better postpone our business until to-morrow, so that the light of day may enable you to exhibit your skill to a greater advantage?" suggested Crooks.

"Oh, the light of the full moon will suit me equally well; added to which I must stick to my word, which was that I would kill you on the happiest evening of your life. A gentleman born never breaks his word, my jovial ex-pirate."

"Curse you, with your ex-pirate. If you are in such a hurry to have a yard of steel thrust into your carcase, I am in just the humour to oblige you. But what about seconds; for if we fight without witnesses, the survivor may run a serious risk of being arrested and tried for murder?"

"What?" laughed Sir Hugh Rowley, "when the dead man will be sure to grasp his bare weapon with a firmer grip than he ever did whilst living," answered Sir Hugh, lightly.

"Well, our mutual hatred will make whichever of us falls keep a firm grip on his sword hilt, even in death, I dare say, so come along; for the sooner I return to my bonnie bride and a cheerful fireside the better I shall be pleased."

"Mrs. Crooks will look bonnier still in widow's weeds, I'm thinking. But will you not don a cloak ere you leave the house, for we read that a dying man suffers more from cold than from aught else, and my charity will go so far as to wrap you up snug and warm ere I return hither to inform Maggie of her bereavement."

"You seem to have a hornet's sting at the tip of your tongue, confound you. But you needn't suspect that I shall suffer from cold, for I've ever found fighting to be warm work, and when I have done with you I shall run all the way home in order to keep the circulation going. Come on, and receive the fate you have invited."

"You mean for me to inflict the punishment I have promised. Our destination is the little sandy hollow a quarter of a mile away."

"You have chosen a pleasant enough spot for your grave, Sir Hugh Rowley," and without any further exchange of taunts or ambiguous compliments the two men quitted the house.

The spot where the duel to the death was to be waged was soon reached, and the full moon shone down upon it from an unclouded heaven.

It was freezing fast, so that hoar frost glittered whitely upon brown bracken and on every tuft of dead heather, whilst the only sound audible was the faint echo of bells from some distant church tower ringing a joyous Christmas peal in honour of the Nativity.

But little recked the two duellists, as they lunged down into the sandy hollow, of that message of "peace on earth and good-will towards men," and neither did the new-made bride, as she cowered over the fire in the dining room of Holly House, seeing in fancy all that was happening out on the moor, and hoping soon to learn that she was a widow, as a welcome preface to becoming the wife of another man, even of him whom she had loved with the one love of her life, which, hap what might, could never be bestowed upon another; and now, presently, she both hoped and believed that she would be able to bestow upon him unbounded wealth as well as her hand and heart.

Meanwhile two bare swords were glittering in the moonlight brighter even than the hoar frost on the bracken and heather.

Sir Hugh Rowley had hoped that his taunts would stir Cornelius Crooks up to such a pitch of fury that he would fall an easy victim; for an angry swordsman ever fights under serious disadvantages.

But now that the business had really commenced, the ex-pirate, if such he really was, had become as cool as the frosty air itself, and Sir Hugh soon discovered that, despite the many lessons he had had from the celebrated London fencing master, he had undertaken a task that he would find by no means easy of accomplishment.

And ere long he began to succumb to the superior strength of his antagonist, whose wrist was one of iron.

A minute or two later his rapier was broken short off near the hilt, and his enemy's was through his body; but, with a curse of mingled agony and despair, Sir Hugh plunged what was left of his broken blade into Cornelius Crooks's coarse, red throat, whereupon the combatants fell dead across each other, whilst the distant Christmas bells still rang on as though in bitter mockery of the dire tragedy that had now been played fully out.

And ever since, on every Christmas night, as was stated at the opening of our tale, that duel to the death is re-enacted in that sandy amphitheatre out on Brandes Burton Moor, but they are spectres and not living men who wage the awful combat, and it is even averred by some that two other forms may sometimes be seen looking on at the death struggle, one being that of a beautiful woman, who shrieks wildly as the younger swordsman is run through the body, and the other the foul fiend in person, tail, horns, cloven hoofs and all, who mopes and grins as though to him the scene was a vastly pleasant and agreeable one.

Sir Hugh Rowley was buried at Southcoats and Mr. Crooks at Brandes Burton, whilst, to the scandal of all Holderness, the widow attended the funeral of her lover instead of that of her husband. As, however, she was now the richest woman in York-shire, she could well afford to outrage all the proprieties, and to wholly disregard public opinion.

As soon as all was ready to receive her she entered into pos-session of the magnificent mansion of Santissima Trinidad, where she assumed almost the state of a queen, and ere long it was rumoured far and wide that she would soon make a brilliant matrimonial alliance, and so console herself for the loss of both lover and husband.

But such predictions are not fulfilled, inasmuch as she had loved once and could never do so again, for her heart was as dead as were the bodies of the two men who to her owed their untimely and tragic ends.

Her wealth and wide estates she enjoyed after a fashion, for she had always taken a keen delight in the exaltment of herself and the debasement of others; so now, year by year, her pride grew upon what it fed on, but little did she suspect that the hand of God was already uplifted, and anon would descend upon her round and milk-white shoulders with crushing force.

For He had determined to make the sea His instrument of punishment, that very sea which had given to Cornelius Crooks his vast wealth was destined to despoil his widow of it all, for:

> "Up rose the ocean from its bed,
>   And landwards drove his billowy car,
>   And headlands, spires, and houses fled
>   Before the elemental war."

writes a Yorkshire seventeenth century poet of that dire catas-trophe which robbed Holderness of hundreds of thousands of acres of land, and swept away all the towns, villages, and scat-tered homesteads which stood thereon.

But this didn't happen in a single day or night, as the verses might lead the reader to believe.

Maggie Crooks's once glorious tresses had changed from gold to silver, and the dimples in her cheeks had turned into wrinkles ere the great and final catastrophe came, whilst instead of one score she counted four score years.

But at the age of thirty her town of Redmore was swept away by the sea; when she was forty that of Tharlethorp followed suit, and scarcely had she reached fifty when the waves overwhelmed both Frismarsh and Potterfleet.

After that, year by year the cold, grey Northern Sea crept on mile by mile, over her other possessions, and towards the great mansion of Santissima Trinidad, which, named after a ship, now seemed to be doomed to meet the fate of one.

When Maggie had so proudly entered into possession of the almost castle, the sea could not be seen even from its loftiest tower, but fifty years had elapsed since then, and now its waves broke upon the sandy shore only a quarter of a mile away from its walls, whilst its owner's landed estate could be more conveniently counted by acres instead of by square miles, as was once the case.

For ten years more the waters crept on and on, till portions of the gardens disappeared beneath them, and it became evident that, with the first furious gale, the sea would attack the mansion itself.

But Santissima Trinidad had grown into Maggie's very heart, as it were, and she could not force herself to flee from the threatened peril.

Then, one dark Christmas night, it came suddenly and unexpectedly.

The ocean drove landwards its billowy car with a vengeance, and all the servants of the house, and there were no less than thirty of them, fled for their lives, and happily saved them.

But their aged mistress refused to follow their example; perhaps because she preferred to die in a palace rather than thenceforth live in a hovel, for, had she left Santissima Trinidad, it would have been almost as a pauper.

So she remained in and was buried with it beneath the waves.

The sea has encroached upon the land more than a league since then, and Santissima Trinidad now lies many fathom deep beneath its waves.

THE FIERY SKULL:

A TALE OF MAGIC AND SPIRITUALISM.

I am an old man now. Not old if you measure the actual years which have passed since my birth; but old if you but know the misery and suffering which have been crowded into those years.

None but God and myself know the misery I have at times lived through. I often wonder that I do live.

This suffering was caused by my own act—the deed done in a moment of frenzy has overloaded my whole life. As I pass, people look pityingly at me and whisper, "There is a man who has suffered." But how little do they know the weary weight of the untold secret which I carry in my bosom. I feel that life must be near its close, and in anticipation of the time when the world's look of horror will not affect me, I write this record of a sinner's life and a sinner's punishment. Look at me now, my hair is bleached as if by the snows of many winters; my form is bent, and my step uncertain.

I was not always this wreck. Memory carries me back to one winter not many years ago. The happy and light-hearted student would not be recognized in the bent and prematurely-aged man before you.

I and my friend Carl Heinemann were the gayest of the students in the University of Hamburg.

No one could know Carl and fail to love him.

His cheerful disposition, and his warm heart won for him friends among all who knew him.

My love for him was more than the love of a brother.

We were inseparable companions. Together we perused old tomes of mystic lore, and together we explored the treasures of antiquity, in which the quaint old city was so rich, and pursued those researches into nature's mysteries in which our souls delighted.

But while Carl's disposition was even to a fault, frank and open, I was naturally sullen and taciturn.

Even with this friend of my soul I could not shake off my gloomy reserve. I could not lay bare the foremost feelings of my heart.

His spotless mind was like an open page, every line of which might be clearly read.

Thus happy in each other's friendship, the first years of our stay at Hamburg passed swiftly, and the horizon of our happiness was bright and cloudless.

About this time there appeared in the town an Italian doctor of celebrity.

His skill brought him many patients, but it was whispered that he was also a master of that more obscure and hidden lore which teaches man to command the powers of Nature and to read the secrets of futurity.

How far he could unveil the secrets that yet lay hidden in the bosom of the future let the sequel show.

The whole city was soon singing with the accounts of his wondrous talent. He had performed a cure which the whole school of doctors pronounced to be no less than a miracle, and as the patient was a great and powerful noble the doctor's fame was established.

Carl and I eagerly sought his acquaintance, and it was by Dr. Montini's invitation that we one evening bent our steps towards his dwelling.

He lived in one of the most obscure and quiet parts of the town. The house in which he dwelt had been in the olden times the house of a brotherhood of monks, and, if vulgar belief was to be depended upon, the doctor and his family were the sole corporeal and yet not its the only inmates.

The shades of a December evening were gathering round, and the pale stars were peeping out one by one, when Carl and I knocked at the old oak door of the doctor's residence.

The door was opened, and never did such a vision of loveliness meet my gaze as when my eyes rested on the girl who answered our summons.

Description is impossible, and even now as I recall my first impressions of Beatrice Montini I can realize nothing but that she was pale and mild and fair.

She seemed enveloped in some pure and radiant atmosphere, and she looked like one of those enchantresses of old whose spells blinded men's vision and laid captive every sense.

She bent her head in answer to our inquiry whether Dr. Montini was at leisure to receive us, and we followed as she preceded us through a long passage and up an old oak staircase.

She stopped before a closed door, which she opened, and entering spoke a few words to the occupant of the apartment, then motioning to us to enter, left us.

As we advanced into the room we noticed a lamp burning on the table, which was strewn with mathematical instruments, and papers on which were drawn strange signs and figures. An antique book with massive silver clasps lay open beside them, and a grim grey skull.

The room was pannelled with dark oak, and hung in places with ancient tapestry, representing scenes in the life of Hermes, the Master Magician.

As we advanced further into the room we became conscious that an old and venerable figure was advancing to receive us.

He uttered some words of welcome in a slight foreign accent, and pointed to seats.

It was Dr. Montini.

He was clothed in a loose dark robe, and had on his head one of those caps denominated skull caps. Below this appeared waving locks of white hair—his snowy beard descended to his waist.

But though the whiteness of his hair betokened age his figure was singularly upright, and the brightness of his eye was undimmed by years. His voice was low and musical, and there was a singular fascination in the old man's presence.

He questioned us kindly about our studies, and listened patiently as Carl detailed to him our research into nature's secrets, and our desire to learn more from him.

When Carl had finished speaking the doctor looked at us long and earnestly. At last he spoke as follows:

"So, young men, you would learn to read the future—to bend the strong powers of nature to do your bidding? Blind enthusiasts, know ye what ye desire? Is it nights of sleepless anxiety—days of unending toil—a craving never to be satisfied—a soul shut out from all human sympathy—an eye that never looks on man without distrust—and seeing in spite of yourself all that you would fain shut from your gaze? This is all your reward! The power ye seek to possess falls with possession, and bids you see in every man a lurking foe, or, if there be one you love, you behold around his path snares which you can see but not remove—sorrows from which you would fain preserve him but lack the power—or even a dreadful death which you can foresee but cannot avert. Be advised, young men; pursue more legitimate studies and forget your present delusion. The pupils of Hermes Trismegistus are not the favoured mortals men deem us."

The doctor's admonition had not the effect he anticipated, for his words only lent fresh ardour to our wishes, and we again repeated our desire to pursue occult studies under his direction.

"Be it so," he replied. "I cannot refuse."

He mused for a few moments, and then turning to the grim, grey skull, uttered some cabalistic words.

The eyes of the skull immediately flashed with fire, and the same lurid glow lighted up the mouth and nose cavity.

Then, turning to Carl, the doctor said, "Thy future lies written as in the pages of an open book. Shall the skull of Hermes tell thee, young man, what he sees there?"

He took Carl's hand, and turning again to the skull, a cavernous voice seemed to issue thereout, saying:—

"I see a youth full of bright promise—a nature formed to enjoy the fair side of life—talents, by whose power you might hold a world captive. But all this fair prospect becomes suddenly obscured. The line of life in thy open hand is dimmed with blood. Trust not the friend of your youth. Behold, love steps in, and thy friend is a traitor."

Those words made a profound impression more from the solemnity of the old man's look and manner whilst the fiery skull was speaking than from the words themselves.

He then approached and took my hand in turn.

A cold moisture started to my brow at the old man's touch.

It was a nerveless touch, and his cold fingers felt like those of a corpse.

He fixed his eyes on mine, and as he did so the fiery skull again wagged its toothless jaws, and in a voice that gradually rose to a shriek exclaimed:—

"I see friendship betrayed, trust broken, and over the pure dream of love hangs the shadow of crime. I see on your brow the blood of Cain. Through a long life remorse dogs your footsteps, and with Cain you cry—'My punishment is greater than I can bear.' The vision passes. My brain congeals again. Accursed, your hand is stained with blood."

As the skull ceased speaking, the inner fire died out and the grim relict of mortality grew cold and grim and grey again.

The old man relinquished my hand, and I tremblingly glanced down at it. Imagine my horror upon noticing a small stream of blood trickling from my wrist to my fingers' ends.

Then before my eyes a horrible vision passed. I saw two men engaged in mortal strife. The uppermost had just passed a knife through the body of his prostrate foe, and the victim's face was that of Carl. As the murderer rose, his form seemed painfully familiar, and when he turned his head, I recognised my own features.

The sight passed away. I approached the window to examine the blood-drops on my hand, and they, too, had disappeared. I tried to shake off a horrible foreboding that seized me, and succeeded in persuading myself that all that had just passed were jugglers and hocus pocus.

We bade the doctor adieu, and days and weeks succeeded each other.

The scene just described gradually became more and more indistinct, and at last, I believe, faded from the minds of both of us.

Every evening we took our way to Dr. Montini's house.

Our studies attracted us as in the first instance, but very soon the beautiful Beatrice proved a still more subtle magnet.

The charm which surrounded her was irresistible, and soon we both of us only seemed to live when in her presence.

The wise old doctor, as skilled in all but the realities of life, seemed not to dream of the result likely to follow from our close companionship with his daughter.

From being so much and so frequently in her society we soon both grew to love her. There was indeed a witchery in her presence that seemed to fascinate the poor victims on whom she cast her spell.

She was equally polite, but cold to both of us; yet both were her slaves. My love for her absorbed every other feeling—my very existence seemed dependent upon her smiles. Yet no word of love had ever passed my lips and she had never bent from her cold stateliness in our presence. She was a queen—the mistress of some potent spell, and we were her enchanted victims.

My passionate admiration was the stranger because I never spoke of it. My secret lay jealously guarded in my own bosom; while Carl, ever true to his frank and honest nature, would discourse in rapturous tones of his idol's charms, little dreaming that I too was her slave.

I believe now that I really must have been the victim of some unhallowed charm. This could not have been love—I was like one possessed. It was madness.

Friendship was forgotten—the very remembrance of old affections was obliterated by this strong image, which effaced all others, and over my love for Carl came the shadow of jealousy.

I looked at his handsome and open face, and the fiend whispered, "How well he was formed to win a woman's heart." As I compared my own unattractive features and my forbidding manners, all better feelings vanished, and hatred alone remained.

I would have avoided him had I dared, but I feared the discovery of my secret, and so I compelled myself to pass all my leisure hours with him as before.

No words can tell the pain I endured when Carl's whole conversation had but one theme—Beatrice.

Thus the time wore on. One evening when we arrived at the usual hour at the doctor's house we were informed by Beatrice that her father could not receive us for a few minutes, and she requested us to wait in her sitting room.

We had been there but a few moments when I was summoned into the doctor's presence.

I obeyed reluctantly, for my evil demon whispered that Carl would be alone with Beatrice.

How I should have valued a few such moments by her side!

I might then have dared to whisper to her of the love that was consuming me; but my fate had no such rapture in store.

Dr. Montini wished to make some remarks on my studies, and from mere remarks he proceeded to long disquisitions on various branches of his mission.

He was evidently unmindful of the flight of time, for more than an hour had passed, when he perceived his forgetfulness, and then he dismissed me and hastily summoned Carl.

He came in. I watched him with the clear-sighted eyes of jealousy. Never had I seen his bearing more proud or his face more radiant. He looked the very incarnation of happiness.

A sick faintness stole over me; my increasing pallor evidently betrayed this, for Carl rushed to my side.

In a moment his strong arms were around me, and he bent anxiously over me murmuring kind and loving words.

His face expressed anxiety and alarm, as he gently inquired the cause of my faintness.

I moved from him as soon as my strength allowed me, and attributed my attack to the heat of the weather and the perfume of some flowers which grew outside the window.

I am sure some evil influence was at work—that some demon took possession of me.

Had I been myself, Carl's generous concern must have disarmed me of all evil thoughts towards him. But now horrible ideas would crowd into my mind, foremost amongst them that if Carl were to die I might win Beatrice.

Then the whisper came, "Other men's deaths have been hastened, why not Carl's? Poison and the sword are both powerful!"

I thrust back the horrible thoughts, but they would recur again and again with fatal distinctness, bringing with them the memory of that awful and almost forgotten vision which had passed before me after the awful prophecy of the Fiery Skull.

The murdered man was Carl. The murderer myself!

I covered my eyes with my hands, and inwardly vowed that I would never become an actor in such a deed.

Dr. Montini noticed the pallor of my face, and kindly advised us to discontinue study for that evening.

To this Carl agreed, and taking my hand begged me to return with him to our lodgings, adding that the fresh air would doubtless revive me.

We left the house together.

When Beatrice heard our steps she appeared at the door.

Carl waited to say a few words to her, while I, sullen and moody, walked on.

Carl evidently told her of my indisposition, for they walked up quickly together and overtook me.

Beatrice kindly expressed her sorrow at my illness, and her hope that the morrow would find me restored to health.

She then smilingly gave me her hand, and left us.

Why was she thus kind and gracious?

The touch of her hand sent the hot blood through my veins.

As I looked at Carl, however, I noticed that he had a rare flower in his hand, which he carried so reverently and gently that I knew it must have been given by Beatrice.

I walked beside him dumb with jealous fury.

He was talking as we proceeded on our way, but I didn't hear one word he said. At last he stopped and looked at me.

"Hermann, my friend, what strange spirit possesses you? You once rejoiced in my happiness, and now when I tell you of the sweet hope which has dawned for me, you look as though you heard me not."

"Liar and traitor!" I cried; "why wear any longer the mask of friendship? Now, I tell you, that I hate you as hell itself. You have robbed me of the one love of my life, and tell me in canting words of your great happiness."

"Hermann, these words are not your own. You are ill. Another time you will be more just. You know that at any time I would sacrifice my own happiness, if by so doing I could advance yours."

"Then prove your words," I cried, madly: "resign all thoughts of Beatrice Montini."

"Never!" he moaned, in a voice of pain. "Even were I removed for ever from her sight, you, Hermann, could never win her love. Even did I resign her, the sacrifice would be in vain. But knowing that she deigned to love me, I should do her wrong as well as myself did I not assure you that your suit would be hopeless. Yet, had you been the object of Beatrice's affections I could have rejoiced in your happiness, even though my own had been for ever blighted."

"Then, if my suit is hopeless, you, at least, shall never win her," I cried, as I suddenly threw my arms around him.

The next instant we were engaged in a mortal struggle.

Hatred lent me strength, while Carl, who only sought to defend himself, grew weak.

I had in my hand a strong clasp-knife, with which a moment before I had been carving a piece of wood as I walked along.

I was mad. I knew nothing but that my rival was on the ground under me, and in the recklessness of my passion I plunged the horrible weapon into his heart.

He turned his eyes once upon my face and died.

The next instant the sight of the dead sobered me.

There lay the friend of my youth.

The years we had spent together passed in review before me.

I recalled his truth and gentleness, and the love which had lain hidden in the madness of the past few months now welled up in a strong stream into my guilty heart.

Beatrice was forgotten. Nothing but the agony of remorse was felt. I took the pale dead face between my hands. I could not weep; but as I kissed the stiffening lips I cried in my agony—

"Carl, my brother, forgive me!"

The place where I had committed this awful deed was near the ruins of an old and disused bridge.

People seldom passed that way, for a murder had been committed there several years before.

The thought of that former crime passed through my mind, but what crime could compare with mine?

There he lay, the friend of my youth, that honest and true heart was stilled for ever. The eyes which but a short time before had looked on me so full of love and gentleness were closed in death; the strong arms which had supported me in my faintness were stiff and cold. I sat through the darkening hours of night. How time passed I know not.

At last, rousing myself from my stupor, I rushed from the spot.

But with reflection came thoughts of self-preservation.

I returned to the place and dragged my victim's body towards the old bridge.

There, under one of the arches, was a deep hole into which the sluggish waters of the river emptied themselves.

I took up my dreadful burthen, and heading carefully across a line of huge round boulders I reached that hole.

Into it I cast the body, and then hurried away.

As I reached my lodgings the neighbouring church-clock struck the hour of midnight.

I threw myself on the bed; tired nature asserted her supremacy, and I slept.

I awoke in the morning with that feeling which I think most of us must have at times experienced.

I felt that some one was near me.

I roused myself and looked round the room, but no one was visible.

But still the consciousness of some one's presence grew stronger, and I heard a sigh behind me.

I rose, determined to ascertain who was my visitor, and as I crossed the room I distinctly heard footsteps following me.

Wherever I turned these footsteps followed mine, but still I could find no one.

I thought I would seek Carl, and tell him of my unseen visitor.

But as I reached the door the horrible events of the preceding night flashed on my mind, and I felt that I was doomed for life to the companionship of my murdered friend.

Tremblingly, I sought my books, hoping by violent study to obtain a temporary forgetfulness of the past.

But no such oblivion could be mine.

As I turned over page after page I distinctly heard behind me my unseen companion turning over his pages also.

Whenever I moved his footsteps dogged mine; if I but turned in my chair or my bed the action was repeated.

And now the strangest part of my tale is to be told.

While I was anxiously awaiting the moment when suspicion must fall on the murderer, a letter arrived addressed to one of the authorities of the University forbidding any search to be made for Carl, and explaining that he had been hastily summoned to a far and foreign country, and that he would probably never return to Germany.

I could have sworn that the letter (which was shown to me) had been written by Carl himself. The peculiarities of the hand-writing were the same.

This letter had the effect of allaying all suspicions as to the cause of Carl's sudden departure from Hamburg.

Years afterwards an old man, who had known and loved me from childhood, told me that he had once written such a letter. He asserted that he awoke at midnight as if in a dream, in which he saw me led to death. He heard a soft voice saying, *"Hermann is in danger."*

In answer to his unspoken inquiry as to how he should help me, this voice said briskly, *"Write!"*

He did not immediately obey the summons, and the voice again, in a tone of pain, urged him to *"Write!"*

He told me that he felt as if he dared not disobey; that he rose from his bed, and, getting his writing materials, sat down, wondering what he must write.

But as soon as he took up his pen and dipped it in the ink, a new spirit seemed to possess him, and his hand was invisibly guided as he wrote the words in the letter I have mentioned.

When he had finished, a weight was removed from his mind, he said, and he heard a sigh behind him and the faint echo of the words, "It is well."

He addressed and sent the letter, though he had not been previously aware of such a person's existence.

Could it be that Carl, whose love for me survived death and was stronger than the crime that separated us, had thus, by some mysterious power granted to him, influenced this old man's mind for my preservation? Oh, wondrous power of human love! Here was my victim in death as in life ever seeking my welfare. The deed which was now so bitterly repented was powerless to sever the bond which had in life united us.

Truly, we little understand the mysteries of that world unseen, yet so near.

I remained for weeks shut up in my room, absorbed alternately in my studies and my own horrible thoughts.

Yet my unseen companion was ever near me, following in my footsteps as I walked, and turning over ghostly leaves as I studied.

At last the desire to see Beatrice grew irresistible.

I prepared to go, but as I passed the mirror I turned to it.

What horrible vision was there?

The reflection which I beheld was that of an old man.

His hair was white and his form bent, as if by the weight of years. I could not believe that this was my own image.

I was in the prime of my youth and strength.

This must be my ghastly tormentor, I at first thought.

But as I passed through the gateway and along the streets, old friends failed to recognise me, and people stared as at a stranger.

I doubted my own identity then, but the longing to see Beatrice was stronger than before. I would see if she recognized me.

I arrived at the house. The door stood open, and I entered. I went into the sitting-room, and there found Beatrice.

I advanced with words of greeting, but she stood transfixed.

The look of horror with which she at first beheld me soon gave way to one of strong indifference.

Her eyes grew fixed and expressive, and she stood as though she saw me not.

I spoke to her. I said reproachfully:—

"Beatrice, have you too forgotten me?"

I attempted to take her hand.

But she drew back with horror from my grasp.

"Touch me not!" she shrieked; "your hands are blood stained. I see the crimson gore enveloping even your heart. Cain, where is thy brother?"

My crime, then, could not be hidden. But I pointed to my bleached locks, and said, "If I have sinned I have also suffered."

Then, seeing the look of undisguised terror and disgust with which she gathered her garments from my defiling touch, I rushed from the house, exclaiming in the words of one of old,

"My punishment is greater than I can bear."

I left the city. Since then I have been a wanderer in many lands; but there is no peace for the wicked. My travels are as in a cycle.

There is but one starting place and one end—the scene of my crime. At the anniversary of that deed I am always on the spot. Sometimes I reach it at noonday, sometimes at midnight. Sunshine or storm I must be there; and there yearly I see that awful tragedy re-enacted—Carl the victim, I the murderer.

I travel far from the scene, yet ever as the fatal day draws near I feel an irresistible will, more powerful than my own, leading me to the old ruined bridge, and there I feel that I must die. Those ghostly footsteps have never left me, and at those hours which were our chosen ones for study I still hear my invisible companion turning over his pages.

Reader, judge me not unkindly. Remember that my suffering, like that of the Wandering Jew of old, has been apportioned to my crime. I am now again on my journey towards the old wooden bridge at Hamburg, I hope and pray for the last time. I cross the channel to-morrow from Walton-on-the-Naze to Antwerp, but I feel that the day of my death is not now far distant, and that there by that old bridge I must this time meet face to face in death the friend who loved me and whom I slew.

TWELVE MILES BROAD.

I don't think I should have been tempted to spend last Christmas Day with Matthew Fallon, the German vigneron, had not the attractions of a promised roast goose been supplemented by those of his little duck of a daughter Gretchen, who chanced to be eighteen on that very day, and whom I hoped to make my wife before 1884 was over.

Thank heaven she is my wife, but though I'm about to write a tale of our brief courting days, I would not for worlds have her read it, lest the horrors which I am going to relate should bring back to her mind so vivid a recollection of the scenes themselves that her reason, which at the time they nearly robbed her of, should again be endangered, and by a mere memory.

Behold me, then, on a burning-hot Christmas Day, leaving my little weatherboard hut, where the thermometer hanging in the shade of the deep verandah marked twenty-nine, and clad only in a coloured shirt and trousers (with a clean collar and a freely flowing necktie, of course) and a broad-brimmed, low-crowned, cabbage-tree hat that had cost me a couple of guineas in the township of Wodonga a week previously, mount a horse that I had paid half-a-crown for on the same occasion—though had he been properly broken in and groomed he would have fetched pounds at any fair or bazaar in England—and giving a crack with my whip, which was two feet long in the handle and fifteen at least in the throng, head him straight for ultra-marine and violet-hued forest ranges, whose lowest spurs were at least a dozen miles away, though the Australian atmosphere made them look not half the distance, and which enabled me to see even the upcurling wreaths of smoke from the homestead wherein I was to be so hospitably entertained.

Heavens, how still the air was. Yet there was something both enervating and depressing in the sharp crackling of the forest leaves in the fierce heat, in the furnace-like glow of the heavens and the silence of both bird and insect life.

When a man happens to be in love, however, and furthermore journeying in the direction of a good dinner, it is his nature to set down as trifles what under different circumstances he might regard as serious disagreeables, and so I scoured the undulating, tree-dotted plains at a gallop (plains of brown grass that had been changed into hay even while it grew, and trees whose sage-green, vertical foliage afforded no shade), and the close of the hour saw me ascending the ranges toward the convolvuli-covered cot of my beloved at a more sedate pace, for the rising ground had taken all the spirit out of my grass-fed nag, and, considering the heat, little wonder.

Ten minutes later, however, he was stabled in a little out-house, and I myself was seated in the verandah with my darling by my side, and a great dish of delicious muscatel grapes and a long-necked bottle of cawarra wine standing on the table in front of me.

How delicious those grapes were, and how cool and refreshing the wine, but of course I had to go and see my presumptive father-in-law, also, whom I found in the little detached kitchen attending to the cooking, which your true German considers to be a man's work—that is, if it is to be properly performed.

Old Matthew was evidently in his element. The goose was already set down to roast in front of an enormous fire composed of two-foot long oak logs, in company with some wild ducks, and the vigneron was now busy in the manufacture of a gigantic peach pie.

It was very evident, despite the friendliness of his greeting, that he didn't want us there, and as nothing more mortal than a salamander or a fiery dragon could have enjoyed his company amid such surroundings, I was very glad when I was almost driven forth, and so had a good excuse for returning to the verandah.

As Gretchen, in anticipation of my coming, had risen at an early hour and got through all her work, even to the laying of the dinner table and the adornment of the Christmas tree (for old Matthew would not for untold riches have omitted a single custom of the "Fatherland" on such an anniversary), she had now nothing to do but sit and talk with me, so that an hour or more passed delightfully away, and a second might have followed in like manner but for the sudden apparition of a dirty, dissipated look-ing fellow, with a blanket and a blackened tin billy strapped to his back, a heavy untrimmed staff in his hand, a stump of a pipe gripped between his yellow fangs, and a stubby beard of a fort-night's growth, who, suddenly rounding the angle of the veran-dah, brought himself to a halt in front of us with a cool remark:

"I seem to nose a good dinner, mate. Roast goose, ain't it? I guess you won't say no to a tired and weary overlander taking a bit and a sup with you on an occasion like the present? Am I welcome? Yes or no?"

"I'm not the boss here, my friend, but as there's a bush inn only three miles along the road, I'd advise you to go on till you get to it, and I don't mind standing half a crown towards your dinner there if you're short of funds," I made answer, for I could see with half an eye that the dirty bushman would be no acquisition to our little family party, for he smelled of bad rum already, and there was a wild look in his eyes and a jerky twitching about his fingers and mouth which hinted plainly that he was within a measurable distance of an attack of delirium tremens.

My offer, however, was received with a contemptuous "You're a pretty sort of cove, you are; a new chum who's got to learn what Australian hospitality means, that's very plain. Who in this free country would think of turning a houseless stranger from his door on a Christmas Day of all days in the year? No, I don't suppose you are the boss, and, what's more, you don't deserve ever to be one, neither, wherefore I aren't going to take 'no' from your lips."

"If I'm not the master here I can very soon take you to him. If he asks you to stay, all well and good, and if the other way, I can then show you the gate," I rejoined, and, springing to my feet, I took him toward the kitchen.

But when we got there, old Matthew Fallon was no more struck with his personal appearance than I had been, and after looking him straight up and down, made an answer to his request with a curt:

"We don't want a stranger at our dinner-table. If you'll take a draught of ale or wine, and a plate of bread and meat, and then go your way, you're heartily welcome, and if you don't choose to do that you can go without."

Instead of accepting the kindly offer and my again proffered half-crown, the fellow began to curse and swear in the most frightful manner, finishing up by throwing down his hat and challenging me to fight.

Being the possessor of a hot temper, I knocked him down at this, and then, lifting him on to his feet again, and fixing his old weather-beaten billycock hat down on his head, I conducted him to the garden-gate, with all his bounce apparently taken out of him, and, gently pushing him through, closed it in his rear, and then said:

"If half a crown's of any service to you, mate, you are still heartily welcome to it, and the bush inn I told you of is away yonder;" and I pointed in the direction in which the shanty was situated.

But the man, turning round on me, gave me a look that I shall never forget till my dying day, and hissed through his clenched teeth:

"To the fiend with your dirty half-crown and with you, too! I'm going to travel in the teeth of the wind, I am. Mark that, in the teeth of the wind, I say; and if before long I don't send you skiddering ten times as fast in a contrary direction, my name's not Jim Baldwin. The goose is cooking, but none of you will set teeth in it this Christmas Day. No, by heaven, that you never shall!" and, shaking his fist at me, the fellow turned round, and shuffled off as fast as he was able.

Of course, I laughed at his threat, regarding it as talk, and nothing more. Besides, I didn't understand his meaning, nor did I consider it to be worth guessing at either. Instead of doing so, I retraced my way to the house, glad to escape from the scorching hot wind that had just begun to blow, and 'neath whose influence the green vine leaves had already commenced to curl up at the edges, and the purple bunches of grapes to shrivel and wither.

One hour later, we were all three seated around the festive board, poor old Matthew Fallon with a great deal of his usual contented and happy look faded out of his rubicund visage owing to the certain destruction of his grape crop if the hot wind, which was by this time roaring as if belched forth from a thousand fiery furnaces, continued for any length of time longer.

He put as good a face upon the matter as he could, however, and grace having been said he was just on the point of commencing to carve the goose when Gretchen suddenly exclaimed:

"There's something more than hot wind raging. Look at the colour of the sky. Hark to those crackling sounds. There's a bush fire somewhere."

Her face suddenly paled, as well it might with such a wind blowing, and the primeval forest of highly combustible gum and turpentine trees extended right down to their little clearing.

Her aspect even more than her words caused me to look around in turn, and directly I beheld the aspect of the sky, and a lot of eagle-hawks circling around in the air, I knew why they had left their nests, and guessed at the deadly peril that was swooping down upon ourselves.

At the same moment I hit upon the solution of what had before been to me a riddle—the parting threat of the vindictive swagman, Jim Baldwin: "I'm going to travel in the teeth of the wind, and the goose that's cooking none of you will ever set teeth in."

Full of the most horrible surmises I dashed out on the verandah, but a single glance was sufficient, and I sprang back into the room again, exclaiming:

"We must up and away; that scoundrel has set fire to the bush, and the hot wind is driving the conflagration down the ranges directly towards us at a speed of, at least, twelve miles an hour."

Gretchen shrieked with terror, and Matthew Fallon dropped the carving knife and fork, exclaiming:

"I'm a ruined man; I shall be burned out of house and home."

"This is no time to think of ruin when life itself is at stake," I rejoined. "Run, man, and saddle your grey mare. I can take up Gretchen in front of me. Each nag will then bear about equal weight. Go! why do you stand still?"

"Because I've lent the mare to a friend and he hasn't returned her yet."

His answer unnerved me, for it told me that one of our lives was sped, and even should I yield up to him and his daughter my horse, the grass-fed animal could never bear such a double burden, old Matthew weighing sixteen stone at the least.

He must have read my reflections in my eyes, for he exclaimed: "Save my daughter, have no thought of me. My dear wife is buried in the garden and I've no great wish to leave her."

There was no time to stand disputing the matter. I made a rush for the stable, Gretchen's shrieking protestations ringing in my ears the while that nothing should induce her to leave her father.

"How shall I be able to tear her away from him?" I wondered as I hurried along; but in less than three minutes I had saddled my horse and brought him to the front, where, slipping the reins around a verandah pillar, I again leaped into the room where I had left father and child.

They were still there, and she seemed to be yet entreating him to escape in her stead, but as I neared them the old man released himself from her tenacious clutch by force, and sending her reeling into my arms, exclaimed excitedly:

"Remember, I hold you answerable both to God and to myself for her safety!"

He then plucked a pistol out of his coat pocket, thrust the muzzle between his teeth and up against the roof of his mouth, and pulled the trigger and fell dead before I was even certain that he grasped anything in his hand. The question was thus definitely solved as to who should be saved and who left behind.

Had not the terrible spectacle caused poor Gretchen to swoon, it is extremely doubtful whether I should have been able to tear her away even then from her father. As it was, however, I whipped her up as I might have done a sheaf of wheat, and carrying her out through the open door-window, threw her across my horse just as though she had been one, and you may be sure that the next instant I was up in the saddle behind her, with no thought in my head except as to how we were to escape.

It was a question by no means easy to solve, for the conflagration was now within a mile of us, and tearing down the ranges at a speed of a dozen miles an hour at the very least.

True, the way to my own homestead still lay open, and I

could see it nestling amid its patches of Indian corn as I trotted
my horse down the hillside, but I did not dare to cross the sea of
waving yellow grass that stretched between, for, if the sparks that
already dropped around us were to ignite that, the flames would
scour the plain at a speed that neither racehorse nor kangaroo
hound could hold its own against for a single mile.

It was maddening to think that the wretch who had done
this black deed could pursue his route with *his face to the wind*
as leisurely as he chose, for the flames of his creating would not
advance half a mile an hour in *that* direction, while we had to tear
along for dear life, with death on the white horse racing almost
neck to neck with us.

But it was no use giving way to anger, for a cool head was as
necessary under the circumstances as either a firm hand or a tight
grip of the pigskin.

The amounts of gum and turpentine in the Australian forest
trees, together with the dry, loose bark of the past year which still
clings to trunk and branch, and in huge slabs strews the ground
all around, renders them almost as inflammable as tar barrels, so
that so small a thing as the sun shining on a broken bottle has
been known to create a conflagration which has blackened and
destroyed a tract of country as large as an English county.

Once clear of the stony ground, the trot was changed to a
gallop, and none too soon, for the fire had been gaining on us at
a rapid rate.

Looking back, a holocaust of flame marked the spot where the
dead vigneron's weatherboard house had stood, but there was no
time for a second glance, for sparks were already falling around
us in a blinding shower, and the aromatic odour of burning gum
and peppermint leaves was almost overpowering. Luckily there
was little smoke, or we should have been suffocated outright.

The conflagration must by this time have been fully twelve
miles wide, and no one can imagine the grandeur or the horror
of the spectacle.

It was as though countless millions of birds with flame-
coloured plumage were whirling and fluttering around vast col-
umns of red hot iron, each a hundred, a hundred and fifty, or two
hundred feet in height, while in all directions these Titanic col-

umns were reeling and crashing to earth with a sound like thunder, sending up fountains and cataracts of sparks to an immense height in the dull red sky, which seemed to glow like a furnace.

Dead or dying birds now dropped around us, flying foxes flapped past on their great leathery pinions, kangaroos came leaping down the ranges, clearing eighteen feet of ground at each onward bound, and more than once I heard the jocund peal of the laughing-jackass, who, poor foolish bird, possessed not sense enough to perceive the danger which even the snakes were endeavouring to escape from.

I was so confused by the noise and the heat, and the uncertainty as to whether my darling Gretchen was only in a swoon or actually dead, that I knew not in what direction I was riding.

But, ere long, hope itself died within me, for my horse commenced to reel beneath its double burden, blood began to tinge its white foam spumes, and the relentless flames were evidently catching us fast.

All seemed red around—the fire was drawing ahead on both sides; it was closing in around us.

But all at once there was a snort, a plunge, and water spurted up and around me. I heard my brave steed's fierce *shriek of joy*, and I echoed it as I perceived that we were breasting a broad stream, and the conviction flashed home to me that it was the river, and we were saved.

We *were* saved, for we gained the opposite bank in safety, and great was my joy on reaching home by a circuitous route many hours later to discover that the fire had not approached within three miles of my little homestead.

It is now Gretchen's home also. She recovered her reason there, but even yet she can never look toward the far away blackened ranges without a shudder and a sigh, so, as soon as I can, I mean to change my farm for one in a different district.

THE HAUNTED SILK MILL;

OR

THE GHOST-GUARDED TREASURE.

CHAPTER I.

"NO WATER WILL QUENCH THOSE FLAMES, AND THE LADDERS
ARE TOO SHORT!"

A s the extraordinary story that I have to tell is something
more than merely founded on fact, I have given the leading
characters therein fictitious names instead of their real ones,
because the stirring events happened only fifty-two years ago,
and they may, consequently, be still living.

The 13th July, 1853, was a blazing hot day in Derby, and a day,
moreover, that was long afterwards remembered, for, at half-past
six in the evening, the thrilling cry of "Fire! Fire!" resounded in all
parts of the town, and from many of the top windows of the six-
storied silk mill, belonging to Mr. Joseph Davenport, in Albert-
street, lurid flames began to rush and roar, whilst hundreds of
the mill hands came tearing forth from every possible exit into
the open space which surrounded the huge building, forming an
excited crowd, which was rapidly added to by thousands whom
mere curiosity attracted to the spot.

"Oh, my God!" exclaimed a beautiful mill girl to a companion,
whose arm she was tightly clutching in her agonised terror, "my
man is perhaps throwing away his life at this moment, and I do

love him so, and we were to have been married next week."

"Joe Need? What on earth cause has he to throw his life away? 'Twas easy enough for everyone to escape from the mill who liked, for the fire's only in the top story of all."

"Yes, I know that, but Mr. Thorpe, of Full-street, got my Joe, and half a dozen more young chaps, to volunteer to go up to that top story to save as much of the silk as they could before the fire reached and destroyed it, and now, more like than not, it has destroyed them. Oh! bother the silk, for though there may be hundreds of pounds worth of it there, it arn't of the value of my Joe's life, at all events to me."

"Now cheer you up, Jane Morgan, for all the floors are of brick, and so fire proof, and no man with so pretty and so good a girl as you are waiting to marry him is going to seriously risk his life for mere silk. Your Joe will go just as far as his duty to his master calls him, but not a single step further, you may make up your mind to that. Ah! and here come the first engines and the escape ladders. That will comfort you, won't it?"

"No water will quench those awful flames in time to be of the least use to Joe and his mates, and no ladder will reach to the dizzy height of those windows, which are seventy feet above the ground, or even more. Oh, Betsy, I'm going back into the mill to find my poor Joe, for I'll make him come away with me or else I'll burn along with him."

"You don't go on any such fool's errand as that, lass," answered Jane Morgan's companion. "Joe Need can get away out of the mill easy enough, I tell you, but you won't find it as easy to get away from me, for I'm about as strong as a young cart horse and you're but a slip of a girl."

And Betsy Briggs clutched hold of her friend with both hands, and held her helplessly in her strong grasp, whilst poor, pretty Jane rent the air with her screams and her heart-rending entreaties to be "let go."

Meanwhile it had been discovered that the fire engines were of next to no use on account of an insufficient supply of water, and that the ladders were far too short, so the firemen began to join two and two together, as rapidly as they could, whilst willing volunteers rushed into the ground floor of the mill, and hauled forth bales of cotton, placing them that anyone who leapt, in their despair, out of a top story window (and by this time only two of the round dozen or so were unlapped by the flames) might fall on their comparative softness and so escape with his life.

But, after the lapse of a few minutes more, with a rattle and a clatter which might have been heard a mile away, the roof of the mill fell in, and, an instant later, a roar as of thunder proclaimed that its descending weight had broken down the brick floor of the top story.

A myriad sparks flew up towards the smoke-canopied sky, a thousand tongues of lambent flame leapt on high as though endeavouring to overtake them, and in the midst of it all arose the cry from at least ten thousand excited spectators of:—

"A man at a window!"

"It's my Joe! My God, it's poor Joe, and there's no hope for him. None!" came a wild wail a second later, as Jane Morgan's tear streaming, agonised, violet hued eyes followed the direction of the great crowd's pointing fingers; and then, with all her strength, for it was now as great as that of a raving maniac, she tore herself away from Betsy Briggs' grasp, and rushed towards the burning mill.

She was almost beneath that seventy feet high window, and only one of the long row of such that was not by this time flame vomiting, when a great wave of fire rushed towards it from within the mill, and to escape death the man she so dearly loved, with an awful cry, leapt into space.

Down he came, turning over and over in his descent, to fall with a dull thud on one of the cotton bales, but rebounding therefrom, he came down the next time on the hard stones, groaned, and fainted.

The next instant the arms of his sweetheart were around him, and her tears were bedewing his scorched and smoke blackened face. In places his clothes were literally scorched off in great patches, and the smell of his burnt flesh was distinguishable yards away.

Tenderly he was borne away, on a stretcher, to the infirmary, where he was promptly attended to by Mr. Gisborne, one of Derby's best known surgeons of that day.

"Oh! will he live? Will he live?" asked Jane Morgan, in tones of piteous entreaty of this gentleman, for she and her friend, Betsy Briggs, had accompanied the injured man to the infirmary and entered it in the rear of him and his bearers.

"Yes, he'll live, my lass," answered the surgeon kindly. "But," he added, with a shake of the head, "his right arm is so injured that it will never again earn him his living."

At this juncture the poor fellow opened his eyes, and recognising his weeping sweetheart exclaimed:—

"Don't worry about me, Jane dear, for I'm all right, and I've done my duty," and then the awful agony that he was suffering caused him to faint away for the second time.

Betsy Briggs saw Jane Morgan home, and stayed with her until she had grown calmer and more resigned to the inevitable. Then making her way to her own humble abode, which lay directly past the mill, she perceived that the fire was at last extinguished, and learnt that no one but Joe Need had been seriously injured thereby, though there had been some very narrow escapes.

Mr. Thorpe, of the firm of Eyre and Thorpe, silk-throwers, of Full-street (he who had called for volunteers to save the silk on the top floor, and himself headed them), escaped, when he saw that all was done that could be done, by tying a handkerchief around his mouth to prevent suffocation from the smoke, and making his way to a window at the Tennant-street end of the mill, where, a ladder being raised (or rather two ladders joined together), he broke through the window and came down without the assistance of anyone, amidst the cheers of the crowd below, whilst another young volunteer in the blazing top story, not daring to leap from a window, notwithstanding that Joe Need had offered to jump first, rushed through the room in the midst of flames, and down the stairs, only a moment before the roof fell in, thus almost miraculously escaping with only a few severe burns.

The fire was got under by nine o'clock without penetrating further down than the top story, but a great quantity of silk and machinery were damaged by the body of water that had been poured through the many windows.

The origin of the fire was never clearly known, but it was supposed to have been caused by the ignition of soot in the tall mill chimney, and sparks flying in through the open windows of the mill's top story, and falling amongst some cotton bales which were stored there; but even a rusty nail that has got by accident into a bale of cotton will sometimes cause it to ignite.

CHAPTER II.

"I WILL SEEK THE HIDDEN TREASURE, GHOST-GUARDED THOUGH IT BE."

Five months and more have elapsed since the burning hot July day on the evening of which the fire broke out in Mr. Davenport's big silk mill in Albert-street.

Derby is now grasped in the icy clutch of a most severe winter, and its poor are in evil case, for there has been a strike amongst the mill-hands and the silk mills have, consequently, been closed for some weeks.

And now Christmas Eve has come round, a sad one indeed for the unemployed, who, or at all events the vast majority of them, lack both fuel and food, and are enduring such hardships as few of them have ever known before.

In the fireless room of a small house, in the working quarters of Derby, are seated three people, Joe Need, with a fire-withered, useless right hand and arm, his deaf and half-imbecile old mother, of whom he had been the sole support up to the evening of the conflagration at Davenport's mill, and lovely Jane Morgan, now looking somewhat thin and haggard from insufficient food, yet full of hope and courage, as, indeed, she has need to be, if she would cheer up her companion as it is her earnest desire to do.

"I tell you, lass, that you must just throw me over, and have done with me, for I should be a selfish beast to hold you to any promise that you made me when I was hale and whole, and so able to work for you. With your beauty and your good and noble nature there's nothing to prevent your marrying well, Jane dear, and I'm not going to stand in the way of it, as I've said oft-times before."

"And you may say it again, aye, a thousand times over, but it will be mere waste of breath, my lad," retorted Jane Morgan with a bright smile. "You're my man, and I mean to keep you. Why, we've loved ever since we were children, and each of our hearts would surely break if it was severed from the other. Besides, I have a scheme in my head, and I mean to carry it out to-morrow night. Now just try and guess what it is."

"Lord, lass, I was never no hand at guessing."

"Well, then, I'll just tell you without your troubling your head. I am going to seek for the hidden treasure in John Lombe's silk mill."

"Why, Jenny," exclaimed Joe Need, with a hollow laugh, "you might as well seek for treasure at the foot of a rainbow. You surely don't believe in any such old wife's tale as that about Mr. Lombe's secreted gold?"

"Oh, yes, I do, and I've good reasons for believing in it, as you will yourself acknowledge by and bye. You know, of course, how Mr. Lombe procured, whilst travelling in Italy, drawings and models of the silk machinery then in use in that country, by bribing two workmen, whom he afterwards induced to accompany him to England, and how he built the great silk mill in the year 1718."

"Yes, yes, lass, all Derby knows that tale."

"Of course it does, Joe, as also that a beautiful woman, called Ida Vitali, was sent from Italy, a couple of years later, to win his love and then to poison him, in revenge for the way in which he had stolen the industry of her nation in order to bestow it on his own."

"I don't see that Mr. Lombe was much to blame, myself."

"No, nor do I, but naturally the Italian manufacturers would, because they exported a good deal of silk to England, and so they would, of course, be great losers by the making of equally good silk here at home."

"Ah, so they would, but go on with your tale, lass."

"Well, the beautiful Italian woman who pretended, some say, to be the sister of one of the workmen whom Mr. Lombe had previously brought over from that country, failed to win his love, but, nevertheless, succeeded in poisoning him. It seems that Lombe had some suspicion that a deadly plot was being hatched against him, with, as he believed, robbery for its main object, and so, shortly before his murder, he secreted most of his wealth (banks being then almost new and not greatly trusted institutions) somewhere or other inside his mill, where it lies hidden to this present day."

"Although during the last hundred and thirty years almost as many people have made eager search for it, I have no doubt, wherefore, Jenny, my dear, how can you hope to discover what so many have looked for in vain? Besides all that, you could not make the search in the day time, and at night John Lombe's treasure is said to be guarded by John Lombe's ghost."

"And wherefore should I fear the ghost of a good man who, at all events in England, never injured man, woman, or child, but was a warm friend to everyone who was in need? Why, considering that we are almost starving, I'd have pluck enough to ask his ghost to point me out the hidden wealth, and to let me take it, for Mr. Lombe hasn't a single living descendant, and of what earthly use can gold be to a ghost? I should think he would be very glad to get quit of it, and so be able to rest quietly in his grave."

"But why should Mr. Lombe's ghost befriend us more than others, my dear?" asked Joe Need, with a wan smile.

"For one reason, because of the heroic way in which you received your dreadful injuries at the call of duty, and because we have loved each other for so many years and were even on the point of being married when dire misfortunes fell upon us, for your misfortunes are, of course, mine also. But I have a better reason for believing that my search will be crowned with success than any that I have yet given you, for just see what is written, in faded ink, on this scrap of discoloured, mouldy parchment, which smells as though it had recently been taken out of some grave."

She handed the tiny document to her lover as she concluded, and with some difficulty he deciphered the following doggerel rhymes:—

> "Whoe'er would John Lombe's riches seek,
> Must be a maid both pure and meek.
> No selfish greed must urge her quest,
> For she must act at love's behest,

No grizzly ghost can do her ill
If these conditions she fulfil,
And perhaps a ghost may point the way
To where old John Lombe's treasure lay,
If she goes on the night of Christmas Day."

"Umph, if a ghost wrote those lines, as you seem to believe, Jenny, he don't seem to me to be much of a poet, or very well up in grammar either," remarked Joe Need (who was better educated than most of his class), when he had finished reading; quickly adding: "But in the name of wonder how did you become possessed of this old, musty, fusty bit of parchment?"

"Ah! that is the strangest thing of all," answered his pretty sweetheart, with an involuntary shudder. The gale that was blowing last night shattered a badly-cracked pane of the window that I was sitting at sewing, and, into the room, with a gust of wind and rain, came what you are holding in your hand. It fell on my very lap, shining all over with a ghastly and horrible light, just as though it had been rubbed with phosphorus."

"As it might have been," observed Joe Need drily. "But, tell me, did you see anything outside the window?"

"I'm not quite sure whether I did or no, because the inrushing rain and wind altogether distracted me. Yet I did think that, for a moment, I beheld a ghostly-looking face, gleaming all over with the same kind of unearthly light as covered that scrap of parchment with the writing on."

"And so, on the strength of the very bad poetry and the shaky grammar you have made up your mind to go treasure-hunting, my brave but foolish Jenny?"

"Yes, I will visit the old haunted silk mill to-morrow night, and there hunt for John Lombe's buried treasure, ghost-guarded though it be," answered Jane Morgan in tones of determination.

"Persuade a woman against her will, and she'll be of the same opinion still; so, as one fool is said to make more, I will accompany you on this treasure quest, my lass?"

"No, no, Joe, for what's written on that parchment scroll says, or at all events implies, that the maid spoken of must enter the haunted mill alone."

"But as it will certainly be locked up, how will you get inside?"

"I've no doubt that a way will be pointed out to me."

"Well, that women have more faith than men is well known. Anyhow, Jenny, I'll go as far as the outside of the mill with you, and I'll give you a whistle, so that if you should find yourself in any kind of a fix you'll have but to use it to bring me to your side."

"That will be very nice indeed, and I thank you for your offer and gladly accept it. But hark, there are All Saints' beautiful bells beginning to ring forth their joyous Christmas peals, so it must be long past eleven by the clock, and therefore high time for me to be home and in bed. I can't wish you joy this Christmas, dear Joe, because no joy comes to them who want bread, but I wish us, one and all, a happy New Year at any rate, and perchance my pluck and faith may win it for us."

"I haven't much hope of it, Jenny, but I won't discourage you, at any rate, by throwing cold water on your daring scheme," retorted Joe Need.

Then, Jane having kissed the old woman, whose deafness had prevented her catching a single word of the lovers' long and strange talk, Joe put on his hat, and saw his pretty sweetheart to her humble lodgings, that were situated a little lower down the same lane, and which she now shared with her faithful friend Betsy Briggs.

CHAPTER III.

INSIDE THE HAUNTED MILL. JOHN LOMBE'S GHOST.

Christmas morning brought to starving Jane Morgan a startling and most welcome surprise.

She and Betsy Briggs had lain in bed till a late hour, so as to feel their hunger and the bitter cold less keenly; but when Jane had dressed, gone down stairs, and opened the door of the cupboard in the back yard, to discover if there was so much as a handful of coal left to light a fire with, she saw at least a hundred-weight of it there, and, wonder of wonders, she beheld on an upper shelf a large, round plum pudding, with a red berried sprig of holly stuck therein, a fat goose, a loaf of bread, half a dozen bottles of ale, and a canister of tobacco; whilst nailed to a yet higher shelf was a strip of calico, running all along it, and bearing, worked in red holly berries, the words:—

"Wishing Jane Morgan, her sweetheart, and her friend, Betsy Briggs, a Merry Christmas and a FORTUNate New Year."

The first two syllables of the word FORTUNate were in much bigger letters than the final one, so that Jane muttered to herself:—

"Now that means something. Fortune? Why it can signify nothing else than John Lombe's hidden treasure, and yet, and yet nobody knows that I have a thought of seeking it except my Joe. Well, whatever it means, it at all events proves that we've some kind and unknown friend, who has provided us with a good Christmas dinner, and who intends that we should all partake of it together, for the tobacco would not have been placed there for me and Betsy, so that Joe was evidently to be of the party."

Jane Morgan then began to wonder how all the good things could have been brought to and deposited in that out of doors cupboard of hers; but it was an easy riddle to solve, for there were heavy footprints in the deep snow, leading direct from, and then back to the yard door, which was always kept merely on the latch, and opened into a back lane; and there was also the track of a single wheel, that of a hand barrow without doubt, going both ways.

Well, Jane did not care to bother her head about the matter any more for the present, in so great a hurry was she to acquaint Betsy Briggs and Joe Need and his old mother with what had happened; the result of which was that, at high noon, for their hunger would not permit of their waiting any longer, the quartet sat down, before a roaring fire, to partake of the Christmas cheer which had been so abundantly and mysteriously provided for them.

Perhaps "grace before meat" was never more thankfully uttered than it was by Joe Need on this occasion, or the health of anyone more heartily drunk than was that of their unknown benefactor, who the quartet had by this time almost made up their minds must be their employer, Mr. Davenport, who was very prone, as all who knew him were well aware, to "do good by stealth," &c.

We need not dwell upon what the assembled friends talked about when the meal was done, and Joe Need was puffing away at what he declared to be "the very primest tobacco he had ever smoked," for the reader will naturally conclude that the conversation was mainly concerning Jane Morgan's intended visit to the haunted mill.

"I've brought you a lantern, with a good length of candle in it, my lass, for only a cat can see in the dark, you know; and here's a double barrelled pistol, which may come in handy as well," Joe said at length, producing the weapon as he spoke.

"But," laughed his sweetheart, "of what use would that old rusty thing be to me? One can't shoot a ghost."

"Nor could you shoot a man with it, lass, for it isn't loaded. No, God forbid that you should ever contemplate taking a human life, Jane, more especially as I'm very sure there's no one in all Derby who would attempt yours. Only, don't you see that if you are being ticed on to undertake to-night's adventure by some practical joker, who might choose to indulge in some rather rough fun at your expense, though of course nothing worse, if you pointed this weapon at his head it would keep him mighty civil until your whistle brought me to your side."

"And me along," put in Betsy Briggs, "for three fists are better than one, and you've only one that you can see, Joe Need. Besides, my arms are as strong as a mule's hind legs."

As the doughty Betsy's heart was evidently set upon going, her volunteered services were laughingly accepted, and, to cut a long story short, at exactly eleven of the clock the party of three set forth for the haunted mill, trudging through the deep snow of the by that time almost deserted streets, with a full moon lighting them on their way, for the gas lamps were so encrusted with snow and frost that their glow-worm glimmer was of little practical use.

The Christmas bells were still ringing merrily from All Saints' lovely Gothic tower, as the adventurers passed its pillared portico, and, five minutes later, they had crossed over to Christy Island, and were standing under the high, dull red brick, many-windowed walls of the haunted mill.

It looked grim and uncanny enough, with its huge and now

motionless water-wheel, that was as much as twenty-three feet in diameter. The water itself was fast ice-bound, the ground around covered with snow, which spread over, as with a spotless shroud, the tree tops on the close neighbouring, beautiful rustic island of Cope Castle.

The little party moved silently on to the door by which the mill hands usually entered the almost century and a half old structure, and here, to the infinite surprise of all three, and somewhat to the chagrin of Joe Need, who, looking upon his sweetheart's undertaking as a fool's errand, had hoped that she would find no way of entering the mill, a key was discovered in the lock.

When Jane Morgan had turned it, and pushed the door partly open, she gazed at her companions and said:

"Now, you must neither of you come a step further. Joe, dear, hand me the lantern, but I shall not light it before I have got inside and closed the door behind me."

She had disappeared almost before the final word had quitted her lips, and the next minute found herself in a darkness so opaque that it could almost be felt, whilst a shrill squeaking, and the scurrying to and fro of many tiny feet told her that there were rats around her by the score, if not by the hundred.

She therefore lighted the candle in her horn lantern as quickly as she could, for she knew that rats, when hungry and in great numbers, would sometimes attack, and even overcome, a strong man, which was a peril that neither Joe Need nor Betsy Briggs had so much as thought of in Jane Morgan's case.

The lantern illumined, however, and handled so that its light flashed, in turn, in every direction, and quickly scared the little rodents into their holes.

And now Jane Morgan hadn't the slightest idea how or where to begin her search. The treasure would, most likely, she thought, be hidden somewhere under the flooring, or behind the bricks in some chimney nook, but in either of such cases her hunt therefore would probably be as vain a task as that after the needle in the proverbial bundle of hay.

Then it suddenly struck her that behind the wainscotting of the counting house might be its most likely hiding place, that counting house in which rumour had it that old John Lombe had spent the happiest hours of his life in poring into his big ledgers and chuckling over his profits.

Well, the counting house of John Lombe was the counting house of the old mill still, and it was believed that no alteration whatever had been made there since Mr. Lombe's day.

It was on the second story, and thither Jane Morgan now hurried, it never once striking her the while that she was contemplating a burglary, or doing anything that was in the least wrong, for was she not looking for the treasure of a man who had died and been buried much more than a hundred years, and who had not a single descendant living?

It was a weird upward journey, for how hollowly her footsteps sounded on the creaking stairs and on the deserted floor. The long rows of windows let in the moonlight, and the reflected glare of the outside snow, casting a strange, unearthly seeming radiance over many wheels, broad leather bands, and complicated pieces of machinery, whilst, dulled in sound by the thick walls, the Christmas peals of All Saints' tower now boomed in her ears.

Arrived on the second floor, she quickly caught sight of the closed counting house door, and then it all at once struck her, and with almost the force of a blow, that it would be locked, the lock a first-class one, and therefore difficult to force, and that she had no right to force it might the task be ever so easy.

But almost as quickly as these thoughts occurred to her, Jane Morgan perceived a thin line of light coming from underneath the door, and a tiny ray escaping through the keyhole as well.

Next a hollow-sounding cough reached her ears, and Jane, "with her heart in her mouth" as the saying is, crept over the mill floor almost as noiselessly as a fly walks upon butter, fell on her knees in front of the closed door, and peeped through the huge keyhole.

What she saw within the room didn't at all tend to lessen her nervousness, for a very stout man, with face and hair as white as snow, and dressed in the quaint costume of George I.'s reign, sat at a desk, apparently deeply immersed in the contemplation of a ponderous and ancient ledger, and totting up long rows of figures by the aid of a candle that was stuck in a brass candlestick, and a pair of horn-rimmed spectacles which sat astride a particularly large and bulbous shaped nose.

"Oh, my goodness, it is John Lombe's ghost!" gasped poor Jane.

CHAPTER IV.

IN WHICH JOHN LOMBE'S GHOST MAKES HIMSELF AGREEABLE.

Perhaps in her momentary terror our heroine uttered those words aloud, or, perchance, she fell half fainting against the closed door.

In any case she must have made a noise of some kind, for the man or ghost, whichever the present occupant of the counting house happened to be, dropped his quill pen, looked around him, and then called out in a hollow, yet not altogether unpleasant voice:

"Come inside, Jane Morgan. I've been expecting you."

Jane knew that ghosts had to be obeyed, or that evil came of it to the bidden, so with what amount of courage she could summon up, which was very little, she opened the door and entered the room, dropping a curtsey as she did so, and remarking:

"Yes, I'm Jane Morgan, and I hope I see you well, sir."

The ghost smiled at this naive greeting; indeed, the smile very nearly approximated to a grin, and then rejoined:

"Thank you, I'm about as well as a ghost who, as doubtless you are aware, isn't able to eat and drink, can expect to be. Now, I daresay you had roast goose for dinner, and I hope enjoyed it, but what attraction would a roast goose be to a mere shadow that is not possessed of even a palate or a stomach?" and the ghost groaned at the reflection.

Thereat Jane Morgan began to feel quite sorry for him, and with her sorrow much of her fear departed.

"Oh, sir," she therefore said, "notwithstanding all your deprivations, I trust that you are happy where you are now liv— residing I mean, and that you are made as comfortable as possible."

"Well, yes, Jane Morgan, it's very nice—very nice indeed, but it has its drawbacks for all that. First of all, I've to wear a gold crown, and I can't say that I find it a very comfortable head gear, at all events not yet; worse still, I've to learn to play on a harp, and not having the least ear for music, that is remarkably trying; but, worst of all, there are no ledgers, or cash books, or coined money of any kind up there, which makes me feel entirely out of my element. Oh, everything's very delightful, Jane, but nothing's business-like. By the bye, you've come here on business, haven't you? You want me to give you some of my hidden store of gold, eh?"

"If it's no longer any use to you, it would be of very great service to me, and to someone whom I love as well," answered Jane tremulously.

"I know all about it, my good girl, and it was to encourage you to take your present step that I sent you some verses. They weren't very good ones, but a ghost is not allowed to write in prose, perhaps for fear that if he were he would be too prosey," and here the spectre actually chuckled.

"Yes, sir, I received your verses," answered Jane, with a smile, for by this time she had lost all fear of her by no means shadowy looking companion. Did you throw them in at my window yourself, may I ask?"

"No, another ghost, an intimate friend of mine, did that. I myself, when I revisit the earth, am not allowed to leave my old mill, and, indeed, I am too happy here to wish to do so. By the bye," drawing from his fob a huge, old, turnip-shaped watch, and regarding its dial somewhat anxiously, "in less than ten minutes I must be gone, for, like Cinderella, I'm bound to depart hence at the first stroke of twelve. As the way in which I disappear is somewhat startling—a mere mortal might think it even terrible—we will finish our affairs at once, my good girl."

As he spoke the ghost opened the lid of the big desk at which he sat, and took thereout an old, mouldy-looking leather bag, which he held out to Jane Morgan, saying:

"There, take hold of this, but be careful not to touch my hand in doing so, for whoever touches a ghost always dies within a year, or, if not then, at some time or other afterwards. That bag contains three hundred pounds, and it is your marriage portion, my dear. And now please go without even stopping to thank me. Depart by the door, I say, whilst I pop through all the floors and the roof, an easy matter for a ghost, I do assure you;" and waving Jane Morgan impatiently away, the spirit of John Lombe next blew out the candle, whereby the counting house was instantly enveloped in complete darkness.

"Thank you, sir, a thousand times, for you have made two people, aye, perhaps even four, happy and comfortable for the remainder of their lives," exclaimed Jane Morgan, hurriedly escaping from the room as she uttered the words.

Five minutes later she had rejoined Joe Need and Betsy Briggs outside the old mill, with the exclamation:

"Oh, Mr. Lombe is an old dear as a ghost, whatever he may have been as a man. He has given me three hundred pounds as a wedding portion—the hidden treasure in fact. It's all in this old leather bag, and if we look skywards for a minute or two we shall most likely see him pop up through the roof of the mill on his journey there, for that's the way in which he always leaves the premises since he's been a spirit."

CHAPTER V.

THE CONTENTS OF THE OLD LEATHER BAG. CONCLUSION.

But though the trio stopped and stared upwards for a good five minutes, no soaring ghost did they behold, so they wended their way homewards, Joe Need declaring, again and again, that, in his opinion, Jane had been finely hoaxed, and though the coins certainly did look like sovereigns (very naturally all three of them had peered into the bag ere this, and even felt its contents), they would all be found to be gilded farthings at the best.

But when the little party had reached Jane Morgan's and Betsy Briggs' rooms, the contents of the bag were discovered to be real sovereigns, and there were exactly three hundred of them, just as John Lombe's ghost had declared.

So the Christmas supper turned out to be an even more enjoyable meal than the Christmas dinner had been, and John Lombe's ghost's very good health was toasted again and again, Joe Need even proposing that they should sing "For he's a jolly good fellow," but his pretty sweetheart laid her veto upon that, lest the term "fellow" might be deemed insulting by a disembodied spirit.

Well, to cut a perhaps already too long story as short as we can, Joe Need and Jane Morgan were married, by license, at All Saints' Church, on New Year's Day, 1854, and within a week after had invested a portion of their fortune in a tip-top tobacconist's and sweetstuff shop, situated in one of the best streets in Derby, carefully investing the remainder.

Of course, the news of our hero's and heroine's suddenly and greatly changed condition in life was soon spread all over Derby, and became the common talk of the town.

Many believed that John Lombe's ghost had been Jane Morgan's benefactor, even as she firmly did herself; but, at length, it was credited by several of the more intelligent townspeople that Mr. Davenport, of the great Albert-street silk mill, had played the role of ghost on that never to be forgotten Christmas day, in order to test the strength of the love which Jane Morgan bore for Joe Need, and to put her courage and unselfish devotion to the strongest possible test ere he secured her future happiness and independence along with that of the man who had proved himself a faithful servant at the cost of most severe bodily injuries.

Joe Need himself at last so firmly accepted this view of the case that he actually called upon Mr. Davenport to thank him for his kindness, but the worthy silk manufacturer rejoined, with a burst of hearty laughter:

"Get along, Joe, my man, and don't make a fool of yourself. I give away three hundred pounds, indeed, not if I know it. Besides, by your wife's account, the ghost she so pluckily interviewed on Christmas Day was as fat as Father Christmas himself, whilst I'm as thin and spare as I well can be."

But Joe Need never relinquished his firm belief that his old employer was also his wife's and his own secret benefactor, and at length even Jane accepted his view of the case. As for our own opinion regarding the bona-fides of John Lombe's ghost, we had rather not offer it.

THE STEEL-BOUND VALISE;

OR

THE MURDER AT THE OLD STONE CROSS.

———————

These are bad days for the Spiritualistic. There has arisen such a practical condition amongst men that it is hard for credulity to flourish. The wizards of the time drive a roaring trade by public exhibition of feats which, not so many years ago, would have introduced them to the stake; and one of their chief delights is to "show up" so-called Spiritualism, to chaff clairvoyance, and poke fun at the mediums.

In spite of their efforts, however, and in the face of a practical generation, a certain number of unaccountable narratives gain the public ear, and not infrequently acquire the public faith in their authenticity; and I believe that human nature still has its old admiration for the horrible, and enjoys a good ghost story over the fire (and before the gas is lighted) as keenly as in the so much bequoted days of superstition. In fact, there can *never* be an unpopularity for the supernatural.

Upon this text, and with confidence in its application, I shall proceed to relate a story which I fancy will puzzle the scientific to explain away, and will mystify the timid half-believer.

In the winter of 18— I had occasion to travel through part of France, charged with a diplomatic mission from high authorities in England to one of the German principalities. The nature of this trust was of sufficient delicacy and importance to induce me to take as companion of my journey a friend (also a secretary in the service) on whom I could place implicit reliance, and to whom I might look with some faith for hearty protection. This was an old colleague who had been my fag at Eton, and who, fifteen years after we had parted as boys, was associated with me in the service to which our inclinations had mutually prompted us. I would explain here (and it seems to me to be important) that our friendship had never, from its earliest date, been characterised by any remarkable sympathy or interchange of sentiments. We were not Damon and Pythias, and had never sworn eternal fidelity, or promised that neither would survive the other's decease. We were capital friends, excellent companions; but as unlike in tastes as we were in appearance. My whilsome fag was a magnificent man (this relieves me from any description of myself), and, had not old fellowship been of sufficient inducement to select him as *compagnon de voyage*, his strength, presence of mind, and courage would have suggested to me that John Markham should share my mission.

I had managed with considerable adroitness to obtain a leave of absence for him at the precise time for which my journey had been arranged, and late in the month of December we were travelling together within two leagues of the German frontier. There were no convenient railways then to expedite our mission, and the distance had to be accomplished by "relays."

Our travelling carriage was a type of its kind which needs no description here; and within its dusky recesses the reader must imagine John Markham and myself huddled in opposite corners, befurred and beshawled in an attempt at defiance of the frost which obscured the windows, and glistened even on the surface of our rugs. The road was so rough, however, that we were compelled to keep our faces uncovered, fearing for our heads against malicious corners of the windows, and, when we could brush the frosty steam from the glass, the prospect of the country—new to us both—was terribly barren and depressing.

"Is there much more of this?" asked John, in grumpish tones;

"because I'm being shaken like a nut in its shell, and there's no getting any sleep in this beastly old jolting rack on wheels!"

"I'm 'extensively confused' myself, as the police always describe a black-eye delivered to one of the force," replied I, in very *staccato* tones, for the road was more than usually rutty at this juncture; "but, as far as I can see, I fancy there's better ground ahead, and then we may get a little sleep."

"What's the time? How bitter the cold is! And *how* I could sleep if this rotten thing didn't oscillate so!"

"It wants four hours of daybreak, John."

"Four hundred thousand fiends!" commenced Markham, angrily, when the clattering of the glass windows and the rickety panelling of the coach ceased, and in a moment more we were smoothly travelling over a good highroad. Weary as we were, the dull rumbling of the liberated *voiture* was as the murmuring of bees that invited to sleep, and in a few minutes we had forgotten the world and the winter in a deep, heavy slumber.

In this slumber I dreamed a dream, and the fashion of it was as follows:—

It appeared to be a lovely night in summer, and I was travelling over a *route* which I had never seen before, and I felt myself transported back to the date of thirty years from 18—; in other words, since I was only nine and twenty at the time of my dream, to precisely one year before my birth.

(These details may seem absurd, or *bizarre,* but must be told amongst other particulars.)

Though I was unacquainted with the road over which I passed, a thousand national signs convinced me that I was in Germany, and when my dream developed and became more vivid I found that I was journeying by means of an antique posting-chariot, and that I had a companion seated opposite to me.

This (how I knew it who shall tell?) was a rich merchant of Hamburg, who was seeking Breslau and the confines of the Grand Duchy of Posen for the purpose of commercial negotiation.

I mention here, parenthetically, that though this has been confessed a *dream*, the minuteness with which every detail was impressed on my mind is very remarkable.

The merchant was a clear-faced, ruddy, jovial man of perhaps forty-five years of age; after the fashion of his compatriots of Holstein he was given to a considerable display of chains, rings, and other matters of portable and ornamental jewellery, while at his feet rested a *valise bound in steel, and protected by three neat-looking locks.*

At certain joltings of the vehicle the comfortable sounds of tinkling metal and rustling paper suggested that the said valise was primed with good gold pieces and rich store of notes and bills on the banks of Berlin and Frankfurt.

In the course of a friendly conversation the merchant admitted with much freedom of trust that there were some three thousand pounds in notes and bills lying in the valise. He did not seem oppressed by the knowledge that this valuable trunk was in the keeping of only himself, nor did it occur to him that such an unusual temptation might convert a carriage companion into a robber. On the contrary, he was quite at his ease, and gaily drew my attention to the beauties of the scenery through which we were passing; he chatted about the chateaus, the forests, the villages in hearty fashion and unwearying voice, his cheerfulness seeming to add to the brightness of the prospect glowing beneath the summer sun.

On a sudden, without a twilight warning, darkness profound and horrible fell on us.

The wind rose and whistled chilly through the open windows of the carriage. In attempting to close them heavy drops of rain or sleet beat upon our hands, and a pale flash of lightning was followed at no long interval by the hoarse muttering of distant thunder. The rain now fell in torrents, and a gust of wind which I shall never forget, blew open the doors of the decayed chariot, which instantly stopped. My eyes, now becoming accustomed to the darkness, rested at this dreadful moment on the faces of a man and woman, one of whom stood at each door of the chariot, their strong eyes glaring through the gloom.

I shudder whilst I recall the fiendish features of this ghastly pair; swollen with passion, and quivering with hate and malice, they seemed to be of that hideous order of the enemies of man which the Arabian fables have called Ghouls. I was petrified and spell-bound to my seat.

At this moment the man, with a satanic grin, pointed his livid claw to the female, and then to the valise, which lay, as I have stated, under the merchant's feet. Instantly, with a ferocious cry, the hag thrust her head into the carriage, and after extracting the valise, directed, in her turn, the attention of the male figure to the jewellery, so fatally conspicuous on the breast and fingers of my companion. Their bony hands fell on their prey, who remained as one dead; and, like horrible vampires, they dug their talons into his chest, and greedy of appropriating each to itself the treasures of his flesh and blood, began to rip the body asunder.

At this sickening spectacle I closed my eyes, but the spattering of hot blood on my face and a horrible cracking sound compelled me to look again, and I saw these demons rending the unhappy man's limbs from the trunk, amidst an infernal accompaniment of laughter. From the dead man's clothing they next pillaged his chains and rings, which the female attached to her own hateful neck and fingers. Then the male made a sign to our postillion (who all this time had remained an indifferent spectator of these atrocities, expressing no compunction, but merely whistling a hunting tune) to descend from the saddle and assist them. The wretch, whose utter apathy was even more abhorrent to me than the ferocity of the two murderers, obeyed at once; and, still whistling his accursed tune, helped to ransack the valise.

This was soon accomplished, and the trio then occupied themselves in disposing of their prey.

The money was transferred to a short sack, and suspended over the shoulders of the female, while the other wretches dragged the dismembered trunk to the base of a large stone cross which stood in the junction of the four roads at which the carriage had been stopped. Lifting up the square stone which formed the base of this monument, they flung the mangled body of the wretched merchant, together with the broken valise, into a shallow pit beneath it, which seemed to have been dug in anticipation of its contents. This over, the trio broke out into a parody of the Burial Service, and at its profane conclusion they uttered a yell of delight. Simultaneously with the echoes it induced came a deafening peal of thunder, the lightning ran snakily along the earth, and the three wretches fell to the ground, and disappeared in the pitch darkness which enveloped the scene, of which no trace remained, save that in my ears still seemed to sound the low whistling of the imperturbable postillion.

The next moment I awoke.

It was still night, and John Markham was lying asleep in his corner of the carriage.

Staggered as I was by the horrible impression left by the dream I did not wake my friend, as I rather dreaded to encounter his inevitable chaff, when I gave a reason for the pallor and terror plainly visible on my face. I touched my repeater; it struck three-quarters after three o'clock. There were, therefore, three hours of darkness to be accounted for by sleep—if possible—or by conversation should Markham be inclined to talk. Candidly, I did not care to coax back slumber, and I was beginning to make up my mind to wake my companion, when with a violent start, which I could feel through all the swaying of the vehicle, he woke, with a face white as the dead, and nervously clutching my shoulder, looked into my countenance anxiously.

"You're all right, Bob, then, old fellow! Thank God! *Whew!!*" he exclaimed, and subsided.

"What is it?" said I hastily.

"Nothing, old man! I was dreaming, that's all! What's the time *now?*"

I told him, and he expressed his surprise. I began to speak, when he said quietly—

"Don't talk to me just yet, Bob; I—I—I'm not awake yet!"

So we travelled on in silence for some minutes; slowly now, for the road had again become heavy.

It was very still, and suddenly *I heard the sound of a low whistling.* I rubbed my eyes; could I be dreaming again? *No!* There was John Markham opposite to me as before—but how changed! He was livid, and his eyes seemed starting out of his head.

"Listen!" he cried hoarsely; "listen! My God! Do you hear it? Do you hear that whistling?"

"John!" I exclaimed. He held up his hand for silence.

It was the hunting tune of the postillion.

"Markham!" I cried; "do—do *you* recognise that tune?"

"Recognise it?" answered he, shudderingly; "listen again!" And again we heard our postillion at his hunting song.

Gradually I began to perceive the mysterious sympathy between us. Hitherto I had taken all Markham had said as part of my own thoughts; I had seen no remarkable affinity betwixt *his* recognition of the air and *mine.*

Before I could speak with a view to investigate this marvellous concurrence of thoughts, my friend leapt up, with a cry of horror, and ejaculated, as he pointed to the road:—

"The Four Roads! The Stone! The Cross!"

I looked in the direction of his finger; there it was, the whole scene, complete in every detail, the story of my dream.

"Markham!" I cried; "this horrible place—that cross—do you recognise *these* also?"

"I saw them," he replied, "in a dream just now! Under that stone lies the mangled body of the Hamburg merchant! Horrible!"

Our dreams had been identical!

When we had passed the hateful spot we spoke more freely: *in no single feature had John's dream differed from mine,* and we were dreaming thought for thought the same moment of time. It was useless to direct either mind from the conviction that the cross roads and their monument had been the scene and receptacle of a cold-blooded murder and its victim; and with this impression fresh upon us we determined to investigate the spot on the first opportunity that offered.

Before, however, a plan had occurred to either of us the carriage stopped for the "relay" at a miserable little *auberge* which served as posthouse for travellers.

We leapt out at once, and were proceeding towards the light which advanced from the portal, when we were suddenly rooted to the spot with surprise.

"Look, Markham!" I whispered, "look."

"THE WOMAN!" said Markham, shivering, *"The Woman of our Dream!"*

There was no mistaking the repulsive, the half human features of THE HAG as she approached us with the lantern dimly gleaming through the wintry gloom.

It *was* the old murderess of the Cross Roads.

The postillion whistled his "air-de-chasse."

"Manners! Fritz!" croaked the old woman, with a multitude of bows to us; "Manners! where is your gentility that you so whistle before gentlemen?"

"Right, as always, Mère Gaston!" replied the postillion with a grin; "always right! but—force of habit, you know—who better? 'tis an old tune, and I whistle without thinking! a thousand pardons to these gentlemen, and to you!"

I looked at the postillion.

He was a very old man; perhaps seventy-five years of age, and I could not help remarking that "he was very infirm for such an occupation!"

"Old habit again!" he chuckled; "I was born on horseback, I verily believe, and I shall doubtless die in the saddle, with a crack of my whip for a requiem, and, to the last, mind you, whistling my favourite air! Aye! Aye! to the last!"

Markham, keeping his eye on the old man, added quickly, *"Struck by lightning, besides, in certain cross roads, at the foot of a solitary stone cross!"*

The postillion seemed petrified at this unexpected conclusion to his speech; his arms fell to his sides, his eyes glared on us, but he did not speak.

The old woman, with a yell of terror sank to the earth, and hid her face in her withered hands.

I rushed to her and picked up the lantern in a moment. This movement on my part raised the postillion.

"Gaston! Gaston!" he shouted. "Help! help!"

An instant more, and Markham had seized the old villain in his powerful grasp, and while I was yet securing the old woman with my handkerchief, another old man came running from the posthouse uttering cries of alarm.

The trio of the Cross Roads was now complete.

Urged by this additional evidence I secured the new comer, who was the husband of the hag, and within five minutes of our stoppage at the *auberge,* we were masters of the ground, having easily captured, at a *coup,* the villainous actors in the tragedy which had formed the subject of our double dream.

So far we had proceeded, when, to our unutterable delight, the sound of carriage wheels was heard. Almost immediately arrived a travelling chariot conveying no less important a dignitary than the magistrate of R——, who, in great annoyance at the absence of the post-horses which should have been awaiting him as "relay," grumbled loudly at the "usurpers;" *c'est à dire* ourselves, and threatened us with the Law!

"It *is* the Law that we seek, Mr. Burgomaster," cried Markham. "You are needed here."

The Burgomaster unrolled himself like a mummy, and descended.

We need not recount his surprise and first expostulations at our detention of these people on the evidence of a mere dream. We stuck to our subject, however, and cross-examined the trio so closely that their confusion aroused suspicion in the worthy mayor's mind at length. Help was obtained, and the gang were detained in prison.

Not to prolong the story, the criminals confessed the murder and robbery of a Hamburg merchant, who, it was then remembered, had disappeared many years before in a mysterious manner. The cross in the four roads was uprooted, and beneath it lay, partly covered by fragments of a decayed steel-bound leather valise, the whitened bones of the murdered man.

The old couple and the postillion were executed at Zerbot soon afterwards.

This was my first and last experience in *clairvoyance.*

BORED TO DEATH.

I am what is vulgarly, if not profanely, called a "poor-devil author."

The clock had just struck nine as my pen gave the last stroke to Chapter One Hundred and Twelve of the "Hobgoblin Husband," a thrilling tale which I contribute hebdomadally to the *Siberian Journal*. By my side lay the unfinished manuscript of that scathing treatise on the political tendencies of the English Channel which subsequently attracted such general attention in the *Diurnal Review*.

Withdrawing my mind momentarily from its preoccupation, I observed that my grate wanted coals—an observation whose correctness was confirmed by a shivering sensation in my limbs.

Rousing myself to the effort which the emergency demanded, I arose from my seat and—my room being unprovided with a bell—went to the door, opened it, stepped out into the hall, leaned over the baluster, and was just inflating my lungs to shout "Bridget!"

I should, however, remark parenthetically that my room was No. 5 of the attic of Mrs. McScrewsby's boarding-house, in Southampton street, Strand. It was Boxing Night, and the other occupants had, two hours before, gone out singly and in groups to the theatre or cheaper places of amusement. Unwonted, almost fearful, silence reigned—a silence that was rendered the more impressive by the fact that the fifth story, immediately below, was equally quiet.

I was, as before intimated, about to break this silence by shouting "Bridget!" when the intended action of my vocal organs was prevented by a sound which just then saluted my ears. That sound was a violent and obstreperous cachinnation. It was not precisely a horse-laugh; I am unable zoologically to classify it.

It broke abruptly upon the stillness with no apparent cause or sequence, and seemed to leave a strong quiver in the succeeding silence.

I had just convinced myself that it was but the product of my own brain, over-excited by the thrilling conceptions just embodied in Chapter One Hundred and Twelve aforesaid, when I again heard it more distinctly than before. Although decidedly masculine in tone, it yet forcibly reminded me of the refrain heard by Jane Eyre in the desolate chambers of Thornfield; and I stared in uneasy apprehension of seeing Grace Poole with her pot of porter, or the livid Mrs. Rochester herself stalk forth from some attic room in Mrs. McScrewsby's boarding-house.

"Ha! ha! ha!"

This time it was a deep, resonant, and hollow laugh, as though forced from the depths of an empty stomach. I fancied that the Demon of Starvation might be exulting over the carcase of some of my unfortunate fellow-attics—perhaps Brown, the unpublished poet in Number 3, or Smithio, the gaunt artist in Number 9.

"Ha! ha! ha-a-a!"

Sonorous and prolonged, like the jubilant howl of a wolf that has just concluded a repast on some unusually toothsome traveller.

I confess that I was frightened. I felt the capillary covering of my head rise and stand in serried array around its bald apex. A chill crept through the marrow of my bones—if, indeed, the bones of a poor devil author can, even figuratively, be said to contain marrow.

I at length perceived that the strange sounds originated in No. 8—Jones' room.

I knew nothing whatever of Jones, except that his inky fingers and untidy aspect had convinced me that he belonged to the literary profession. The settled gloom of his countenance and compression of his bloodless lips, together with a strange twinkle in his eye, had given me the impression that he was harbouring some dreadful purpose. I had always instinctively shrunk from Jones.

Now, however, fully determined to learn the source and nature of these mysterious explosions, I proceeded to No. 8. The door stood open, and I timidly looked in. There sat Jones in his solitary chair before the empty grate, habited only in a ragged dressing-gown. He held a newspaper before his eyes, and would alternately read something therein and give utterance to a yell of laughter.

Thinking him intoxicated, I was about to retire, when, seeing me, he rushed forward to greet me.

"Ah! come in, Mr. Polhammer! Delighted to see you! Come to congratulate me, I suppose? Happiest moment of my life! He's done for—yes, he's done for at last! Ha! ha! ha!"

"Who's done for?" I asked, bewildered.

"Ah! true, you don't know. Read that. Ha! ha! ha!"

Thrusting into my hand an *Evening Standard*, he pointed to an obituary notice:—

"DEATH OF AN EDITOR.—We regret to have to announce the demise of Archibald Pippin, Esq., the late well-known and accomplished editor of *Bullion's Monthly*. He has been for some time declining, and expired last night."

Here followed an eulogium on the talents and virtues of the deceased.

"Been some time declining! Ha! ha! ha! Sit down, dear fellow, and I'll tell you the facts of the case, confidentially."

I would gladly have retreated, but Jones had button-holed me, and placed himself between me and the door. So, with the best grace possible, I sat down on the bed.

He rubbed his hands together and laughed again, but then, with an effort, became quiet, sat down in the chair, drew it in front of me, leaned forward until his glaring eyes almost touched mine, and began:

"Sir, I was born a genius. I manifested that genius when not yet out of my cradle, by crying only in poetic feet. I made verses before I could talk distinctly, and was an acknowledged poet at six years of age. When I reached manhood my productions were the delight of my native parish—I am a native of the north of Scotland, sir. They were eagerly sought for and lauded by the editors of the *John O'Goat's Journal*, the *Shetland Miscellany,* and the *Orkney Literary Monthly*. Poetry gushed spontaneously from my inkstand. No subject was too lofty or too profound for my prose; I dwelt in a heaven of imagination, sir, from which I looked down with placid contempt on the puny efforts of those whom the world calls great.

"It is ever a necessity of genius to love and be loved. It was my fate to adore Arabella Muggins—an angelic creature, with languishing eyes and glossy black ringlets—the daughter of a timber merchant in my native village. Arabella adored me in return. We plighted our mutual faith and sought the paternal benediction.

"The sordid Muggins, insensible to the charms of poetry and the dignity of genius, called me a beggar, and forbade me, with threats of personal violence, ever again to visit his daughter.

"That night I formed a resolution. I managed to have an interview with Arabella, and communicated my resolution to her.

"'Arabella,' I said, 'your father accuses me—with truth—of being poor. There is here no adequate pecuniary reward for literary genius. To-morrow I will go to London, where wealth is the recompense of merit. I will write for the magazines, and receive the magnificent sums which the publishers delight to lavish on contributors. I will produce books whose multiplied editions shall pour gold into my now empty pockets. I will purchase a villa at Kew, where the banks of the silver Thames are dotted with the suburban palaces of literary men. Then I will return, exhibit to your father the evidences of my opulence, and again sue for your hand. Think you he will then refuse me?"

"Arabella approved of my resolution.

"With one passionate embrace, the memory of which will ever haunt me, we bade each other—as we thought—a temporary adieu. Oh! what bliss then loomed up before me! It was all blasted by—— But he's done for! Ha! ha! ha!"

"I came to London—it was just a year ago—took rooms, and devoted myself to intense literary labour. Even genius needs money. To supply my immediate necessities I prepared articles for the magazines. Having first devoted several hours to the study of my subject, I penned a trenchant satire on city life. I also produced several poems, and a scathing review of contemporaneous literature. I took these to the office of *Bullion's Monthly,* inquired for the editor, and was ushered into the presence of Pippin.

"I conversed freely with Pippin, communicated to him something of my history, plans, and aspirations, and added some valuable suggestions with regard to the management of his magazine.

"Pippin said that, as a matter of form, it would be necessary to examine my manuscripts before paying for them, but promised to send me the money as soon as they should have been approved. I returned to my room and waited for the remittance, of which I stood in need, my landlady and laundress having suggested the payment of their bills.

"Three weeks passed, and the money came not. In the meantime my landlady and laundress had become urgent. Thinking the remittance might have miscarried, I decided to call upon Pippin. As I entered the office he quietly opened a drawer—to get my money I supposed. You may imagine my astonishment and indignation when he produced and handed to me my manuscript, on which were endorsed the words 'Declined with thanks.'

"My first impulse was to throttle Pippin. My second emotion was compassion for a man so lamentably destitute of literary appreciation. Bestowing upon him a glimpse of withering contempt, I left the office and carried the manuscripts to *Pressman's Monthly*. There they met the same fate.

"In the meantime my landlady and laundress had become even more clamorous.

"My articles were afterwards successively rejected by *Tinsel's Monthly* and *Fizzle's Monthly*.

"In the meantime my landlady and laundress had become belligerent, and I had been driven to change my quarters.

"During the months which had now elapsed I had not been idle. I completed a book—a poem in forty cantos—a poem whose success I confidently expected would cause Milton, and Shakespeare, and Byron to rise from their graves out of sheer envy.

"With triumphant emotions I bore it to the publishing house of Sheep and Calf, and left it for the inspection of their manuscript reader.

"At the appointed time I called to complete the arrangements for its publication. Messrs. Sheep and Calf informed me that their manuscript reader had reported unfavourably of my book.

"Under this unexpected blow I only found breath to demand, 'Who is your manuscript reader?'

" 'Archibald Pippin, Esq.,' replied Calf.

" 'Pippin of *Bullion's Monthly?*'

" 'The same,' said Calf.

"The whole mystery stood revealed. I rushed out into the darkness of gathering evening, and strode homeward. Torrents of rain deluged my head and streamed down my back, but could not cool the fever of indignation within. The object of that indignation was Pippin. Pippin, moved by base envy of superior genius, had first rejected my articles. Pippin had doubtless instigated other editors to do the same. Pippin had now committed his crowning outrage by condemning my book.

"I passed periodical depots, where the next month's magazines were for sale, filled with common-place trash—that my brilliant productions were excluded was the work of Pippin. From bookseller's windows gleamed, in crimson and gilt, the inferior works of weak authors—that my great epic poem had no publisher was due to Pippin. Other literary men were dwelling in the midst of luxury, and breathing the incense of adulation, while I, Adelphus Jones, was plodding umbrellaless through the storm, to encounter the yet more formidable tempests of my unpaid and indignant landlady—for this I had to thank Pippin.

"I reached my cheerless room. On my table lay a letter from a correspondent in my native village. It informed me that Arabella, having waited six months for me to fulfil my promises to her, had at length yielded to her father's solicitations and had become the wife of another.

"My cup of bitterness was full, my ambition crushed, my hopes blasted, my love blighted. Henceforth I could have but one object in life—revenge on Pippin. Towards morning—it may have been a dream—I thought a demon perched on my bedside, and whispered to me a suggestion. That suggestion I adopted, and arose at daybreak with a fully matured resolution, a resolution to the accomplishment of which I have since devoted every energy of my being. That resolution was—let me whisper it to you—to bore him to death.

"The modus operandi was to visit him frequently, provided with a liberal supply of manuscript. This I would read to him by the hour, under the pretence of asking his criticism or submitting it for his acceptance. I generally paid my visit to him about noon, the hour when the energies are beginning to flag after the labours of the morning, and prolonged them until I saw that he was reduced to the extreme point of irritability and exhaustion.

"Within a few months I began to observe unequivocal tokens of my success in Pippin's increasingly haggard countenance and look of ill-concealed terror, with which he would greet my approach.

"Pippin did not yield to his fate without some struggles; but against a determination such as mine his struggles were impotent. When driven to desperation, he gave orders that I should not be admitted, but I gained access to him by means of ingenious disguises. When he changed his quarters I was sure to trace him unerringly, and penetrate his retreat. Neither remorse nor a bailiff ever dogged a victim more indefatigably than did I mine.

"Never did doting parents watch more eagerly the returning bloom on the countenance of an invalid child than did I the encroaching ravages of terror and anguish on the visage of Pippin. Oh! it was glorious to note the deepening and lengthening of the wrinkles, the sinking of his eye, the increasing cavity of his cheek. Never was trill at the opera house such dulcet music to my ear as was the feeble, sepulchral tone with which he complained of loss of appetite, qualms, chills, vertigo, and sleepless nights.

"At length he took to his bed.

"Yesterday I called at his house. Lest I should not be admitted, I hastened to his room without announcing my name. Assuring the anxious friends who surrounded his bed that I had come to amuse and divert him, I seated myself beside him and read forty pages of manuscript which I had prepared for the occasion. I then entered into a detailed narration of my early history.

"When I had thus entertained him for several hours, I observed that his countenance became agitated with violent convulsive twitches. He asked in a scarcely audible voice, but with that wild intonation which always characterised him, if I would not defer the remainder of my interesting recital until another occasion. But assuring him that I was quite at leisure I continued my narrative.

"His countenance became yet more violently agitated, and his eyes flashed with the lurid light of a fast-expiring taper. He sprang from his bed, and, with a sudden spasmodic movement of the hand, followed by several equally-sudden movements of his foot, impelled me out of the room and down the stairs. He then bolted the door after me.

"I knew that exertion would be fatal to him!

"The next morning I met the undertaker coming from his house with a happy countenance. We grasped hands and rejoiced together.

"I carried the tidings to the *Evening Standard* Office in Fleet street, and waited patiently for its issue. I seized the first copy obtainable, and bore it in triumph under Temple Bar and down the Strand home. I read it aloud, and shouted in my ecstacy as I walked along. People stared at me, and doubtless thought me mad. They little dreamed"—

At this moment the terror and disgust excited in me by Jones' recital reached its climax. The malicious gleam which his eyes shot into mine filled me with a shuddering apprehension that he was about to repeat upon me the horrid experiment whose success had filled him with such fiendish exultation. The bare idea caused my flesh to creep and my bones to quiver.

Suddenly thrusting him away with a violent effort, I made a rush for the door. Winged by fear, I fled through the hall, over-throwing several of the lodgers who were just returning from the various theatres. I reached my apartments in safety, and bolted the door behind me. I dreamed fearful dreams all night, from which I awoke with the horrible expectation of seeing Jones seated beside me, intent on *boring me to death*.

When I looked in the glass that morning I found that three hairs in my left whisker had turned from their original red to snowy whiteness.

I immediately removed to the attic of another boarding-house, in which I now pen this narrative.

THE SPECTRE HORSEMAN:

OR,

HAUNTED WYE-COLLER HALL.

A CHRISTMAS STORY.

———————

CHAPTER I.

The cold, bright Christmas of 1644 was destined to witness unwonted festivity, as well as a terrible double tragedy, at venerable Wye-Coller Hall, which still uprears its grey and blood-stained walls some six miles distant from the huge, grimy, manufacturing town of Blackburn, in Lancashire.

For the star of King Charles I. was, at the time, in the ascendant, and that of the Parliament on the wane, Bolton having been lately captured, after a furious assault, Liverpool taken, after only a three weeks' siege, and the Roundheads driven, for the most part, into the adjoining county of Yorkshire, on all which accounts Sir Roger Cunliffe, a doughty Royalist, was able to turn his thoughts once more upon his ancestral home and his beautiful girl wife, who was young enough to have been his daughter, for of neither had he been able during three stirring months to obtain so much as a glimpse, a hard lot for an uxurious old gentleman who had only been wedded for just double that period.

Sir Roger Cunliffe, of Billington and Wye-Coller, was a stalwart sexagenarian, of haughty mien and fiery temper, who drank hard, swore hard, loved and hated with equal fierceness, was more ready to settle an argument with his sword than with either tongue or pen, and was accustomed to have his own way in everything.

Thus had he won the beautiful Barbara Benson for his wife, not a whit heeding that she did not love him, though she had told him so plainly, for love him he resolved to make her, ere she was a year older, by honeyed speech, presents, and the granting of her every desire in the first instance, and if those means failed, then by harsh words, and, maybe, the thong of a whip, for Sir Roger believed thoroughly in the truth of the old saw that "a woman, a dog, and a walnut tree, the more you beat them the better they'll be."

But, of course, such extreme measures would only be adopted as a last resource, and when his own love had began to cool somewhat. For the present he would still play the role of the ardent lover rather than that of a husband, and he would fill the old Hall with guests from Christmas to the New Year, proud to show all and sundry that he had won to be its mistress the loveliest girl in Lancashire, though, of course, making no mention of the fact that the poverty of her parents had induced them to sell her to him, "will she nill she," very much as though she had been a horse, a dog, or any other as easily disposed of chattel.

The only individual who could have stopped the nefarious monied bargain, had he known of it in time, was Barbara's only brother, Hector, but he was away at the wars, fighting on the Parliamentary side, even before Sir Roger had made his sister's first acquaintance, and when he next returned to his home, on a hurried visit, the sacrifice was consummated, and May and December, for more than a month, been merged into one.

Barbara had certainly exchanged poverty for wealth, and, at the worst, one tyranny for another, and so it is just possible that she was tolerably contented with her lot.

At all events when Wye-Coller Hall rapidly filled with its glittering Christmas guests, not one of them could detect the least trace of unhappiness in her lovely countenance, and she played her part with a courteous and kindly grace which delighted as well as somewhat surprised her lord, considering the quiet life which she had led previous to her marriage.

Her conduct pleased him greatly at first, but his satisfaction therewith did not last very long, for, by the arrival of the morning of Christmas Eve, the old baronet had grown mighty jealous of a young cavalier, by name Reginald Mowbray, who had come to Wye-Coller in the train of Lord Molyneaux, and who the "green-eyed monster" prompted him to believe, hovered about his wife, and paid her far greater attention than he had any right to offer or she to accept.

What made the matter all the worse was that the individual in question was a remarkably handsome fellow, and only a couple of years older than Barbara, wherefore Sir Roger resolved to keep a close watch on them both, and, as a consequence, ere the day was half over, his first vague suspicions had changed, and not without reason, into a firm conviction that Reginald Mowbray was making hot love to his wife, and that not at all to her disliking.

For he had discovered them walking in the grounds alone together, and, following them unperceived, had lain himself behind a bush when they at last came to a halt, and from this place of concealment had heard much, though not quite all (for the somewhat choleric baronet was somewhat deaf), of the following conversation:—

"My poor little Barbara, why did you allow yourself to be forced into this hateful match?"

"Because, Reginald, there was no help for it. Father's arguments in Sir Roger's favour were unanswerable by reason that he punctuated his discourse, as he is wont to do, with his stick. 'Tis said to be a silly thing to jump out of a frying-pan into the fire, but I was glad enough to leap out of the fire into the frying-pan, and there to receive soft words in lieu of hard blows, for Sir Roger at all events is kind to me."

"But, my darling, you can never grow to love such a grim and grey old curmudgeon."

"Alas! never, for what girl could teach herself to love a man forty years older than herself?"

"Nor can you teach yourself to respect your husband, I much fear."

"Oh, no, not even that, because he drinks so hard and swears so terribly. Yet, whilst he continues to be kind to me I can at all events endure him."

"My poor, dear little Barbara," and here the handsome young cavalier clasped the beautiful Lady Cunliffe in his arms, and kissed her on the forehead, "I would have given my very life to have saved you from such a fate. I who have always loved you so dearly——"

But Sir Roger stayed to hear no more, fearing that if he lingered a moment longer he must rush forth from his hiding place and slay his wife and her undoubted lover where they stood, and, as Reginald Mowbray had come from the Hall without his sword, that he decided would look too much like murder, whilst the killing of his wife would not only cause him to be regarded as a monster, but also make him to be mocked at as an old fool for having believed it to be even possible that a lovely girl in her teens could ever be taught to love him.

"No," muttered Sir Roger to himself, as he hurried along, scarcely knowing in what direction his steps were bent, "I must quarrel with and slay the young cockscombe on some other pretext, and, by the devil's horns, be the pretext good, bad, or indifferent, he shall not live to hear the Christmas bells ring out to-morrow."

CHAPTER II.

UNMASKED!—A DEADLY SWORD THRUST.—UNUTTERED WORDS.

Sir Roger Cunliffe passed the rest of the day he scarce knew how. His wife he avoided as best he might, lest she should read in his face the dark thoughts of his mind, and warn Reginald Mowbray of his peril, urging him to seek safety in flight, and, perhaps, even offering to accompany him.

The worst of it all was that he had to wear a mask before his guests, nearly a hundred in all, many of whom he knew neither by name nor by sight, inasmuch as he had invited the most important of them to come to Wye-Coller Hall with all their following, and noblemen like the Earl of Derby, Lord Molyneux, and Lord St. Albans, never went anywhere without a considerable retinue of esquires and pages, who, being of gentle blood, were entitled to all the privileges of guests whilst the mere troopers and men-at-arms were relegated to the servants' hall.

So Sir Roger, whom, as a mere baronet, the great nobles of the party had honoured by accepting his invitation to spend the merry Christmas-tide at Wye-Coller, had to smile when he would fain have frowned, to utter soft words instead of indulging in blasphemy, as he had a far greater inclination to do, and to amuse and entertain his visitors whilst his thoughts were bent upon "battle, murder, and sudden death" rather than on sport and revelry.

Worse than all else the day wore on without the offering of any valid excuse for picking a quarrel with Reginald Mowbray, and running him through the body as the natural sequence thereof.

Grand was the feast spread in the baronial hall of Wye-Coller that night, whereat Sir Roger Cunliffe and his lovely girl wife presided as the very embodiment of hospitality, the former with much mock joviality, and the latter with consummate grace.

At an early hour, however, the ladies retired from the festive board, for in those days, and even up to a hundred years later, a feast always degenerated at the last into a saturnalia, in which songs were sung and ribald jests bandied to and fro that no modest woman could have listened to and thereafter remained pure and unsullied in mind.

The entire company had become flushed with wine, and, to his credit be it said, Reginald Mowbray with shame also, when Sir Roger Cunliffe observed something about the young cavalier which caused his keen eyes to flash fire beneath their grey beetling brows, and then made him spring to his feet and shout out:

"I call upon Mr. Reginald Mowbray to fill his goblet, and then, upstanding, to drain it to the health of his gracious Majesty the King."

This speech caused a murmur of surprise to pass round, inasmuch as the health of the king had been drunk by all with the usual honours at an earlier hour of the evening.

Reginald Mowbray, however, smiled pleasantly, and, doing as he was requested, or rather as he was ordered, exclaimed, "I wish his Majesty our King the very best of health, and long life in addition;" and was then about to raise the brimming goblet to his lips, when Sir Roger, glaring like a tiger baffled in its spring, exclaimed in a voice hoarse with rage: "Stay, sir, that is not enough. You must drain your goblet not only to the health of the king, but also to the confusion and destruction of his enemies."

Upon hearing those stern words, the face of Reginald Mowbray suddenly paled, for he felt that he was detected, and, moreover, caught in a very death trap.

For a moment, and only for a moment, he hesitated, then said in clear, calm tones: "I cannot and will not drink destruction to the king's enemies, because I have friends and even relatives amongst them, as doubtless have many other of your guests, Sir Roger Cunliffe," and as he finished speaking he replaced his goblet of wine on the table untasted.

His words and action met with the approval of many, and some hesitated not to openly declare it, but the madly jealous baronet of Wye-Coller, who, to do him justice, would have taken the same course had he not suspected what he did, and, indeed, was very nearly sure of, sprang from his seat, and with half-a-dozen strides reached the back of Reginald Mowbray's chair, where, clutching hold of his long cavalier's love-locks, he tore the wig, for such it was, from off his head, revealing by the act a mass of closely cropped brown hair, the universal wearing of which had given the king's enemies the nickname of "Roundheads."

"A crop-eared spy!"

"A rebel within the Royalist lines!"

"To the nearest tree with him!"

"Oak and rope, that is his fittest fate!"

Such were the shouts and cries that immediately rose on all sides, as the hundred or so of guests leapt to their feet in the wildest possible indignation and excitement.

More slowly Reginald Mowbray, as he had called himself, rose to his feet, saying quite calmly as he did so: "My lords and gentlemen, you may hang me if you like, though if you knew why I came hither I think you would find the reason a sufficient excuse. My love for——"

But at that juncture Sir Roger Cunliffe, fearful that his rival was on the point of making him a laughing stock by some reference to his own former relations with the fair Barbara; even, perhaps, by declaring that they had once been betrothed, but that she had been wantonly sacrificed to her father's cupidity and the weight of her old husband's money-bags, wherefore he had only come to Wye-Coller as young Lochinvar once repaired to Netherby:

"To tread but one measure, drink one cup of wine," ere he bade farewell to his lost love for ever, etcetera, and etcetera; fearing some such exposure as this, we repeat, Sir Roger Cunliffe suddenly struck the young man across the face with the back of his hand, exclaiming as he did so:

"Leave your excuses unmade, and then, instead of a felon's death by the rope you shall die as a gentleman, sword in hand, for I will do you the honour of spitting you on my own good blade. What, would you still speak? Are you then a coward, as well as a rebel?"

A terrible fate was it that thus prompted Sir Roger Cunliffe to effectually seal Reginald Mowbray's lips, who, under the circumstances could, of course, only bow to the inevitable; nor did he do so altogether reluctantly, for he reflected that, could he but make his beloved Barbara Sir Roger Cunliffe's widow, happy indeed would be her future lot as compared with that of being his wife.

Sir Roger was too impatient to shed his rival's blood to propose that the duel to the death should be fought out of doors, by torchlight; indeed, nothing would content him but that it should be waged on the spot, where there would be plenty of light to see by.

His proposal was, of course, agreed to, so an ample ring was formed, away from the supper table, and drawing their long rapiers, the combatants at once set to work, Sir Roger Cunliffe with the utmost fury, and Reginald Mowbray, with cool self-command.

Both were skilled swordsmen, five minutes swift play of their blades made that fact evident to the spectators, who could see, as well, that their host's evidently ungovernably ferocity placed him at no small disadvantage when opposed to one who was playing the grim game of life and death as calmly as though he was merely engaged in a friendly contest at chess.

But, as it happened, fate was against the younger man, for, in delivering a lunge in carte, his foot slipped on the polished oak floor, and before he could recover himself, Sir Roger Cunliffe's rapier flashed under his guard, driven with such force that the blade, entering his chest, came out through his back a good three inches and more.

As he fell, Reginald Mowbray apparently strove to say something, but a rush of blood from his mouth choked the words in his throat, and, in another moment, life had fled.

Sir Roger Cunliffe dragged his rapier out of the prostrate body, and clashed it back into its scabbard, reeking with gore though it was.

Then, without addressing a word to anyone he turned on his heel, and strode out of the banquet hall, from thence across a dark and gloomy corridor, and then up a wide, black oak staircase, whose balustrades were massive and quaintly carved.

He felt the while that his vengeance would not be complete until he had told his wife that he had slain her lover, and had gloated over her grief.

CHAPTER III.

A DEMON'S DEED.—THE HOOT OF THE HORNED OWL.

Sir Roger Cunliffe found his wife asleep.

The light of a full moon, streaming in through the heavily mullioned window, shone full upon her exquisitely-chiselled features, on the long fringed lashes which rested on her rounded cheeks, on the perfect contours of a plump, alabaster-white arm, that lay outside the bed-clothes, and on the rippling masses of wavy, golden hair which strayed over the pillow in unconfined luxuriance.

What a contrast did that fair young creature present to her burly, grey, and grizzled spouse, with his tiger-fierce eyes, penthouse brows, a bloated face of almost the hue of beetroot, owing to past dissipation and present passion, which latter was, in a moment more, worked up to a yet more violent and perilous pitch by his observing tears on his wife's pale cheeks, and hearing her utter softly in her sleep the word "Hector."

Thereat he could control himself no longer, but, seizing hold of that lovely exposed arm with so powerful a grip that his fingers sank deep into the tender flesh, he shook his wife roughly awake, hissing into her ear, as her lustrous, violet-hued eyes unclosed, and met his own fierce gaze with a shrinking glance of mingled surprise and terror—

"So you were dreaming of Hector, were you? Well, when next you sleep dream of him skewered on my rapier, for at this moment he lies as dead as butcher's meat on the floor of the banquet hall, and 'twas my good steel which laid him there."

"You brute! You monster! Oh, Hector, my dear, my beloved Hector!" was all that the poor young thing could shriek out, in a wild agony of mingled passion and grief; and those were the last words she ever uttered, for they stirred Sir Roger to such an ungovernable degree of fury that he again drew forth his fatal rapier, and therewith committed a crime, cruel and foul enough to have made the angels weep in heaven and the demons laugh in hell.

With one hand pressed hard against her mouth, to still her apprehended shrieks, he plunged the weapon again and again into her milk-white and palpitating body, that was exposed to his remorseless steel, owing to his victim having tossed aside the bedclothes in the extremity of her agitation; nor did he cease from his fiendish task until the exquisite form of the fair girl, whom six short months ago he had sworn at God's altar to love and cherish, had given its last agonised quiver, and lay still in death.

Then, with a groan of equally agonised remorse, for he had never intended to do her any bodily injury when seeking her presence, he cast his accursed weapon on the floor, and stared into vacancy with the expression of a man who had just awoke from a horrible nightmare.

Even as he did so he heard a hoot, which was again and again repeated, and, glancing towards the window beheld, perched outside, on the stone sill, and staring into the death chamber with its round, expressionless, amber-hued eyes, a great, brown, horned owl, the infallible death-omen of the Cunliffe family, and which, whenever it hooted thrice, indicated the extinction of the last of the race, which was—himself.

As the conviction was driven home to him that his crimes were already on the point of being avenged, he thought of the old rhyme—

> "Say not 'tis false! I tell thee, some
>   Are warned by a meteor light,
>   Or a horned owl, flitting, calls them home,
>   Or a voice on the wind by night."

As the lines of fate recurred to him, the owl spread its wings and flew away, whilst the faint echo of bells from the distant tower of St. Bartholomew's church at Colne announced that a Christmas morn had again arrived.

But the mellow sound brought no assurance of "Peace on earth and goodwill to men" to the murderer in that ancient wainscotted bed-chamber of Wye-Coller Hall.

Shaking all over with superstitious terror as much as from utterly futile remorse, Sir Roger Cunliffe felt that if he would escape from being stricken with sudden madness he must at once seek human companionship, so he rushed headlong out of the death chamber, and, a few minutes later, staggered into the banquetting hall, his eyes wild and staring, and the usual beetroot redness of his coarse, fat face changed to a sickly grey.

And there he was destined to make the most dreadful discovery of all, for scarcely had he shown himself, when Lord Molyneau approached him with a very grave expression of countenance, and an open letter in his hand, saying—

"I fear, Cunliffe, that I have some very distressing news for you. In searching the body of your late antagonist, on the chance of finding some treasonable papers, we discovered this letter, which reveals the melancholy fact that the man you slew was your wife's brother, Hector Benson, and that he came hither, by the connivance of a young gentleman in my train, called Ralph Ffolliot, solely in order to see his sister, to whom he seems to have been greatly attached, and to whom, being a proscribed rebel, he could only hope to obtain access through the practise of some such ruse. Ffolliot was, alas, too drunk to render an explanation that would have averted the dire mistake, until it was too late to be of any use."

What pen shall describe Sir Roger Cunliffe's feelings upon receiving this wholly unlooked for information, and, as he realised that he had murdered an almost bride, whom he actually madly loved, in a fit of perfectly groundless jealousy.

Oh! why had not her "fool of a brother," as he mentally dubbed him, declared himself, and so have saved his own and his sister's lives; but the next moment Sir Roger remembered that he himself had acted in such a way as to render it absolutely impossible for the young Parliamentarian to have done so without cowardice being attributed to him as the reason thereof, for he had even told him to his face that he would regard him as a poltroon if he uttered another word.

The double murderer then read the letter which Lord Molyneaux tendered him.

It was indeed one from his dead wife, beginning: "My only and dearest brother Hector," and approving of his scheme "to visit her at Wye-Coller, disguised as a Cavalier, since he could not hope to approach her in any other character," and so on, a simple, touching and loving epistle, over which Sir Roger could have wept, only that he had forgotten how to shed tears many a long year ago.

When he had got to the end he felt and looked like a man mazed.

"What is to be done?" asked Lord Molyneux, as he and many of the more distinguished of the guests crowded round the miserable man. "Can we manage matters so that your sweet young wife may never learn that her only brother fell by her husband's hand? We are all friends here, and will religiously keep the dreadful secret, of that you may rest assured, Cunliffe."

"Thank you, my lord; but I beg of you all to suffer me to leave you for a little while, so that I may think the matter over calmly," and as the silent circle of deeply-sympathetic friends opened to let him pass, Sir Roger staggered rather than walked across the hall (shudderingly passing close by the corpse of his late antagonist, as it lay still stretched upon the black oak floor), passed out through a distant door, and from the moment of his disappearance was never again beheld by any one as a mortal man.

Five minutes after he had quitted the banquetting hall those who were therein (some of them laying out the corpse of the dead Parliamentarian on one of the tables that had been hastily cleared for the purpose), heard, above the faint sound of the Christmas bells of Colne, the thunder of a horse's hoof-strokes upon the hard frozen ground without.

Surely its rider rode as never rider rode before. "Even if the devil was pursuing him," someone observed, "no man would have galloped so recklessly in the dead hours of the night."

Much they all wondered who he could be, but many rightly guessed when, on the following morning, the dead body of Lady Cunliffe was discovered, with every evidence that she had been foully murdered as well as by whom, for Sir Roger's bare and bloodstained rapier still lay upon the bedroom floor where he had cast it down in his too late remorse.

CHAPTER IV.

IN THE DEVIL'S KEEPING.—THE SPECTRE HORSEMAN.

Poor Lady Cunliffe and her brother, Hector Benson, were buried in the same grave, a few days later, and as there were no coroners' inquests, or post-mortem examinations in those days, the manner of their deaths was (so that no disgrace should fall upon the last member of an old and honoured Lancashire family) kept a profound secret by one and all who had become acquainted therewith.

No search, for the same reason, was made for Sir Roger, for it was felt that his had been no premeditated crime, but the outcome of a sudden and uncontrollable passion, born of acute jealousy, as also that his conscience, living, would punish him in a far more terrible manner than the law could do, even at the hands of its last dread exponents, the torturer and executioner.

'Tis said, though how it came to be known is somewhat of a puzzle, that, on leaving Wye-Coller Hall, Sir Roger Cunliffe rode, at a furious gallop, to the hut of an old witch, daughter of the famed Mother Demdike, who lived in a miserable hut at the foot of Pendle Hill, which rises hard by Colne, and offered her an immense sum of gold if she would grant him the gift of utter forgetfulness of everything that had happened to him during the past year.

The witch, 'tis reported, replied that she was not powerful enough to work so potent a spell, but that if he would accompany her to the top of the mountain, she would summon to his aid one who both could and would.

Sir Roger, the narrative goes on to state, greedily accepted her proposal, and dismounting from his exhausted steed, walked beside the ancient crone to the hill-top, whereon she repeated the Lord's Prayer backwards, and then uttered some sort of weird incantation, with the result that the Devil suddenly appeared before the twain, and that in his most awful form, for—

> "O'ertopping Sir Roger, gigantic he stood,
>   None can picture a figure more fell,
>   His eyes were the deep, crimson colour of blood,
>   And his breath was the vapour of hell."

To this awful and infernal being the baronet of Wye-Coller repeated his prayer for the boon of forgetfulness, at last offering his very soul as the price thereof; but the fiend laughed at and mocked him, saying "his soul was his already, and that as he had put him to the trouble of travelling so great a distance at midnight, he would have to pay toll with his body also."

Then there ensued a most terrible struggle, 'midst the crash of thunder and incessant flashes of lambent lightning, whilst many witches, besides she who had conducted the doomed murderer thither, careered round and round the hill-top, astride of broomsticks.

Amidst such awful surroundings what could mortal strength do against demoniac power?

The struggle was, consequently, a brief one, and, in the course of a few minutes Sir Roger was secure "in the devil's keeping," who whisked him from off the mountain's summit into the sulphur-laden air, and bore him shrieking away to his own fiery realm, and 'tis said that for months afterwards human footsteps and the deep dents of cloven hoofs marked the spot where that fateful fight had taken place.

But even from hell's dark domain the doomed Sir Roger was to be allowed, for all time, at the midnight of each Christmas Eve, to revisit, as "A Spectre Horseman," the scene of his double crime, and at the period of his ghostly ride from Pendle Hill to Wye-Coller Hall the residents of the district never venture from their homes.

At the appointed hour the ghastly horseman can be heard dashing past those homes at full speed, and the few who have been bold enough to peer forth from behind partly-opened shutters have seen him, mounted on a coal-black steed, attired as a Cavalier of the olden time, and brandishing a bare and blood-reeking sword.

On reaching the front of the haunted hall, he dismounts with a heavy sigh, the great door flies open, whereupon he enters his old abode, ascends the stairs, and strides into the chamber in which he murdered his young and lovely wife.

Then awful shrieks ring forth, and presently the ghostly figure reappears, hastily remounts his equally ghostly charger, adorned with its old-world trappings, and rides back to Pendle Hill by the same route as he came from thence, and on its summit the devil is ever waiting to receive him.

OUR FELLOW LODGER;

OR,

THE ADVENTURES OF A CHRISTMAS EVE.

When, after a four years' study of my profession in the country, I went to London in order to gain some knowledge of town practice and acquire a familiarity with the Law Courts, previous to going in for my examination, I had lost but little of that faith in the romantic and marvellous which was the marked feature of my boyhood. The dull pages of Blackstone, and the still drearier ones of Ayckbourn and Roscoe, had not destroyed the results of those three years of illness, when, confined to my couch, I had revelled in all the glorious romances of Scott and Bulwer, and from them created an ideal world of my own. No; at one-and-twenty, my creative fancy still invested everything unusual with the garb of romance, and in every one I met of strange mien or eccentric habits, I was prepared to discover a living mystery.

I and a friend, who was going in for examination at the same time, and who, moreover, had been an acquaintance of childhood, resolved to lodge together, both for the sake of economy and the pleasures of mutual companionship and study, and we were not long before we found what we thought would suit us to a T.

Our chosen apartments consisted of a handsome three-windowed drawing-room, tastefully furnished, on the first floor, and a large double-bedded room directly behind, and communicating therewith by means of folding doors. The house was situated in a quiet street on the Surrey side of the river, only a minute's walk from Westminster Bridge, and consequently in convenient proximity to the Houses of Parliament and the Law courts.

Think not, gentle readers, that I am going to weary you with a narrative of student life, which, with its unvaried monotony, could neither amuse nor interest—but I am about to tell you of a strange adventure which befel me during my stay in Theluson Street—an adventure so fearful that for years its memory has been engraven on my heart.

The only lodger in the house besides ourselves was a medical practitioner at a neighbouring hospital. He occupied the ground floor, and was familiarly spoken of by our landlady as "young Doctor Norton." With that rigid reserve that distinguishes all classes in London, and which countrymen so readily fall in with, we had occupied our apartments many weeks without making any attempt to scrape an acquaintance with our fellow-lodger; while he, on his part, exhibited equal indifference. One evening, however, my friend having gone out to a dinner party, leaving me alone, I grew weary of my books, and made up my mind to while away a few hours at Astley's. Unable to find my latch-key, and Mrs. Draycott, the landlady, not having another, I ventured to send her to the down-stairs lodger, to ask him, with my compliments, if he was not going out that evening, to lend me his. When she returned, she told me that Doctor Norton was very happy to lend me the key, and then added in a whisper, "I suppose you will be back by twelve sir, for the doctor will want it again then?"

"Did he say so?" I asked.

"No sir, oh no; but then he always goes out at that hour and returns again about four. La, sir, I don't suppose he's missed doing so for the last three years."

Promising to be back before the time named, and to place the key on the little table in the hall, I went to the amphitheatre; but neither the attractions of the stage, nor the excitement of the arena, could fix my attention that night. I kept thinking of Dr. Norton, for the few words carelessly uttered by our landlady had exalted him in my brain to no less than a hero of romance, and satisfied my craving appetite with a theme for wonder and unravelment.

I was home long before twelve. My friend had not returned, and as the moon shone brightly, I did not light the gas, but drawing aside the curtains and pulling up the Venetian blind, sat by the window and gazed into the street.

Just as the clock on the staircase struck the hour, I heard Norton open his door, cross the hall, and then the front door closed gently behind him, and, muffled in great coat and wrapper, I saw him descend the street with a slow and thoughtful step, and turn sharply around the corner in the direction of Westminster Bridge.

His partiality for midnight strolls, to say nothing of Doctor Norton's appearance, in itself was sufficient to excite a curiosity such as mine. Young—he could scarcely have been twenty-five—handsome and well formed, there was yet a wild wandering expression in his full and piercingly black eyes that seemed like a herald of approaching insanity. This, with his thin bloodless lips, and a face which stern in its intellectual beauty of chiselled feature was, nevertheless, pale as that of a corpse, ever reminded me of Bulwer's Eugene Aram. Not once in the many times we had met on the staircase or in the hall, had I seen him smile. A cloud of care seemed to rest on a brow which bore more lines than the youth of its possessor would authorise.

When talking over the matter at breakfast with my friend, next morning, I met little encouragement in my romantic ideas.

"Pooh, Arnold, how you will make mountains out of molehills. Norton belongs to St. Saviour's; I suppose he goes to visit the wards."

"There, you must be wrong, Cammick, for that is the work of the surgeons who live in the hospitals," I replied; "besides, if 'twas not so, they would not expect a poor devil to be out of his bed from midnight to four a.m. every night for three years."

"Well then our hero is a gay Lothario, walks the cafés, sups at Sally's, or Kate Hamilton's, waltzes at the Pic—you know it does not open until one a.m., and,"—

"Nonsense, Tom," I exclaimed, interrupting him, "if you have looked into the man's face once, you would know him to be no such character."

"Quite as likely at least to be that as any that you have selected for him. But make him Neapolitan refugee, French conspirator, housebreaker, resurrectionist, or what you will, only be silent, for I've got to grind up Smith's confounded chapter on 'Constructed Trusts' for class to-night, and I don't care a rap whether he's Garibaldi or Nana Sahib."

Cammick's *badinage* only stimulated my longing desire to unravel the mystery that surrounded the person of our fellow-lodger, and I resolved that on the very first opportunity I would follow and watch the proceedings of the doctor, be the result what it might.

One evening, therefore, when a friend dropped in and persuaded Cammick to accompany him to the opera at Covent Garden, and afterwards to sup at Evans's; on the plea of a headache, I escaped making one of the party, and knowing what going to Evans's meant, and that Tom would not see Theluson-street again till pretty well up in the small hours, I determined this very evening to put my plans into execution.

Taking a bottle of port from the cupboard, and placing it with a glass on the table, I wheeled the sofa towards the fire, lighted a cigar, threw myself amidst the cushions, and was soon fast asleep. My slumber must have lasted for hours, for I was roused by the clock on the staircase striking twelve. Springing to my feet, I threw off my dressing gown, and putting on my coat, cloak, and hat, I fished a short but strong oak stick from an obscure corner, and was prepared. I had only just time to toss off a couple of glasses of port, when, as usual, I heard the doctor's door open, his light springy footsteps cross the hall, and then the click of the patent lock, as the front door closed behind him. Turning down the gas, I sprang down the staircase, and gained the street in time to see Norton turn round the corner towards the river, as when last I watched him.

It was a clear frosty night, and, as I gained the bridge, keeping cautiously some twenty yards in the rear of him I followed, the unclouded moonlight streamed down on the stately Palace of Westminster, and flashed down from the gilded galleries of the great clock tower.

"Confound this, if the doctor looks back he can't help seeing me, and may guess my purpose," I muttered to myself, for not another being was in sight, and there was light enough to read by. But the doctor did not look back, but seemed almost to glide over the broad pavement from which he never raised his eyes.

The river crossed, he increased his pace, and darting into some low, intricate, third-class streets that lie huddled within a stone's throw of the Houses of Parliament, where I had some difficulty in keeping him in view, he at last came to a halt before the door of a house that stood in one even more wretched than the rest, and knocked twice.

As he did so, he looked sharply both up and down the street, but I slipped within the shadow of a doorway on the opposite side, and so escaped observation. From this retreat, I saw the door slowly open, and the weird witch-like form of a very old woman appear in the aperture. Then, I noticed that neither did Norton address her, nor did she speak to him, but making way for him to pass, again closed the door.

As yet, all had gone well, but how was I to penetrate the mystery? Not certainly without danger; without discovery—impossible. I was resolved not to abandon it, however. In my present dress Norton would scarcely recognise me, even if we stood face to face. I would assume the character of a detective, which would account for my intrusion. So boldly crossing the street, I laid hold on the handle of the door through which the doctor had passed. It was unfastened, so I walked in and found myself in a sort of kitchen; in the broad fireplace sat the old woman who had unbarred the door for the doctor; she was smoking a short black pipe, and on the table beside her stood a guttering candle. She saw my entry, and was about to scream, but, crossing the room at a bound, I had my hand on her mouth, while I whispered in her ear, "Police, but no harm meant to you. Here's half-a-sovereign; pretend to sleep, when you wake you will find another. Where is the man you just let in?"

The piece of gold had its usual effect; the old hag pointed to a trap-door at the other end of the room.

Once more warning her to be silent, I advanced towards it, and discovered that a long step ladder conducted to a cellar beneath, against the wall of which was thrown the reflection of a light, as though it came from an apartment beyond. Wrapping my cloak tighter around me, and drawing my hat over my eyes, I cautiously descended; and, when I gained the cellar, I discovered that my surmise was correct, for the rays of light came through a glass door on the right, through which I could witness all that was passing within, without much risk of a discovery.

The room was of moderate size and whitewashed. Its furniture consisted of a table, a couch, a few chairs, and a large mirror. I could not see all the room nor could I see Norton, but I saw his reflection in the mirror, and that was enough. His hat, overcoat, and wrapper, were thrown aside, his hands were tightly clasped behind his back, and he appeared to be earnestly gazing at a large glass case which stood in a niche before him.

Whilst I was wondering what this case might contain, Norton stepped on one side, and I saw reflected in the mirror, the form of a lovely girl attired in the costume of a ballet dancer, with her hands crossed on her bosom. Although to all appearance in the full bloom of youth and beauty, there could be no doubt but that this creation of loveliness was a corpse, and I felt an icy chill of horror run through my veins, when I beheld the doctor draw a key from his pocket, unlock and throw back the lid of the glass sarcophagus, and again and again passionately press his lips to those of the dead girl. Indeed my horror became so great, that I involuntarily uttered an ejaculation loud enough to catch his ear. Hastily closing the lid, he advanced towards the door. I had neither the strength nor the resolution to move; my courage and bravado had all left me, and when I felt his hand on my shoulder, and saw the lamp which he held in his hand flash full on my face, I could have sunk into the ground for very shame.

Norton's whole countenance was working with strong emotion, and his voice was broken and harsh as he said, "I recognise the features of Mr. James Arnold, my fellow-lodger, and a gentleman whom I have heard highly spoken of by a mutual friend, Mr. John Taylor, who walked the hospitals with me, and who passed at the same time. I have heard of your love of the romantic and the unravelling of mysteries; I presume you thought you should discover one by tracking me hither to-night?"

"I confess, sir, that I did," I replied, regaining in some degree my composure, "but now that the first excitement is over, my heart tells me that I have acted improperly in trying to pierce a secret such as yours, and that I owe you an apology."

"Perhaps so; but, pray, don't make one; you acted from impulse. Had I been you, I might have done the same. I certainly wished to keep mine a secret from all men; but as you have witnessed so much, you shall know all. It will relieve my heart, and I know that you are a man of honour, who will keep my secret until my death. After that event, which can't be long, you may tell the tale to whom you will."

He took my hand as he spoke, and led me into the inner room, right up to the glass coffin.

"Is she not beautiful?" he said, pointing to the corpse. "Look at her, Mr. Arnold, and I will then tell you my narrative."

And I did look; yes, looked until I was fascinated, even by the beauty of death. But it was not like death; no one would have thought that aught graver than a light and refreshing slumber closed the eyes of the lovely girl, who lay so cold and still. It was, indeed, an instance of wonderful embalming. The complexion was that of a fair brunette, and as clear as it could have been in life; the features were of the most chiselled beauty; the lips small and well-shaped, while the heavy glossy masses of her rich brown hair flowed over and below her white shoulders and the full and beautifully-formed bosom, which was partly uncovered by the rich ballet dress, in which her exquisitely proportioned form was clad, her round white arms displayed the firmness and elasticity of life itself, and her small hands and tapering fingers were crossed on her breast. Yes, while I gazed at her, I forgot that I was looking at a corpse; I forgot the presence of Norton, and murmured to myself, "how lovely! beautiful as an angel!" and other unconscious expressions of admiration.

Suddenly the voice of the doctor recalled me to myself. I left the coffin, and placed a chair by his side. "Mr. Norton, I can half guess your story," I said; "nevertheless, if its narration will not call up too many painful memories, I should like to hear it from your lips; mine, you may rest assured, will keep it an inviolable secret."

"Sit down, then, and you shall hear it," was the reply, and as I obeyed the request, the doctor began his tale, as follows:—

"It is now some ten years ago since I left Plymouth and came up to London to walk the hospitals, and prepare for my medical examinations—as gay and thoughtless a youth as ever the sun shone on. My father, a country practitioner of Devonport, in whose surgery I had passed the first three years of my studies, allowed me £100 a year to cover all expenses, with an assurance that he could afford no more.

"Never shall I forget the poor old governor's last words as we walked up and down the platform of Plymouth railway station, while waiting for the train:—'Always remember to go to church on a Sunday, my boy—'twill go far to keep you in the right path during the week; and shun, as you would destruction, those dens of infamy, the casinos and music halls. People who frequent them are all trotting down stairs as fast as they can go, and they will meet no hand in their course to turn them around and point upwards.'

"I promised obedience to these instructions; and, upon my arrival in London, I kept my word. Devoting my every energy to the study of the profession, I frequented no place of amusement but the theatre; and it was while performing as Columbine in a pantomime at the 'Grecian', that I first beheld one, whom to look upon was to love—my own Athalie. Ah! Mr. Arnold, had you seen her then, a light spiritual creation of beauty, you would not have wondered at my sudden love; and when, a few days later, after great difficulty, I managed to get an introduction to her, I discovered that these charms of form and face were allied with a perfect education, and a fascination of manner and deportment calculated to grace the very highest society.

"I need scarcely tell you that, after a short acquaintance, we became engaged. I learnt that her real name was Jessie Wilmot, and that her father and mother were both dead. The former was a captain in the army, her mother's father had also been the same; but, though an only child, her parents had been able to lay aside very little of their income; and, upon the death of her mother, three years before, when she was only fifteen, she had been driven to seek her own living; and, under the name of Athalie de Bourg, had found it on the stage.

"Never shall I forget the happiness of the first few months of our betrothal; Jessie, for I always called her by her real name, lived in quiet but humble lodgings at Annett's Crescent, Islington, from which my rooms were scarcely half a mile distant; and all through the lovely summer-time, we used to wander before breakfast in Regent's Park; and in the evening I used to call for her, and take her to the theatre, and then go home for a few hours to study, and ever be at the stage-door the minute the ballet was over, to guard her home again. Yes, those were happy times; but yet I longed for the day to come when, my examination all passed, I might, as a duly qualified physician, offer Jessie a home as well as a heart, and obtain my father's sanction to our union.

"I had never yet broken the matter to him, for I knew that, like most country gentlemen, he had not an exalted opinion of the stage, and would consider my engagement as a folly, a delusion, a step to be strongly censured and condemned. 'It's no good telling him now,' I thought; 'I will stay until some opportunity occurs for him to see Jessie; then he cannot disapprove of my choice.'

"Alas! Mr. Arnold, that opportunity never came. One evening, when I called to accompany her to the theatre, I learnt that she had already started, as she intended calling to see a sick ballet-girl, a favourite of hers, on the road.

"That night I was at the stage door, anxiously awaiting the close of the ballet. My Jessie did not come out first, as was her wont. I asked a danseuse whether Miss de Bourg was at the theatre? She replied in the negative. Wildly I walked to her lodgings, dreading I knew not what; and my terror was increased by learning that she had not returned since she left to attend the play.

"To shorten my tale, three days passed without bringing me

any clue to aid me in the discovery of the lost one. My health and spirits gave way before so terrible an affliction, for I had used every effort without avail. But a more fearful ordeal was yet before me. On the fourth morning after Jessie's disappearance, I walked into the dissecting room of the hospital, and Jack Lowe, a fellow chum of mine, who was smoking a short black pipe with his back to the fire exclaimed, 'Hallo! Norton, we are in luck's way, my boy—the most beautiful subject for dissection that I ever set eyes on. Poor girl! she was picked up in the New North Road last Friday night, and brought to the hospital at once, but even our cleverest men could do nothing for her, and she died last night. As no friends claimed her, of course, old Proctor pounced upon the body for the dissecting-room, and there it lies still warm. I think I never beheld aught that was human so beautiful before.'

"As he spoke, he pointed to the body, which, covered with a white cloth, lay on the green-baize dissecting table. Smiling, in spite of all my inner torture, at Lowe's words—who ever dealt in superlative—I advanced mechanically towards the table, and raised the covering. Oh, heavens! my head seemed suddenly on fire—my brain whirled—for my gaze rested on the face of JESSIE WILMOT, calm and placid as if in sleep.

"Never shall I forget that terrible agony. For a moment I gazed intently at the beloved features—the next, without word or groan, I fell senseless on the floor.

"I have little more to add. When consciousness returned, I claimed the body, as a friend's, and obtained leave to remove it. I learnt that Jessie had been brought to the hospital in a faint, and never recovered her senses until a few minutes before she died. She was then too feeble to speak, but drew her last breath with a smile on her lips.

"Reason with myself as I would, I could not make up my mind to part with the body. Jessie looked so calm and beautiful in death, that the mere thought of the black coffin and the hideous grave were unbearable. Two years before I had learnt the art of Russian embalming from a native of that country. I succeeded in obtaining the very Columbine dress in which she had first won my heart. You see she is clad in it now. A few leaves and simple spices preserve the body from the slightest trace of decay—they have done so for three years—their power would continue for ever. But it is not needed: while I live, I have my Jessie by me, and every night I come to gaze upon her sweet face. But it will not be for long—my health is failing—in a few more weeks I shall come here to die. Yes, to die; with my arms clasping that sarcophagus; and I have requested in my will that Jessie and I may then be buried side by side.

"Mr. Arnold, you know my story. I am now going back to Theluson Street; perhaps you will accompany me?" And, casting one more glance of deep affection at the beautiful corpse of his beloved one, he led the way from the room.

Arrived in the upper apartment, we found the old woman still sleeping, or pretending to sleep, by the fire; and I managed to slip the promised piece of gold under the candlestick, unperceived by my companion, while he was securing and locking the trap door.

In another half-hour we were at home. Taylor had not yet returned; but, dispirited and sick at heart, I retired to bed—not for the sake of sleep or rest, but to ponder in the darkness over all I had heard and seen of a fellow-being's agony and despair.

And a few months later, poor Edward Norton did die beside the corpse of her he loved; and I, whom he had made his executor, saw that the wishes of his will were carried out. He and his beloved were conveyed to Plymouth, and buried side by side in the old churchyard at Stoke, beneath the venerable yew tree that shadowed the graves of both his parents.

So ended the early career of "OUR FELLOW LODGER." My promise of secrecy expired with his decease, and with a few changes of name and locality you have his tragic history.

TALE OF TWO CHRISTMASES.

CHAPTER I.

WHAT THE SNOW CONCEALED.

Christmas is being kept as it has not been observed for nine long years in the great hall of Samlesbury.

The yule log burns on the wide, open hearth, the coloured candles are lighted in dozens upon the long, feast-laden table, the minstrels are playing in the carved, oaken gallery, and holly and other evergreens decorate the wainscotted, antler and armour bedecked walls. The guests consist entirely of men, no woman having crossed the threshold of Samlesbury Hall since the death, in child-birth, of its last beautiful nineteen-years-old mistress, nine years ago.

Since the loss of wife and babe, Sir John Osbaldiston, the owner of Samlesbury, has never been seen to smile, but he does so now, though with an evident effort, for he has given this feast in honour of the departure on the morrow of his young brother, Richard, for Bombay, there to fill a promising post in the East India Company's service, for Sir John is desirous that Dick's last evening in the home of their ancestors shall not be a sad one.

John and Richard are the last of their name and race, and though their births were ten years apart, they have ever been fondly attached to each other; the sturdy, plain-featured baronet having been, as it were, a father as well as a brother to the strikingly handsome first boy and then youth as the only being left for him to care for.

So at this Christmas feast he tries his hardest to be merry too, and with a success which deceives all but Richard, who, for his part, with a life of adventure before him, thoroughly enjoys himself amongst the jovial, fox-hunting squires who have been his life-long comrades, so that song succeeds song, interspersed with toast and jest, until, at 11 o'clock or so the revellers depart for their respective homes.

"And now I suppose it's off to bed, old man," queried twenty years old Richard of thirty years old John, when, at last, they were left alone.

"Well, no, my boy," responded the baronet, with a sigh that he could no longer repress, "the full moon shines brightly on the white snow and so I am going for a stroll down the elm avenue in order to get the fumes of the wine out of my head and the noise of song and laughter out of my ears."

"Say, rather, to give way once more to your morbid thoughts and unavailing grief. Surely, John, nine years are more than enough in which to mourn the loss of even the loveliest and sweetest of wives. Ere now a sensible man, without the least slight to the beloved dead, would have wooed and won another bride, if only for the sake of saving one of the oldest and most famous of Lancashire families from becoming extinct," answered the younger brother, reproachfully.

"Be that thy task, Dick," was the rejoinder. "I would not wrong any woman by giving her my hand when my heart will lie for ever buried under the churchyard sod; that is, unless she returns to me."

"Returns to you? Who? What do you mean?"

"Coralie's last words to me were: 'Don't grieve overmuch, dear John, for I will come back to you, even on earth, though perhaps not for many years!' It was a strange saying, but as for the meaning of it——"

"Good God, if the words signified anything they meant that she would one day return to you, not as a ghost, but re-incarnate in mortal flesh and blood," interrupted the younger brother, in accents of awed emotion.

"Richard," answered Sir John, gravely, "do not let us think that, to an all merciful God, anything is impossible. Let it suffice that unless Coralie comes back to me I shall one day go to her, unfettered by any other earthly tie. And now I am off, since for the last hour and more some mysterious power has been drawing me in the direction of the elm avenue and I can resist it no longer."

"May I go with you, John?" asked Richard.

"My dear boy, I shall be only too glad of your company," was the response, and five minutes later the brothers, wearing long cloaks, had left the hall behind them and had entered the elm tree avenue.

The white snow lay deep upon the ground and weighed down the lighter boughs of the trees, but the sky was clear and studded with stars, whilst the full moon shone so brightly that surrounding objects were plainly discernible.

The night was so still that a faint echo of the Christmas peal of bells being rung in the parish church of four miles distant Preston could be plainly heard.

"Those bells are speaking of peace on earth and goodwill amongst men," said Sir John Osbaldiston, thoughtfully. "Well, Dick, God has given me peace at last, and there is goodwill and warm brotherly love between us two at any rate, wherefore I suppose I should feel contented with my lot."

"John, the merciful God who has at last given you peace may also, in His own good time, bestow upon you renewed happiness. But what form is that hovering amongst the trees yonder? It is surely a woman, clad in flowing raiment as white as the snow itself."

"I both see her and recognise her, Richard," answered the baronet, in solemn tones. "It is our ancestral ghost, the famous White Lady of Samlesbury Hall; she whose lover was murdered by her fierce brethren before her very eyes because his was a different faith from hers and theirs, and who afterwards and very speedily, died of a broken heart. She always appears to one of our race to give warning of a birth or a death in the family. I saw her last on the night wherein I lost both wife and child, and I believe that for some especial purpose she has lured me hither to-night."

Richard Osbaldiston made no answer. Of course, he knew the history of the family spectre, but he had not the least desire to make its personal acquaintance.

Unwilling to be thought a coward, he walked on in silence by his brother's side, with his gaze fixed upon the White Lady, who, as they approached, presented the aspect of a beautiful girl of some eighteen years, with a face as white as the loosely flowing garb she wore, and eyes and hair of the deepest black.

She pointed downwards to a little mound of snow, which seemed to have a slightly undulatory motion, but, in a moment more, she had disappeared from view, and just where she had seemed to stand grew a stunted tree, with one scraggy, down-drooping branch pointing to the exact spot that the spectre's outstretched hand had just done.

"Only a vivid imagination after all, conjured up by the moon-light and the snow—a mere tree instead of a ghost," began Richard Osbaldiston, but his brother interrupted him sternly with—

"It was the White Lady in the first instance, Dick, and she drew us hither with a will that was stronger than an iron cable. Ah, she pointed at that little hillock of snow, and it seems to me as though it has a slight movement in it. My God! can there be some living thing buried beneath it who would have perished but for our coming?"

Sir John threw himself down on his knees ere he had finished speaking, and began with eager haste to scatter abroad the snow mound.

A minute later he rose to his feet with a little girl clasped in his arms.

"A child, and still living!" he exclaimed excitedly. "We must back to the Hall with all speed, Dick," and wrapping the little one up in the folds of his thick cloak he started homewards at a run.

CHAPTER II.

"IT WAS THE WHITE LADY, OUR FAMILY SPECTRE."

Arrived home, Sir John Osbaldiston kicked the smouldering logs on the great hearth-stone into a blaze, unrolled his cloak from around the little form it had so snugly enclosed, and revealed to view the loveliest nine-year-old girl that his eyes had ever gazed on.

She was thin and meanly clad, but her eyes were as blue as forget-me-nots, whilst her hair hung about her in a cataract of golden curls. A minute more and a flush as pink as the petals of a wild rose broke through the hitherto death-like pallor of her cheeks, and gazing inquiringly around her she murmured softly:—

"Where am I? I want to go home to my mother."

"Drink this wine, little one, and then you can tell us where your mother lives; and when you have had some food, we will carry you to her," answered Richard Osbaldiston.

The child drank the wine, and it immediately restored her, whereupon Sir John asked:—

"How came you to get buried in the snow, Golden Locks?"

"Mother was ill, dying, I heard someone say, so I stole out of the house to find a fairies' ring that I know of. It is a dark circle worn in the grass by the fairies' feet as they dance round and round. I went there because 'tis said that whenever a mortal child appears amongst them the fairies will grant her whatever she may first ask for, and I wanted to beg them to make mother well again. But the fairies' ring was covered deep with snow, and when I had worked hard to clear it away with my hands for a long while I got all numbed and fell down and went to sleep. Oh, it was wicked of me to do that, for now my darling mother will have to die," and the little maid burst into tears.

"Suppose that it being too cold for the fairies to come out to-night, they asked my brother and I to grant your wish in their stead. Now, don't cry, but eat, and then we will carry you home and do every whit as much for your poor mother as ever your friends the fairies could."

The child seemed to believe all that was said to her, nor did she require any pressing to partake of food.

But whilst she ate she was able to talk, and, asked how she fancied she could find her fairies' ring when the ground was covered with snow, she answered that she remembered exactly where it was, because of a queer-looking tree close beside it with the end of one scraggy branch pointing straight down to where the fairy ring was.

Next she made the extraordinary statement that just before

she went asleep, as she called it, a beautiful lady, with a face as white as her dress, bent down and tried to clear away the snow from off her, but that her hands seemed to be like vapour, and so not to have the power to remove a single flake; discovering which the lady rose to her feet, and stretching out her arm towards Samlesbury Hall, appeared to be impatiently beckoning to someone to come to her assistance.

"Ah, it was the White Lady, our family spectre. Did I not tell you, Dick, that I was forced to go to the avenue to-night by a mysterious power I could not resist, and that child's life has been saved thereby," remarked Sir John.

The younger brother gazed at him wonderingly as he asked:

"Is it possible that you notice nothing strange about her—that, in fact, this lovely little creature is the exact copy of what your dead wife was at her age?"

"Yes, I perceived it at a glance, and did not my dying wife tell me, with her last breath, that she would one day return to me? Well, she has now come back to earth to be my daughter instead of my spouse, for if she lives and consents to my now deepest desire, I intend to adopt this heaven-sent darling as my own child, and to make her my heiress in due course."

And when, an hour later, Sir John Osbaldiston and his brother, the former carrying the little maid once more warmly wrapped up in his cloak, and the latter a basket containing a bottle of wine and some nourishing food, entered a miserable cottage on the outskirts of Samlesbury village, it was to learn, from a dying woman, that "Golden Locks," as the baronet had taken to call the child, was not hers, but a foundling she had found, as a tiny babe, abandoned upon her doorstep, and who, as she was then in easy circumstances and just left a childless widow, she had brought up as her own.

She was evidently grateful for Sir John's offer, and declared that she could now die happy, which before the dawn of day she did.

Then the child was carried back to Samlesbury Hall, the brothers calling on the way at the cottage of an old woman who had once been their nurse and persuading her to accompany them.

Thus it was that ere sunrise, the pretty foundling, still weeping bitterly over the loss of her foster mother, lay in a comfortable bed, and, notwithstanding her grief, she soon sank into a dreamless sleep.

Meanwhile the brothers smoked and talked about this new and most interesting addition to the family.

"I shall leave for India with the comfortable knowledge that a veritable sunbeam has at last penetrated through these for long years sombre walls," observed Richard, with a smile. "The good God could not have bestowed on you a more precious Christmas gift John, and you must treasure it as a sacred possession. What are you going to call the little angel, who is a perfect miniature of your own lost wife?"

"I shall bestow on her my dear wife's maiden name of Coralie Clitheroe. Now that she has come back to me as a little child I will not rob her of her proper name."

"When ten years have passed away you may be able to persuade her to exchange it for your own, even as the first Coralie did," suggested Richard.

"God forbid that I should ever do her so cruel an injustice," retorted Sir John Osbaldiston. "What, unite her sweet youth to my crabbed age? Why in ten years I shall be over forty, and fatter and uglier than I even am at present; but Dick, my boy, you yourself at that time will be only thirty. What then if I educate and train Coralie so that you shall find it an easy task to win her when she reaches a marriageable age? When my wife was a young girl you were in love with her as well as I."

"That I certainly was, and whilst yet so small a boy that I had to mount on a high stool in order to reach her lips under the sacred mistletoe. I was at school when you married her, and when the news reached me that I had lost her I could positively eat no dinner that day. Now could a healthy and usually voracious schoolboy give a deeper proof of his affection than going without his dinner?" answered Richard, laughingly.

"Dick, perhaps one day I shall be able to give you a wedding breakfast to make up for that lost dinner. That Coralie will grow up into a most lovely woman I have not the least doubt, and it will be for you to preserve our name from becoming extinct and to prevent our old family seat from passing into the hands of strangers."

"I thank you for your kindly intentions at any rate. But as I have to start for Liverpool en route for India, in five hours time, I think I'd better devote four of them to sleep and begin about it as quickly as I can," and so saying, Richard Osbaldiston threw himself down upon a couch, and within five minutes was snoring sonorously.

CHAPTER III.

IN WHICH NINE YEARS PASS AWAY.

After Richard Osbaldiston's departure Samlesbury Hall assumed a changed aspect, for a motherly soul, the widow of a clergyman, was engaged as housekeeper, and her accomplished daughter to be little Coralie's governess. Female servants were also hired in the place of men, so that the old mansion soon assumed an aspect of homeliness that it had not known for many years. And the little, once half-starved orphan changed under these wholesome influences, which rounded her cheeks, planted pretty dimples therein, bestowed on her witching smiles and merry laughter, and taught her to sing as joyously as the birds of the air.

She became the caged sunshine of that hitherto dreary house. Sir John bought her every conceivable toy, and when both house-keeper and governess declared that he was going the right way to utterly spoil the child, he on one occasion made answer:

"Everyone tried to spoil my dear wife when she was nine years old, so lovely and so sweet was she, but she proved to be unspoil-able, and so will my present little Coralie, for she takes after her in disposition as closely as she does in face and form."

So the lovely child gradually changed into a girl and then into a maiden fair to see, whereupon Sir John bethought himself of what years ago he had expressed to his brother as being the dearest wish of his heart, namely, that one day he and she should marry, and so preserve the name of Osbaldiston from becoming extinct.

He therefore had a miniature of Coralie painted by a celebrated artist, and sent it out to Richard, who in due course acknowledged its receipt, declaring that he had never looked upon so lovely a face save that of one whose memory must be ever precious to them both. He added that he was daily shaking a shower of gold from the "Pagoda Tree," and hoped to return to England in three years more a wealthy man, by which time Coralie would have arrived at the marriageable age of eighteen, when he would gladly claim her for his wife if fortunate enough to win her love.

So Sir John began matchmaking, telling his adopted child what a noble, generous, and handsome fellow Richard was, but never referring to his secret desire, for Coralie was still only fifteen, and therefore too young to think about marrying.

But when her fifteen years had grown to seventeen, Sir John's advocacy of Richard's cause grew less strong, because he began to feel that it would be a bitter trial to surrender Coralie up even to a brother, for it was no longer a father's unselfish love that he felt for her.

"It would break my heart to be parted from her," he would muse, "but then why need we be parted, for if I make a free gift of Samlesbury Hall to Dick and his wife I am very certain that they will suffer me to end my days therein, so I shall see almost as much of my darling as I do at present."

Coralie had never possessed any boy or girl friends, for the Osbaldistons were too proud to mix with their inferiors in social position, and of equals they had none living near enough for their young people to become Coralie's intimates, so that Sir John was still her sole companion.

But she never grew tired of her guardian's society, for so she had begun to call him, at his own request, for he had by now told her whom he wished her to wed, and had declared, with a dismal attempt at laughter, that it sounded silly to call the brother of the man she was to marry by the name of father.

Now, though Coralie delighted to gratify Sir John's every whim, this one did not please her, for the idea of marrying Rich-

ard Osbaldiston became more and more repugnant to her with
each passing month.

The frequent letters which he now wrote her were read only
once, and then petulantly torn to fragments; his many handsome
presents were barely looked at ere they were laid aside, and Coralie regarded his at length rapidly approaching return home with
absolute dismay, never guessing that her "dear guardian" was
contemplating his advent with much the same feelings.

And then at last a letter came to Sir John from his brother
which brought matters to a climax, for it stated that Richard
hoped to arrive at Samlesbury Hall on the day after Christmas
Day, and that he trusted that he should find his dear old John and
his lovely bride that was to be in the best of health and spirits.

CHAPTER IV.

THE SECOND CHRISTMAS NIGHT.

The Christmas night that will embrace the closing incidents of
my story was an exact copy of the one nine long years back on
which its opening events were narrated.

Sir John Osbaldiston in his clumsy way tried to make Coralie laugh by jokes about the coming of the bridegroom on the
morrow, but a child might have perceived that his jocosity was
forced, and Coralie was decidedly irritable and depressed in
spirits.

"Guardian," she at last broke forth with, "don't for goodness'
sake keep on sounding your brother Richard's praises, for I'm
sick of having them continually drummed into my ears. I wish
that he was bringing a wife home with him instead of coming
here to seek one."

"Ah, my bonnie bird, you'll be singing quite another tune a
few days hence, and will be drumming his praises into my ears
instead of I into yours," answered the baronet.

"Oh, you dear, well-meaning old goose, why will you remain
blind when you might so easily see?" retorted the lovely girl, and
seating herself on Sir John's knee she burst into a flood of tears.

A couple of hours later she made the odd request, for it was a bitterly cold night.

"Guardian, I want you to take me for a moonlight walk over the frozen snow, and go with me down the old elm avenue to the spot where you found me buried when I was a child, and I wish you to talk of nothing else all the way there and back."

"Dress yourself warmly, and it shall be as you desire," answered Sir John, and a few minutes later the middle-aged man and the eighteen years old maiden were arm in arm, seeking their strange destination.

As on the Christmas night of nine years ago the air was calm and still, and the faint echo of the joy bells from Preston's distant church tower could be distinctly heard. The spot they sought, pointed straight down at by the drooping branch of the old tree that had once told a half-starved little girl where to search for her snow-buried Fairies' Ring, was at last reached, and the strangely-matched pair gazed at it in silence.

At last Coralie said:

"It was you, and not your brother, who found me, who lifted me out of my white grave, and bore me to your home wrapped snugly in your warm cloak, and it is you, and not Richard, who have made Samlesbury Hall an early paradise to me ever since. Oh, guardian, you have always loved me, aye, and you love me still, so why are you so resolved to give me away to one who has scarcely ever seen me, and whom I could never, never care for as I do for you?"

There was almost agony in her tones, but Sir John was still obtuse, and so made reply:—

"Yes, I know that you love me as though I was your real parent, my darling, but Richard is young and singularly handsome, and as a father I must provide you with the most fitting husband I can find."

"And you think that a young girl can care for nothing but youth and good looks in a husband; and, because you are grey-haired and plain-featured you believe that no other kind of love than a daughter's can ever belong to you. Oh, you foolish guardian, don't you know I long ago discovered that you had learned to love me with a very different affection from that of a father for a child, and that, with the purest unselfishness you have tried to overcome that love, for my sake as you imagined, while all unknown to you I have grown to love you even as you love me, but until matters reached a climax was too shy to say so."

"Coralie, that is absurd. Why I am forty years of age, and you in the first bloom of youth. I'm as ugly as a satyr and you are as lovely as an angel. Oh, I cannot believe my ears. Coralie, it is cruel of you to make a mock of me," exclaimed Sir John.

"A mock of you? Let *this* prove that there is no mockery in my words," was Coralie's reply, as she threw her arms around her guardian's neck and kissed him on the lips. "I love you, and can never love anyone *but* you. For nine long years you have been father, mother, and big brother to me all in one, and now I ask you to become my husband."

"Coralie—why—you mean it. You actually mean it. Your eyes tell me so as well as your lips. Oh, I do believe that you have made me the happiest man in the world; but my poor Dick, what a death blow this will be to him."

"Not a bit of it, old fellow," exclaimed a merry voice close by, "for poor Dick wants a sister much more than he does a wife, and you are about to give him one whom he will love very dearly. You see, I arrived home half a day before I was expected, and having sent on my luggage, the whim seized me to make for Samlesbury Hall through the old elm avenue in order to recall the memories of a Christmas nine years ago. Do you remember, dear old John, how on that night you told me that your dying wife had promised to one day return to you in the flesh. Well, if there is any truth in the doctrine of the re-incarnation of the mortal body she stands beside you now. I have heard every word that you have said to each other from behind a tree trunk, and I congratulate you both from the very bottom of my heart."

What need is there to continue our story further.

Suffice it to say that a week later Sir John Osbaldiston was married to Coralie in the chapel of St. Leonard at Samlesbury village.

CPSIA information can be obtained
at www.ICGtesting.com
Printed in the USA
LVHW011403221122
733723LV00006B/256